STAGE-STRUCK
By Suzanne Stokes

Tuesday, 28th October

Rose Grayson rushed into her house, slamming the door on the gale and driving rain. Her heart was pounding and she was sick with fright. To make matters worse, now that she was late there was no time to back out; the cat had to be fed, and she had to change her clothes.

'I can't do this!' she yelled at the bedroom mirror. 'What am I, some sort of masochist?'

Hurriedly she stripped of her blue uniform dress, dragged her jeans off the hanger, wriggled into them and pulled on a thick sweater. Unable to stand Min's persistent meowing she pounded down the stairs to feed her before returning to the bedroom mirror with a frustrated squeal because her mane of curly Titian hair had corkscrewed out of control in the damp weather. Cursing, she dragged a brush through it, applied lipstick and almost jumped out of her skin at the loud hammering on her front door.

Clearly, Lauren had arrived.

'Rosie - come on!' she called through the letterbox. 'I'm drowning out here!'

'Coming...' Rose clattered downstairs to open the door. 'Oh my God, what are you wearing, it stinks?'

Lauren, Rose's dear friend and neighbour, was huddled into an aged Afghan coat she had pounced on with glee at the local Oxfam shop, and which was now soaking and smelled like a wet camel.'

'Sorry about the pong.' Lauren grinned, stepped inside, dripping all over the hall carpet.

'I'm sorry too – I've changed my mind. I'm not coming to the audition.'

'Rosie...' Lauren paused, then took her friend by the shoulders. 'Do try. I know it's in the church – but it's not your church. And we're doing a pantomime, not King Lear.'

'It still spooks me. Look, my hands are shaking, and I feel ill.'

'If I were your patient what would you advise me to do?' demanded Lauren. 'Face up to my fears or bury my head in the mud?'

'Sand,' muttered Rose. 'And I'm a children's nurse not a shrink.'

'Well, if you don't come I can't go either. My car won't start...which means I shan't get the part I want ...' She lowered her head to hide a smile.

Stage Struck

Rose gave her a shove. 'Blackmail! Your car never starts. Oh, God. Well, all right. But not the coat. Call the vet for it tomorrow - leave it in the bathroom till we get back and you can borrow my Barbour.'

'Okay.' Lauren smiled. 'It is a bit lively.' Removing the coat, she revealed a lime green sweater topping the orange skirt.

'You look like traffic lights!' Rose relaxed and laughed. 'How can you live in colours like that?'

'Colours like what? Come on, we're going to be late.'

Rose headed her little red Skoda for the local Methodist Church Hall where the audition was to be held. 'You have no idea how nervous I am – especially about going into the church. I don't know how you persuaded me into this.'

'It will be good for you, Rosie. Honestly, its fun. And when you've been through a rough time – and Lord knows you have – something outside of your normal life gives you a lift. They're an interesting crowd. In fact, some are *very* interesting. If you were a psychiatric nurse instead of a Sister on the kids' ward, you'd have a field day.'

'Sounds scary... I think I'll just drop you off outside and go home.'

'Don't be daft. Try to calm down and don't think about going into a church. After all, it's only a building.'

'You're right. Sorry. So, tell me about some of these mad people I'm about to meet.'

'Better if you find out for yourself. I don't want to prejudice your first impression. But one person I hope you will like is Clive.'

'Clive? You haven't mentioned *him* before. Have you been holding out on me?'

'No. Well, not really, he's just... well, kind of a friend.'

'What kind of a friend? Come on...tell.'

'Well, we've been on a few dates. He's really nice but it's nothing serious. I don't do serious, you know that. I'll introduce the others as they pitch up.'

They pulled into the car park at the Methodist Church in the centre of the High Street where the Sipton Amateur Dramatic Society - unfortunately known as SADS - rehearsed their shows.

Rose and Lauren pushed open the heavy oak door and went into the stone-pillared foyer. To the left was a passage to the church hall and to the right the Minister's office; straight ahead lay the church. The glass doors separating it from the foyer had been left open, but it was quiet and darkened. The smell of old hymn book and the lingering perfume of flowers left after Saturday's wedding wafted out. Rose stood for a moment almost overcome with fear and ready to run. Her breath caught in her throat, she felt sick and began to tremble violently. 'I can't...' she whispered.

'Yes, you can. We're through here, not in the church. Just don't look if it upsets you.'

Lauren took her arm and led her away into the large church hall with its polished parquet floor. Pinned round the walls were pictures painted by the Sunday School children. At one end was a small stage hung with dusty red velvet curtains, and at the other end was a little kitchen with a hatch through which the smell of coffee drifted. In the kitchen a diminutive woman in her sixties was pouring hot water into the green Beryl Ware cups without which no church canteen would be complete.

'Hello, Patsy,' Lauren greeted her. 'Need a hand?'

'No, thanks, but a longer pair of legs would be useful.'

Drawing nearer, Rose realised Patsy was a little person standing on a specially constructed platform so she could reach the counter.

'This is my friend Rose - she's new,' Lauren told her.

'Nice to meet you, Rose.'

'Patsy is our mother figure. She's an artist, sculptor and formidable seamstress.'

'And I play small parts on stage – very small parts.' She chuckled. 'Coffee?'

Rose smiled gratefully. 'I would love one – thanks.' Her breathing had returned to normal, and now she looked around with interest.

Lauren pointed to a couple in their mid-forties who were obviously in the throes of a confrontation. 'That's Mason and Candy Fairfax; Mason's directing the pantomime.'

Almost nose to nose, but speaking quietly, their body language indicated that some vitriolic exchanges were taking place. Mason was about six-foot four and towered over Candy who was slim, blonde and spitting feathers.

'They fight – often.' Lauren shrugged. 'But they probably have a great time making up.'

As they watched, Mason walked away from Candy who stared angrily after him. With an almost imperceptible stamp of her foot, she turned and headed for the Ladies.

'I'll go and see if she's all right. Are you okay here for a moment, Rose?'

'Sure.'

Rose sipped her coffee and surveyed others who were coming into the hall chatting, shaking out wet umbrellas and hanging up dripping coats. Among them was a middle-aged, red-faced, paunchy man who greeted everyone as 'darling.' To her alarm he spotted her standing by the kitchen hatchway and homed in with a fatuous smile.

Stage Struck

'Hello, darling,' he gushed, breathing whisky fumes in her face. 'I'm Winston James. You're new, aren't you? I would have remembered you if I'd seen you before – especially with those legs. Wow, they go right up to your bum, don't they?' He reached out as if to pat her rear and Rose jumped back in alarm.

'Rose,' piped up Patsy from behind the counter, 'could you come round here and give me hand, please?'

'With pleasure.' Ros moved quickly out of groping range into the tiny kitchen.

'Leave her alone, you old lech – and here's a black coffee,' Patsy snapped at Winston, who gave her a shameless grin. 'Rose, you could wash up those few cups, if you wouldn't mind. They have such a deep sink here that if I fell in I'd drown.'

Rose laughed. 'Lauren says you're also an artist?'

'Yes – I paint, but sculpture is my real love. I have a little studio at home and I teach at the local art school two days a week. What about you?'

'I'm a Sister on the children's ward at St. Mary's.'

'What an emotional job that must be.'

'Yes – but I love it.' Rose contemplated the little lady and wondered how many traumas she had been forced to deal with in her life. "How long have you been a member of the group?'

'More years than I care to remember. These people are my surrogate family.' She gave a pixyish grin. 'I may be only four-foot-three, but they don't seem to notice. Aye, aye, Mason's marshalling the troops. I have a feeling it's going to be an interesting audition. There are a few people here I haven't seen before, which is good. We desperately need new blood.'

They moved into the body of the hall where chairs had been arranged in front of the small stage, and they both sat with Lauren who had saved their seats.

Mason had arranged papers and scripts on a table. He stood up, ran his fingers through his hair, cleared his throat and the chatter died away.

'Thanks to all of you for coming, and welcome to Lauren's three friends...er... John Reese, Clive Pearson and Rose Grayson who are new here tonight,' he said, consulting a piece of paper. 'My name is Mason; this is Candy my wife and our choreographer.' He glanced at her but she avoided his eye and stared frostily into the middle distance. 'For those of you who are newcomers, we perform our shows at the Library Theatre, but all rehearsals will be here. Due to a number of unforeseen circumstances we're starting rehearsals nearly four weeks later than usual which means this is going to be seat-of-your-pants drama. Probably there will be dramas all the way.'

'No change there then,' whispered Lauren to Rose.

'It means, if you are cast,' continued Mason, 'you're going to need to learn your words in double-quick time. If we need to cram in extra rehearsals you will be expected to make the effort. As long as we work together, we can still put on a show to be proud of.' He paused, shuffling through his notes and Candy yawned beside him and glanced at her watch. 'There will be fifteen performances over three weekends starting on Boxing Day and we usually sell out, so nearly two thousand people will get to see the show. It finances the rest of our year, enabling us to try more adventurous theatre which may not put so many bums on seats. So we'll waste no more time. I want to start the proceedings tonight with Act One, Scene One, where Jack the Jester and Mrs. Mixit, the dame, meet in the village square.'

Winston began to rise from his seat, his hand out for the script but Mason avoided his eye and asked Gary Jones to read Mrs. Mixit and Clive Pearson to read Jack. Winston sat down, his face like thunder.

'Winston thinks he has a divine right to be dame,' Lauren told Rose 'This could be interesting.'

'Excuse me,' the man next to Rose leaned across her to speak to Lauren. 'Why is the cook played by a man?'

'You're American!' Rose exclaimed, and then blushed, having stated the obvious.

'Sorry ma'am, but I sure am.' He grinned, exaggerating a Texan drawl.

'Well,' Lauren whispered back, 'you see, in pantomime the dame is always played by a man, and the principal boy is played by a girl. Just watch, you'll get the hang of it. Clive didn't tell me he was bringing you along. Rose, this is Clive's flatmate, John.'

'Hello,' Rose responded. 'Are you going to audition – have you done this stuff before?'

'No, Clive's the drama queen. I'm just here to watch. And I'm not really flat – it's just an illusion.'

'Ssh, the director is about to yell at us for jabbering,' Lauren mouthed at them.

Gary and Clive took scripts and began to read.

'Hello, children! I'm Jack the jolly jester. Welcome to the Kingdom of Keepumlarfin,' began Clive, and it was immediately plain that he knew what he was doing as he capered around the stage. 'Hello, Mrs Mixit,' he continued. 'That's a smashing frock.'

Gary took a deep breath and plunged into, 'I got it at Matalan at fifty percent off their twenty-five percent off the previous cheapest price which was forty percent cheaper than the week before sale. It was so cheap, in the end they paid me to take it away.'

Nobody laughed. His timing was off and he read it like a man. After listening for a few moments, Mason interrupted. 'Thank you, chaps. Clive, would you continue and... John, would you have a go at Mrs. Mixit please.'

Winston, who had risen expectantly from his seat, sat down with a scowl.

'Oh, boy,' muttered John. 'I have to read this like a woman, huh?'

'No, a man playing a woman – it's not the same thing. Go for it. Imagine yourself with a big bust and long bloomers under a voluminous dress,' giggled Lauren.

'Oh, boy,' he repeated, heading for Mason and taking the script.

They began again and the magic of theatre suddenly transformed the chilly church hall to the spring celebration at Keepumlarfin. Perhaps, because they were friends, Clive and John were already at ease with each other. The jokes flowed and the image of the tall, handsome Texan dressed in a wig, with red cheeks, batwing eye lashes, kiss-me-quick bloomers and a bosom of gargantuan proportions was instantly before them.

Those watching rocked with laughter and no-one doubted that this year Winston James would not be playing dame. He knew it too, and his already florid cheeks glowed with rage. Angrily, he rose to his feet. 'Mason – I demand the right to read for this part,' he spluttered.

'Winston, of course you may. Does anyone else want to read Jack?'

No-one spoke, so Clive continued as the jester and they began again. But Winston read badly, over-played the scene and the banter between them produced only an embarrassed silence from the gathered members of the group.

'Thank you, Winston.'

Gratefully Clive and Winston handed back their scripts and sat down.

'Now we need the terrible twins, Hansel and Gretel. Lauren – will you read Gretel, and Steven you can be Hansel.'

Rose had never seen Lauren perform before and was astonished to see the transformation in her friend as she and Steven ran a series of gags which, although corny, brought shrieks of laughter from the small audience, and the parts were cast.

'Right, we'll take a short coffee break, folks.'

The group drifted to the hatchway where Patsy was once again presiding over tea and coffee.

'You astonish me,' marvelled Rose. 'I had no idea you could act like that.'

'What about you, Rosie – are you going to have a go?'

'Good Lord, no. I'll be happy helping backstage or something. I'd be completely out of my depth.'

Stage Struck

Just then Mason approached them and glanced admiringly at her long legs. 'Ah, Rose, I do hope we can persuade you to try out for Robin Hood.'

'No, no I'm sorry, I've never been on stage in my life. A few dancing lessons when I was five convinced my parents I had two left feet.'

'Shame,' he said, laying a hand on her arm. 'Do think about it. There's a first time for everything, you know.'

'I suppose so.' Rose blushed, and was suddenly conscious of an increase in her heart rate.

'Mason – a word, if you please.'

'Oh, dear,' he sighed, turning round. 'What can I do for you, Winston?'

'You know bloody well, you shit.'

A silence fell, as the group collectively braced itself for the inevitable.

'Winston, there's no need to use that sort of language. I understand that you're disappointed you obviously are not going to be playing dame this year – but it's time the group evolved a bit. New talent must have a chance. And we could benefit enormously from your experience and advice.'

'The people of Sipton *expect* me to entertain them at Christmas, Mason. You can't cast a bloody Yank.'

'I'm sorry, but I just have.'

'Then I hope you live to rue the day, and that the whole production falls flat on its face!' Scarlet with rage and humiliation, he stormed across the hall and out into the rainy night, banging the door behind him.

'Poor man,' groaned John. 'I feel terrible.'

'Please don't,' Mason reassured him. 'Unfortunately, he's an alcoholic and totally unreliable. It's unfair on the rest of the cast who work so hard to make the show a success. We have to work together, and he's not a team player any more.'

Somewhat subdued, everyone returned to their seats to resume casting, and Rose was asked to read the part of Robin Hood, the principal boy. Panic stricken, she tried to decline, but Lauren gave her a gentle shove and an encouraging smile.

Taking a deep breath, Rose stepped forward and took a script from Mason. 'Verruca the witch has cast a spell and put her dim-witted son Scaliban to sleep next to Lady Marian, with the idea that both will fall madly in love with the first person they see when they wake - hopefully each other. But Robin Hood wakes Marion first – and of course Verruca is foiled. Just relax, Rose, no one is judging you. We all had to start somewhere.' He smiled kindly at her, his dark brown eyes behind horn-rimmed glasses willing her on. 'As you come on stage,

Stage Struck

Scaliban is snoring loudly. Lola – please read the part of Marian and Jason, will you be Scaliban?'

Lola, uncurled from a graceful pose on the floor and accepted a script. 'Thanks, Dad.' She gave him a cheeky grin and went lie on the small stage.

'Okay – here goes.' Rose walked up onto the stage and looked back at the small audience. Lauren waved and gave her a thumbs-up. Taking a grip on her nerves, she plunged in. 'Hello, children. I'm Robin Hood. My word, what have we here? Beauty and the Beast by the look of it; I do believe this is Lady Marian, the Baron's daughter. Oh, isn't she pretty? But why is she asleep here with this horrible hairy heap? She looks so peaceful, perhaps I shouldn't wake her. Do you think I should wake her?'

'Yes,' yelled the audience. 'Wake her!'

Startled, she laughed and lifted Lola's hand to her lips.

Lola stirred, woke and came to life as an enchanting heroine who instantly fell in love with Robin Hood.

The parts were cast and Mason beamed with pleasure. 'We are doing well tonight. Now, we need a Verruca.'

As if on cue, the door to the hall flew open and a gust of wind seemed to carry in a tall, willowy woman, aged perhaps sixty. She had dark hair, more eye make-up than was flattering, a slash of bright red lipstick and wore a fur coat.

'That's Maureen Clarke.' Whispered Lauren. 'She's chairperson of the group and she's a battle-axe of the first order, but her heart's in the right place.'

'Mason, I'm late.'

'Maureen, you are.'

'Do you want me to read?'

'I do. Verruca, the wicked witch.'

'Typecasting me again are you?'

'You said it.'

'All right. A script would be helpful.'

'Didn't think you'd need one.'

'Swine'

With a twinkle in her eyes, she grabbed a script and, fur coat billowing, swept onto the stage.

'Candy – can you be Tabitha the cat please?' Mason asked her shortly and moodily she joined Maureen, crouching in a corner, licking her paws.

'I smell children,' began Verruca, for Maureen had already moved into the character, adopting a slight stoop and using her long fingers to gesture. 'Ugh, I *hate* children; nasty, smelly, noisy little beasts. What are you all doing here? Don't you know witches eat little children?'

The audience booed enthusiastically and Verruca hissed back at them. 'All right, all right, I'm only joking! Come here, Tabitha I'm going to have to teach you to be a really bad cat, otherwise you're no use to me and I shall dump you back on boring old Dick Whittington…'

The part was cast and Candy agreed with a shrug to be the cat whose only lines were to meow, but who nevertheless was responsible in stringing the show together.

'Fantastic! We have a cast,' said Mason, rubbing his hands delightedly. 'Leo and Gillian are to be the punk baddies – I agreed that last week as Gillian is away tonight. Anyone not cast is automatically in the chorus and will need to go to dance and music rehearsals as per your printed schedules, so thank you everyone. Rehearsals for actors begin on Thursday, here promptly at eight o'clock. Anyone going to the pub?'

'I'm not,' snapped Candy. 'If I take the car, can someone give Mason a lift home?'

'We can,' piped up Lauren. 'That's if it's okay with Rose – we're only a couple of streets from Mason's house - do you mind, Rose?'

'No, of course not.'

Candy flounced out, banging the door behind her and Mason pulled a face. 'Put it down to hormones,' he grumbled. 'Come on, the first round is mine.'

A few people declined, but as well as Lauren and Rose, Clive, John, and Patsy trooped across the road to the aged, oak-beamed Fox and Rabbit, and gathered round the open fire in the lounge bar. Mason ordered the drinks and joined them.

'That,' he beamed, 'was a very successful audition. Rose, I'm sorry if you got rather press ganged into playing Robin Hood but you read very well and you look great.'

'Well, thank you - I'll try not to let you down.' She found the colour rising to her cheeks again, and wondered how Candy could be so nasty to her adorable husband. Hastily she looked down, aware she was staring at him.

'And John – it's hard to believe you've never performed before,' Mason continued. 'Or have you?'

'Barber shop – I sang in a barber shop group back home in Houston. But I must admit I never saw myself in bloomers. They'll have to be long ones - I'm six four!' He laughed delightedly at the prospect, his near-black eyes twinkling. 'Just wait till this gets back to the office, Clive.'

Stage Struck

'Perhaps we should keep quiet about it for now, mate – we'll be awfully bored with the ribbing by Christmas.'

Clive was a little shorter than John with fair hair, deep blue eyes and a square chin with a dimple. Off stage he seemed more serious than John. He did tell them that he hailed from the West Country, worked for a large city bank which meant travelling to London with John each day, and that for the moment the two of them were sharing a flat in Sipton.

'I'm looking for a house to buy,' he told them, 'but after my divorce it will have to be very modest.' He didn't elaborate, and pain flashed across his face at the admission.

'Have you done a lot of acting?' Rose asked. 'You seemed so at ease this evening.'

'I've travelled a lot for the bank – lived in several countries, and found the local amdram groups an instant entrée to a social life. So, wherever I go they're my first port of call. John has just come over from the States, and I'm recently back from Dubai so we decided to flat share until we get ourselves sorted. We worked together in Singapore several years ago and kept in touch.'

'He's a fine actor, Rose,' John chipped in. 'Like you, I'm just a beginner, but Clive has a great list of achievements: Macbeth, Henry Higgins, Toad…'

'Toad?'

'Of Toad Hall. Wind in the Willows.'

'Oh, of course. That was my favourite story when I was a child. My dad used to…' she faltered.

'He read it to you?' John asked kindly, aware she suddenly had tears in her eyes.

'Yes.'

'It's my round,' Patsy declared, and rising went to the bar, reached up, and banged on it with her umbrella to attract attention.

Paul, the barman, leaned over and grinned down at her. 'Hi, Patsy – what can I get you?'

'Same as they all had last time, please.'

'She's a wonderful person. I wish I had half her character,' said Rose, struggling to regain her composure.

'She's a mainstay of the group,' Mason told her 'We all love her to bits.'

'Will she be in the show?'

'Yes, in the chorus - and she's going to be Scaliban's teddy bear.'

'I'm so glad I came tonight.'

'Yes, Rose, so am I,' Mason replied quietly.

Half an hour later they said their farewells, and Mason climbed into the back of Rose's car. In the enclosed space she was acutely aware of him and relieved when she dropped him off at a large detached house in a well-heeled street quite close to her own. Bidding the girls farewell, he walked towards the house grim-faced. It was in darkness, and since there was no car on the drive, Candy had obviously not returned home.

'What's going on with those two?' asked Rose as she pulled away.

'Married blitz, I'm afraid.'

'Is he seeing someone else?'

'I doubt it – but who knows? With the haranguing he gets at home he's ripe for it, poor bloke. What did you think of Clive?

'I liked him. He's really sweet.'

'And John – dishy or what?'

'They are both…nice.'

'Nice? They're rather better than that!'

'Lauren, I just want a mixture of new friends and I did enjoy this evening in spite of my initial anxiety. Let me take it at my own pace.'

'Sorry – it's just that I want you to be happy again.'

'I know, and I'm getting there. Just give me time. Do you really think I can carry off Robin Hood?'

'Yes, of course you can. Look, I know it was hard for you to go into the church tonight – but each time it will get easier.'

'Do you want to come in for a coffee?'

'No, thanks – I'll just collect the yeti from your bathroom and go home. I have an early meeting. But the first rehearsal is in two days, so I'll see you then.'

Rose went to bed that night with her head full of the evening's events. But as she fell asleep her dreams were uneasy, and at two o'clock she woke with a shriek, shivering in a cold sweat. It was happening again.

***

Candy left the audition fuming. The rain had stopped, but wet leaves on the pavement caught her by surprise, and she slipped and sat down suddenly in a puddle. It was the last straw and tears streamed down her face as she struggled to her feet, brushed the worst of the debris from her coat and climbed into the car. She had a painful bruise on her hip, her sodden clothes clung damply around her legs and she'd snapped the heel off her boot.

Nick had promised to come this evening – he was the stage manager and should have been at the audition. She'd been looking forward to seeing him all day and now she felt let down, disappointed and humiliated. She was sure now that he was avoiding her.

If he dumps me, she told herself, pulling away from the kerb, I'll make certain he never works with SADS again.

Putting her foot down hard on the accelerator, she roared along the high street towards her friend Sarah's house, where she hoped a glass of wine and sympathy would be available.

But Sarah didn't seem very pleased to see her – in fact she popped her tousled blonde head round the half-opened front door and peered out, impatient at Candy's insistent knocking.

'Candy! What on earth are you doing here at this time of night?'

'It's only ten o'clock. Please can I come in? I need a friend. I simply can't go home yet.'

'I'm sorry, but it's not a good time. You haven't been in an accident, have you? You're covered in mud and stuff.'

'I fell over. I'm okay, but I need someone to talk to.'

'Sorry, love. Can I call you in the morning? I have someone here right now.'

'Well, I don't mind if you have another friend there…'

'Candy, much as I care about you, I can't minister to your problems right now. Go home and have a large gin and tonic.'

'I'm sorry. I'll talk to you tomorrow.'

As the door closed she heard Sarah say, 'Oh, God, that's all I need,' and the low tone of a masculine voice replying.

So that was it - Sarah also had a lover. How she envied her oldest friend. She was single, well, divorced to be precise, and had the freedom to do as she chose with whomsoever she chose, and no-one else to consider.

Sulkily, Candy returned to her car. She simply couldn't bear the idea of going home yet, so after a moment's thought she decided to drive past Nick's house. If there was a light on she would knock and make the excuse that she was worried about him as he hadn't turned up at the audition. Why, oh why had she allowed herself to get so deeply involved with him? She drove slowly, thinking back to the night she met Nick Harrow, nearly six months ago.

As a new member of the group he had turned up at a rehearsal of a play in which she had the lead, and he'd been roped in as assistant stage manager. She had been instantly attracted to him, and so it seemed, he was to her. He struck a romantic figure – handsome, in his early forties, with thick, dark hair, deep blue eyes and a tan. He had a hundred-watt smile and a trim body which he kept in shape by running and swimming.

Stage Struck

She had to admit he would have had to be stupid not to realise she fancied him, and a week later he had asked her for a lift home as his car was being serviced. When he kissed her before getting out of her car she had been astonished at her own reaction. Her heart rate soared, something inside went into meltdown and she had kissed him back passionately. Since there was no reason to rush home that night as Mason was at a company dinner, she had agreed to go into Nick's house for the standard offer of a cup of coffee. But of course they got nowhere near the kettle or Nescafé. She left a couple of hours later, hoping she'd have a chance to shower away the lingering scent of her new lover before facing her husband. She knew she had a glow in her cheeks from the excitement and some exceptional sex, and she felt alive, feminine and attractive for the first time in ages.

Candy smiled at the memories; the stolen moments – the secret phone calls – the way he called her 'Flower' when they were making love. The careful cover-ups of a clandestine affair had all been part of the fun at first. Nick made her laugh, bought her silly presents and told her she was beautiful. She felt she connected with him at an intellectual level because sometimes after making love they would lie in bed talking about music, drama and art...and then he would start to touch her again. Nick was an earth-shattering lover, and even though she was now shivering with cold, the memory of his touch sent a warm flush through her body. But she had never intended to fall in love with him, it had not been part of the game plan, and when it happened the effect on Candy was cataclysmic. The affair took over her every waking thought; she could hardly bear to be in a room - let alone a bed - with Mason, and she began to fool herself into believing that Nick felt the same about her.

When, as seemed inevitable to her, Nick asked her to move in with him, how would she ever find the courage to tell Mason? She knew her husband would be devastated, but theirs had been a minefield of a marriage, and her volatile, tempestuous temperament had not worked well with Mason's more considered, gentle approach to life. Her passionate nature embraced every aspect of her being. When she wanted something, she wanted it instantly, whether it was a new car, or to have the dining room decorated. Mason would always do things in his own time, having organised them perfectly first, and it drove her insane.

'Can't you ever do anything spontaneously?' she had stormed at him once.

'It seems to me,' he yelled, 'that when *you* do things spontaneously, I end up doing them all over again. Properly.'

'Are you saying I'm incompetent?'

'No, Candy,' he said through gritted teeth, 'but you never think things through before you jump in and commit yourself. Consequently, I usually have to come and sort out the mess you've made.'

And she knew he was right, which was even more infuriating. Her affair with Nick was a case in point, as she had not even considered the ramifications of her actions on her children or Mason. She had wanted Nick and plunged into the relationship without a backward glance.

But during the past two weeks things seemed to have changed. Nick had become cooler, ended phone calls quickly, made excuses when she had wanted to see him, and it frightened her.

She bit her lip, hoping it was just her imagination playing tricks. Switching off her headlights, she coasted the car to within sight of Nick's house and parked under a tree in deep shadow. His car was not in the drive, and the house was in darkness except for the porch light.

'So where are you, you bastard?' she muttered.

For an hour she sat there, getting colder and colder, her wet clothes sticking clammily to her skin. At last, just after midnight, she saw his Land Rover approach and watched as he parked it at the kerb by his house. She could see him in the streetlight talking on his mobile phone and laughing. As he finally emerged from the car she considered going over to him and asking what the hell he was playing at. As he disappeared inside the house, still chatting on his phone, she started her car and drove home, feeling uncomfortably like a stalker.

She crept into the silent house. Mason had left the hall light on for her, but had gone to bed, and judging by the fact that Lola's old banger was parked outside, she too had come home early and turned in for the night.

Shivering, Candy made herself a mug of cocoa, and called Nick's mobile.

It rang three times before he answered sharply, 'Hello, this is Nick Harrow.'

'It's me, darling,' she whispered. 'Where were you tonight? I missed you.'

'Candy! Its half past midnight – I've been asleep for hours. I didn't come tonight because I had some work to finish here for a meeting tomorrow. I did call Mason – didn't he tell you?'

'No, he didn't.'

'Oh. Well, I'll be in touch in a day or two and maybe we'll get together.'

'Maybe?' she said frostily.

'Go to bed, Candy – you'll get bags under your eyes.'

Stung, she rang off. He was lying through his teeth and she was shocked to the core, and sick with terror. It was all going wrong.

Stage Struck

She began to shiver violently again. Creeping into the bathroom, she undressed while running a bath. She checked her hip in the mirror and knew that by tomorrow she'd have a most unattractive bruise. Climbing stiffly into the bath, she lay down and gloomily surveyed the length of her shapely body, now turning lobster red below the surface of the water. At forty-four, she knew she looked good and her dance school – her pride and joy – kept her in shape as well as providing a reasonable income. But old age was lurking in the corner waiting to pounce, and she viewed that prospect with horror. The years seemed to fly by and in no time at all she'd be sixty-something, probably a grandmother; no-one would fancy her then.

With a self-pitying moan she climbed out and dried off. But even though she was now physically warm, she continued to shake. Dressing in a robe from behind the bathroom door, she went back downstairs and poured herself a large brandy. Watching the clock approach one-thirty, she sat on the living room floor by the flame-effect gas fire that had seemed so desirable and now looked really naff.

It was obvious. Nick was about to end the affair, otherwise why had he lied to her? But only two weeks ago he'd been so passionate she was afraid Mason might notice the small bruises on her lips and breasts, and had taken great pains to use lots of lipstick and avoid being seen naked by him for several days. How could Nick love her like that and then turn cold almost overnight?

The fear of losing Nick made her feel queasy and as always when she was stressed, her breathing became difficult. Fishing in her handbag for her asthma inhaler she wondered for the hundredth time why she had allowed herself to get into this mess. What would she do if he dumped her halfway through the bloody pantomime and then she had to see him every night? It would be excruciating.

There was only one thing for it, she decided – she had to get out of her involvement with the show, and hope against hope that Nick would realise he missed her and ask her to move in with him

'Oh, it's all *your* fault, Mason,' she muttered, rising slowly to her feet. 'If you had paid me more attention, none of this would have happened.' But in spite of her attempts to justify what she was doing, she felt a stab of guilt as she slid into bed beside him. He had been a good husband, and in the early days she'd been deeply in love with him. Now she felt affection and concern but the passion had long gone. His hands upon her were predictable and when they made love she found herself thinking about what shopping she needed, who she had to phone the next day, and whether Lola might scrape through her 'A' levels. It was the one time she would not allow herself to think about Nick. It seemed disloyal – but to whom, she wasn't sure.

Mason stirred and turned towards her, half opening his eyes. 'Where did you go?'

'Sarah's.'

'Why?'

'I didn't want to go to the pub. I hate dissecting the show after a rehearsal. Lord knows, it takes up enough of your time as it is. And I don't want to play the cat. I'll do the choreography, but otherwise I don't want to be involved. The kids from my dance school who want to be in the show can be trained at class until the last two weeks, so from now on you can count me out of rehearsals.'

'What the hell's the matter with you, Candy?' he asked.

'Nothing. I'm just sick of the drama crowd.'

'They're our friends.'

'Well, I'm sorry, but I'm burned out. I've been involved with the last three productions, either on, or backstage, and I can't face another ten weeks of going out two nights a week to a freezing church hall.'

'Fine. I just wish you had said so before and in a reasonable manner. And why did you have to cause a row at the hall about pre-casting Gillian and embarrass me in front of everyone? I know you don't like her, but it's my job to cast the show, not yours.'

'I'm sorry, Mason - you're right.' She tried to back down hastily. 'It's me flying off the handle again, isn't it? I can be such a cow.'

'Yes, you certainly can, and I'm sick of it. It's like living on the side of Mount Etna.'

'Perhaps it's an early menopause. My hormones…'

'If that's the case, your menopause started when you were twenty-two.'

'Mason!'

'Oh, shut up and go to sleep. I have to leave on the seven o'clock train for Manchester, and I'll be staying there overnight – thank God.' And he turned away and pulled the bedclothes up to his ears, shutting her out.

Stage Struck

Wednesday 29th October

When Candy woke the next morning, Mason had gone. His accountancy firm was flourishing and he often travelled around the country to meetings or to secure new business. He must have slipped away before dawn and Candy wished she'd had a chance to make her peace with him, before he left. He was hurt, and she knew he had good reason. For all his faults, she was sure he had never cheated on her or let her down, and she had the grace to feel bad about it - for a short while at least. But soon her anger at Nick's behaviour reasserted itself, and as she made some coffee, trying to wake herself properly, she wondered whether she dared call him again.

She woke the children, and fifteen minutes later they clattered down for breakfast.

'Mum,' said Leo around a mouthful of toast, 'can I book my driving lessons now? It's my birthday in a couple of weeks.'

'I do know that,' she replied, fondly regarding her son.

'Keep death off the road, I say,' chimed in Lola with a grin at her brother.

'You had lessons at seventeen -'

'And I passed first time,' she replied, pulling a face at him. 'I bet you don't.'

'Enough.' pleaded Candy. 'I can't cope with this so early in the morning.'

'I'm not surprised, after the late night you had,' snapped Lola, casting her a withering look.

'Gillian starts her lessons this week,' Leo interrupted. 'I'd be sick if my girlfriend passed before me.'

'I don't know what you see in that little tart,' complained his mother. 'She looks as if she's stepped straight off the set of Twilight? Ghastly.'

Leo stood up and faced her furiously. 'That's your opinion and I wish you'd keep it to yourself. You're just jealous because she's young and talented.'

'Do you want driving lessons or not? If so, you had better change your attitude - and your girlfriend.'

'Come on, baby brother,' said Lola, dragging him by the arm. 'Let's go. Be grateful you're allowed a girlfriend.' She glared at her mother. 'I'm supposed to be a recluse. What happened to sexual equality?'

'Leo doesn't have to study as hard as you to make the grade,' Candy snapped, 'and he doesn't have exams in a few months.' And anyway I couldn't stop him, Candy muttered grimly to herself as the front door slammed.

Stage Struck

From the wide kitchen window she watched her children climb into Lola's battered Golf and drive away. How did she manage it? Why couldn't she keep her mouth shut?

She loved Leo so much – even more than Lola, if she was truthful. Good-looking to a fault, he had a string of girls calling for him, which he found something of a nuisance as he was totally smitten by Gillian Cornwall, who wore micro-mini skirts, revealing most of what God had given her, sometimes dyed her hair pink and wore more eye make-up than Alice Cooper. Not what Candy had in mind for Leo at all. But, she allowed, Gillian was a very talented actress and dancer, which was why Mason was so keen to have her in the show.

Lola at eighteen was a leggy blonde and the image of her mother at the same age. Candy often looked at her daughter with envy, because she had her whole life before her. All the fun, the excitement, the boyfriends, the challenges, and Candy hoped she would not marry at a ridiculously young age as she had done. 'Play the field, my darling – break a few hearts before you settle down.'

Lola wanted to be a professional actress. Her dream was to go to drama school and become a performer because she knew she was a good dancer and had a passable singing voice. But a few days before she'd been distraught to overhear her father comment to her mother that her acting skills left a lot to be desired.

'She just needs training,' Candy had defended her spikily. 'And good direction.'

'She needs to go to university, get her degree and a career first. Then she should just enjoy drama as a hobby – she'll never make it big.'

Another row had exploded between them. Neither of them had been aware that Lola was listening outside the door, tears pouring down her face.

At school break time, Lola cornered her friend Stella and poured out her fears.

'They fight all the time, even in front of other people, and I'm sure that one day one of them will just up and go.'

'But you're grown up now,' Stella said. 'You'll be off to university -'

'Drama school.'

'Okay, drama school. And Leo is nearly seventeen. If your parents can't stand each other, what's the point of them staying together?'

'Daddy would go to pieces if she left...' Lola flushed and lowered her head. 'Promise not to tell anyone, but I know she's seeing someone.'

'Oh Lola, you poor thing.' Stella touched her hand. 'Are you sure?'

'Yes.'

'Your mother must be mad to play away because your dad's a hunk. He'd find someone else in no time.'

'Stella! I couldn't bear it. I'd hate her.'

'Who's lover boy – any idea?'

'Someone from drama, I suppose.'

'How exciting.'

'Exciting? It's horrible. I thought all those people were our friends, but one of them is threatening to ruin my life.'

'I wish my parents would do something out of the ordinary,' mused Stella. 'They're so boring and predictable. Are you still seeing Alex?'

'Yes – when I can. It's difficult because boyfriends are supposed to be off limits until after the exams.'

'Maybe you should stand up to them.'

'If you understood the stress levels in our house already, you would know that is the worst thing I could do. They'd ground me completely.' Lola picked up her bag. 'Come on – we're late for Geography.'

By lunch time Candy had cleaned the house, put the washing on the line and walked past the telephone about a hundred times, willing it to ring. Nick knew her routine, and until recently had always called her about mid-morning from his office. But now there was a resounding silence. Panic rose up in her throat again, constricting it, and a lump seemed to have formed in her stomach. She reached for her inhaler and tried to calm down. Perhaps he *was* in a meeting. Perhaps he had been telling the truth last night, after all, and merely popped out for a late takeaway after working all evening. But he hadn't been carrying food bags, and he certainly hadn't been asleep for hours. And who was he talking and laughing with on the phone at that time of night? The questions fired off in her mind like rockets, and in the end she collapsed in front of daytime television in an attempt to give her tortured mind a rest.

When the phone did ring Candy almost hit the ceiling. Frantically, she hunted for the TV controller, turned the sound down and grabbed the phone. 'Hello?'

'Mummy, it's me – are you all right?'

'Lola.' Her heart sank like a piece of lead. 'Yes…yes, of course I'm all right – why?'

'Nothing really – but you were so late home last night, and you looked like death this morning; I didn't want to say too much in front of Leo.'

'Oh... I just had a late night at Sarah's house – had a couple of drinks and we forgot the time. But thank you for caring.'

'Mummy, I do know...'

'You do know what, Lola?'

'Oh, nothing. I'll see you at dance class after school.'

Candy put down the phone and sat staring at the wall. Could Lola possibly know about Nick? She was an intuitive girl, and until recently they had always been very close. Perhaps she had guessed. And if *she* had guessed, was it possible Mason also had his suspicions?

Suddenly Candy's world seemed to be closing in on her – and once again she reached for her inhaler.

Stage Struck

Thursday 30th October

Full of trepidation, Rose drove herself to the first rehearsal. She had highlighted in pink all her lines in the script, and tried to learn a few in her lunch break at the hospital, much to the amusement of her staff nurses, Sally and Joan.

'Principal boy!' Joan had giggled. 'Fishnet tights and thigh slapping. Ooooh I can't *wait* to see that. We'll organise a coach party to come to see you!'

'Oh, dear,' she said, smiling, 'I knew I should have kept it to myself.'

It seemed that everyone knew about her part in the pantomime, and she was being teased unmercifully. Even Doctor Katz now said, 'Come along, Sister, show a leg,' when he wanted her attention on a ward round. But they were all supporting her, as they had done through her sorrows and troubles and she was grateful for their affection.

She parked the car and walked down the High Street towards the church, her heart beat rising with every step. Taking a deep breath, she opened the church door, steadied herself and then, pinning a smile on her face, moved purposefully past the entrance to the main church into the hall, where Patsy was presiding over her coffee cups.

'Rose,' she greeted her. 'They were taking bets on whether you would come back tonight. I know you were pushed in to taking part. I'm so glad you decided to give it a go.'

'I haven't slept well since I agreed to it, Patsy. But here I am, and in need of a strong black coffee, please.'

Mason came into the hall a moment later and Rose tried not to stare at him too hard. He looked pale and tense; his eyes were tired behind his glasses, but he managed a smile when his glance fell on her.

'We'll start in five minutes. I need a coffee first.' As Mason approached, Rose felt her heart thump rather hard in her chest. 'It's so good to see you. Is Lauren here?'

'Not yet – she had a meeting in London, and she's coming straight from the station.'

Plainly, Candy had not arrived with Mason, and Rose wondered whether their row had escalated into something more serious.

The noise level rose as more and more people came into the hall, among them a good looking man with immaculately cut dark hair and a Colgate smile. Rose almost expected to see a twinkle emerge from his mouth with a *ting*.

'Who's that?' she asked Patsy over the counter.

'Nick Harrow our Stage Manager – a bit of a smoothy but he's a good SM.'

Nick looked around as if seeking someone then, with a slight shrug, came over to the counter and dazzled Patsy with a grin. *'Café noir, s'il vous plait.'*

'Mais oui, Monsieur,' replied Patsy, handing him a cup.

'Where's the beautiful Candy?' Nick casually asked Mason.

'She's not going to be involved – too tired, she says.'

'Really?' He raised his eyebrows, and moved away thoughtfully.

Just then Lauren burst into the hall, still dressed in her business clothes comprising tailored trousers and suede jacket with elegant Chelsea boots, her hair almost tamed into a jet black bob. 'Sorry I'm late.'

'Who is this?' joked Patsy. 'I've never seen her before.'

'Okay, okay' grumbled Lauren. 'I didn't have time to change.'

'You've got legs, and a waist – and pretty feet in ordinary boots,' joined in Rose with a laugh. 'You look gorgeous!'

'Oh, give over – I hate this stuff – it's so uncomfortable.'

The rest of the cast had arrived, so Mason called them to order, and the rehearsal began.

'John – you're going to hate this, but I've brought you a rehearsal skirt. You move differently when you're dressed for the part, and it will help you to believe in the character. Sorry, mate.'

'Oh, boy,' grinned John, tying on the wrap-around batik skirt. 'I'm sure glad my mother can't see me now. Clive…Clive come on, we have to start.'

Clive was preoccupied with looking at Lauren, but she was oblivious to his gaze as she scanned her own lines.

'Sorry …right….um... Hello everybody, I'm Jack the jolly Jester… Well, say hello Jack…'

For an hour they practised the first two scenes over and over and by the time she had been through her own first scene twice Rose was feeling more confident. Mason encouraged her, explaining she needed to breathe from her diaphragm if her voice was to carry through the theatre. He showed her how to turn the correct way on stage, and pointed out the audience would hear her better if she faced front. But it was all done in good humour and she loved it.

Lola was a bit subdued but gave her all as Lady Marian. However, Rose was aware that the young girl was watchful, her eyes assessing others in the room, especially the men and particularly Nick Harrow.

When they broke for coffee Nick came up to Rose and introduced himself formally. He had a pleasant voice and a firm handshake, and although he clearly checked out her face and figure with approval, he didn't make her uncomfortable.

'Will you be coming to our annual dinner dance?' he asked. 'I'm organising it this year, and wishing fervently that I hadn't agreed to do it. It's on the thirteenth of December, before the panto preparations get too frantic, and while everyone is still speaking to one another.'

'Well,' she said, hastily checking her shifts in her diary, 'yes, thank you, it sounds like fun. Is it posh frocks?'

'Absolutely. We have about fifty members plus partners, but most of them never put their heads over the parapet except for a booze-up. I always see people at the party I thought had died.'

Rose laughed. 'Count me in. Have you asked John and Clive? They're new too.'

She introduced them, and in the end Clive and John said they would only go if Rose and Lauren agreed to accompany them, and a deal was struck.

'Who are you going with, Nick?' asked Lauren.

'You'll have to wait and see, my flower,' he teased her. 'Right, I need volunteers to build and paint the sets. We have a store behind the church where all the flats and large props are kept, together with most colours of paint and rather hairless paint brushes. Since we have to take everything outside into the car park to paint it, I want the work done in the next week or two before the weather gets any colder. Names please, for next Saturday?'

Clive, John and Mason volunteered so, after a glance at each other, Lauren and Rose agreed to go along too.

'Great. Lunch will be my treat at the pub afterwards.' This won him a few murmurs of thanks. 'We meet at ten o'clock, so bring a thermos of something hot. I have to leave now, Mason, work to finish for tomorrow, but I'll see you all at the weekend.' He waved and left, and the rest of them regrouped to finish blocking out their moves.

Maureen had a streaming cold which gave her a magnificently croaky voice and Mason liked it so much he asked her to keep it in the character.

'But Mason' she protested. 'I saw Verruca as more of a Cherie Blair....'

'No, Maureen, she's a full on, warts-and-all witch – with a croaky voice.'

'If you insist.' She shrugged. 'You're the boss.' And with no further argument turned to put a spell on Lady Marian, frightening a small child who had come to the rehearsal with her mother. The little girl howled and had to be taken out of the hall.

'You see, Mason, you'll have half the kids screaming for their mothers.'

'And the other half loving it. Do you have that effect on the kids at school? The head teacher with the hex?'

'When it suits me.' Maureen gave his a wicked smile. 'Let's say they don't mess me about. Are we finished for the night? I need a large scotch and a warm bed.'

'Yes – you can certainly go before you start an epidemic. Chorus - please stay for half an hour with Jo, who's going to do some of the choreography in the Maypole scene. Please learn your lines. Thanks everyone.'

Lauren and Rose approached Mason as he was leaving.

'Is Candy all right?' Lauren asked.

'I don't know. She's behaving very oddly - even for her. She says she's done three shows in a row and has had enough. But Jo is a good choreographer, and Candy is still going to teach the little ones at her dance school, so we really don't need her. We're just short of a Tabitha Cat at present. Any ideas?'

'Sorry, I haven't.'

'Rose - any nubile nurses at your hospital who might come along?'

'I'll ask around.'

'Thanks – see you on Tuesday.'

Nick left the rehearsal feeling very relieved that Candy had dropped out of the show. Perhaps she was going to accept the inevitable ending of their affair with more grace than he had anticipated. He'd been trying to cool things for a couple of weeks. It had been fun but he was becoming tired of her insatiable need for attention. She questioned his every move, and last night he'd lied to her instead of telling her that he'd been out for a curry with some friends from work. She would have wanted to know who he had been with, and where, and it exhausted him. It was like being married.

He was also worried that she was becoming careless about concealing their affair at home. The last thing he needed was for Mason to find out and make a scene at the drama group. Since coming to Sipton, the group had formed the main nucleus of his social friends, but he knew they would instinctively side with Mason, and he would be severely castigated by them. It was, he knew from experience, always tricky getting out of relationships, especially with married women. He had to let Candy down gently – try to make her think it was her idea to finish it; which was why, with Mason and the children safely at rehearsal for at least another hour, he decided to call her.

'It's me,' he whispered as she answered the phone. 'Are you all right? Mason said you had dropped out of the show.'

'I am extraordinarily well,' she slurred down the phone. 'Very well indeed…in fact I can't remember when I've been weller.'

'Candy, my flower, you've been drinking.'

'I have. So what?'

'So I think an early night would be a good idea? Drink lots of water and get some sleep.'

'And waste the rest of this very good bottle of wine? No, no – but you could come and share it with me. I'm sitting here drinking it with nothing on except my mascara. Doesn't that tempt you, Nick? It always used to.'

'Oh, God. Look Candy, I'll be there in a couple of minutes – for Pete's sake put on a nightdress or something.'

'Why should I put my clothes on when you're coming round? You'll only take them off again, you naughty man.'

'Believe me, Candy, I won't. I just want to make sure you're tucked up in bed before the family get home and you say something we'll both regret.'

'I'll be waiting.' She hung up.

'Oh, shit. Stupid, stupid, stupid. I must have been mad to get involved with her.'

A few minutes later he parked just down the road from her house and walked up to the door carrying a briefcase with a clipboard in his hand.

Candy opened the door with a giggle. She stood, stark naked, with the porch light shining on her. 'Are you pretending to be the insurance man?'

'Candy, for Heaven's sake, get in out of sight and put some clothes on!' He shoved her into the hall and closed the door.

'Nick – Oh, I've missed you so much.' She flung her arms round his neck and kissed him, and in spite of himself, Nick dropped the briefcase and clipboard and kissed her back. She really was a very sexy woman, and the feel of her soft skin aroused him instantly.

'Candy,' he croaked, pushing her away, 'I can't – not now. Mason and the kids will be back soon, so please be sensible. Look, get dressed while I make you a black coffee. You're going to give the game away if you're not careful, and then we'll all be in trouble.'

'Well, maybe it's time they knew about us. I mean, we can't go on like this, darling, can we?' She hiccupped. 'I love you and you love me, so I think it's about time we moved in together.'

'What?' he gasped. 'Candy, you know that isn't possible.'

'Why not? You're living alone, and I don't want to be with Mason any more. I want to be with you. It's time. I shall tell him tonight – that's what I'll do. The minute he walks through the door.'

'No, Candy, you won't.'

She sobered up instantly. 'What do you mean?'

He braced himself. This was not how he would have chosen to handle things and he really didn't want to hurt her, but now he had no choice.

'Candy, I don't want you to move in with me. We've had a lot of fun, and I think you're gorgeous and very desirable. But I'm a solitary being which is why I've never married. I like my own company and the freedom that goes with it. I never wanted the wife and two-point-four children – or a live-in mistress, and I still don't. I'm sorry.'

'You bastard.'

'Yes, you're probably right.'

'Are you dropping me?'

'I think it's for the best.'

'No!' She began to cry – deep wracking sobs, and in spite of himself he put his arms around her. 'Please don't do this, Nick. I love you so much. I need you.'

'That's the problem, Candy. I hate to be needed. I'm a very selfish person.'

She turned away, picked up a glass of wine from the coffee table and threw it over him. To his consternation, she then picked up the bottle, which was almost empty, and advanced on him threateningly.

'Candy, don't be stupid. Put it down.'

'Make me!' He grabbed her wrist but as he wrested the bottle from her she flung her arms around his neck and, pulling his face down, began to kiss him frantically. 'Just once more, Nick, please, darling, just once more, and I swear I'll let you go in peace.'

He was lost. Within a few seconds he was undressed and she was pinned under him on the sofa.

It was over very quickly, and Nick sat up dressing hastily as Candy lay, laughing softly at him.

'You see, darling, you can't resist me.'

'That was absolute madness. Now get dressed or go to bed and for heaven's sake don't even *speak* to Mason until tomorrow when you're sober.'

'Okay, but only if you promise not to end it between us. Honestly, Nick I can't handle it. Mason would know, because I can't hide my feelings.'

Stage Struck

'That's blackmail. I'll call you tomorrow morning.' He rushed upstairs and found a dressing gown behind the bathroom door which he flung at her. 'Put this on, for God's sake, or you'll have some very difficult explaining to do if Lola and Leo come through the door and find you like that – never mind Mason.'

Sulkily, she picked it up, and he hoped she had the sense to put it on.

He retrieved the briefcase and clipboard from the hall, slammed the front door, ran to his Land Rover and drove away, hoping desperately he hadn't left any tell-tale signs of his presence in the lounge; he had dashed out too quickly to check properly.

This really has to stop. He wondered how on earth he could extricate himself gracefully. Candy – aptly named, he thought irately – was becoming like a sticky sweet paper he couldn't shake off.

***

Clive and John left the rehearsal and went across to the pub. A roaring fire blazed in the grate and they both moved close to it with their drinks.

'That hall was like a freezer. I was glad of my skirt tonight.'

Clive laughed. 'Keep your voice down or I'll pretend I'm not with you. Anyway, what do you think of Lauren?'

'She's delightful, and it's good to see you taking an interest again after the divorce.'

'I've only been out with her for a few weeks, on a casual basis. She's a great girl, lots of fun, but not as easy to get to know as you might think. Oh, look who's just come in. Isn't it the bloke who didn't get the part of dame?'

Winston went up to the bar and ordered a drink, then looked around for someone to talk to.

'Don't look at him – perhaps he won't remember us,' said Clive quietly, turning his back. But the tall Texan beside him was hard to forget, especially for Winston, and a moment later he headed in their direction.

'Good evening.' Uninvited, he pulled up a chair at their table. 'You got my part in the pantomime, didn't you?'

'Um, well, I got the part of dame certainly,' replied John, 'and I'm sorry if that's a problem to you, sir.'

'It was ridiculous giving it to someone else. No-one in the group has my experience. I've been playing dame for twenty years.'

'Then perhaps you could give me some tips?' asked John hopefully.

Winston shook his head and knocked back a large whisky. 'No, you can sink or swim, and I expect you'll sink. The group is going down fast. It's not what it used to be.'

'Why is that – er – Winston?' asked Clive.

'Arrogant young bunch now – think they know it all. Those of us with age and experience are getting side-lined.'

'But surely new young people are the life blood of any group, aren't they? What else do you do in the society? Apart from play dame.'

Clive had a feeling John had opened a Pandora's Box, and that no end of nasty things were about to emerge.

'Well, recently I played the lead in *Pygmalion*.'

'Professor Higgins?'

'No, Doolittle, and I've been in dozens of other plays over the years. I should have gone onto the professional stage, but somehow the right opportunity never came along.'

He then regaled them with the experiences of more than twenty years on the amateur stage, claiming to have played everything from Mark Anthony to Sweeney Todd.

'Do you direct or stage manage?' asked Clive.

'Good heavens no. I'm an actor.'

'Ah. Can I get you a drink?'

'Large scotch, please.'

Clive went to the bar and stood looking back at the lonely man whose whole life had been rendered worthless because he hadn't got a part in a pantomime. Loneliness was a scourge he too had suffered after Daisy left him and he shuddered at the memory. They had been married five years, travelled the world with the bank, and he thought they had been happy. But one day she'd left a note to say she had fallen for someone else, and that their marriage was over. He had been inconsolable, unable to comprehend that she had been seeing someone and he hadn't a clue. It was several months before he tracked her down, and discovered she had left him for another woman.

Those had been the worst days of his life. With great relief, he accepted a year-long posting to Dubai, during which time the divorce was finalised. His return to the London office meant it was time to settle down, buy a small property and move on with his life; the time for grief and regret was over. So, here he was in Sipton with his old colleague John, the only person outside his family who was aware of the true reason for his marriage break up. And he knew he could trust him implicitly.

John had never married. At thirty he said he still wasn't grown up enough to cope with a serious relationship. There had been a number of girls over the years, one or two of whom had lived with him for a time, but as the product of a fractured home, John was in no hurry to repeat his parents' mistakes. Marry in haste, repent forever, was his motto.

'At leisure, surely?' Clive had corrected him.

'I think my version is more accurate,' John replied wryly. 'My folks are still at war and they've been divorced for sixteen years. I still feel like a tug-of-love baby.'

'Neither of them married again?'

'Oh, sure – my dad's on his third try, and Mom married a pig who knocked her about. I sorted him,' he reminisced with relish. 'Now she's living with a hat designer.'

'Good heavens. My life seems quite banal by comparison.'

Now Clive looked at the kind-hearted American who was trying to mollify the aging actor, and thought how lucky he was to have him for a friend. He carried the tray of drinks over; Winston took his without a thank you, and downed it in one.

'Do you live close to the centre of town?' John asked Winston, obviously desperate to find a topic of conversation away from the drama group.

'I have a flat at The Brambles. I used to have a big house at West Common, but when Peggy died there was no point in keeping it. Too many memories.'

The Brambles was an exclusive development half a mile from the high street, mostly occupied by young executive commuters who needed a place close to the railway station. Clive couldn't imagine Winston fitting in there at all.

'Do you have children?'

'A daughter, Jackie – and a son.'

'And do you see them often?'

'No.' He stood up abruptly and moved away. 'And I don't like to talk about my private life with people I don't know. Goodnight to you.' He walked stiffly to the door with a brief salute to the barman. Through the window they watched him cross the road to the Sipton Wine Shop from where, a few minutes later he emerged, carrying a heavy brown bag and headed for home.

'I would hate to end up like him, poor guy,' John said. 'He's sure hard to make friends with, but he's lonely, and it seems like the drama group is his family now.'

'He's certainly a sad character, and I bet he does have a wealth of experience he could share.'

'If he's ever sober long enough. How old do you think he is?'

'Maybe mid-sixties – not ancient. There's obviously a problem with his kids which is making him very unhappy,' Clive mused. 'Perhaps we should try again to get him involved with the show. I'll talk to Mason next week.'

Stage Struck

Winston let himself into his silent flat, shut the door behind him and leaned on it with a sob. The encounter with those two young good-looking men who had stolen his whole *raison d'etre* had left him drained of everything except anger.

Patronising creeps. 'Get out of my life,' he howled. 'How dare you rob me of the only thing that has meaning for me any more?'

He was certain he would probably never play dame again. He'd had his day and everyone knew it. His friends at SADS would despise him, especially after his outburst at the audition, and he groaned aloud.

What a fool! At last he wiped his eyes and poured half a tumbler of scotch then, on second thoughts, filled the glass to the brim.

***

After the rehearsal Mason agreed Leo and Lola could go on to meet their friends at the bowling alley, if they promised to be home by midnight. Too exhausted to go for a drink with anyone, he had gratefully locked the church hall door and dropped the key into the caretaker's cottage on his way home. He was not looking forward to seeing Candy; she had been in a foul mood for nearly a week and his patience was getting very thin. He hardly knew her any more, and wondered what had happened to the extrovert, happy, ever optimistic girl he had married.

He opened the front door in time to glimpse Candy in a bathrobe disappearing around the top of the stairs.

'I was about to have a bath,' she called down. 'I knocked a bottle of wine all over me. Sorry – I was going to share it with you when you got home.'

'Never mind.'

Mason went into the lounge and was amazed at the disarray. There was a wine stain on the carpet, a bottle lay on its side on the floor, and the loose cushions from the sofa were tossed onto the coffee table. What *had* she been doing?

Irritably, he threw the bottle in the kitchen bin, replaced the cushions and sprayed stain remover on the wine mark. Finally, he turned on the TV and collapsed in the sofa in front of it. News of a bomb in the Middle East, a sportsman who had taken something illegal, and reports of a falling stock market, followed by adverts offering him fifteen different types of insurance was all that was on offer - apart from a choice of game shows and a depressing soap. Bored, he switched it off, put on his favourite CD, poured himself a scotch then stretched out on the sofa and tried to get comfortable. But hard as he tried, the cushions seemed to be fighting back, and finally he stood up, pulled them all off and plumped them up. This sofa, which had seen nineteen years of family life, was lumpy and in need of replacement.

But it had seen happy times, he recollected with a smile. Leo had probably been conceived on it, the family had often cuddled up together on it to watch a video, stuffing their faces with take-away pizza, and the children had used its cushions to build all manner of make-believe worlds when they were small. The squashy old sofa was part of the family. Perhaps if they just had it dry cleaned it could stay a bit longer. He patted it affectionately and closed his eyes, letting the sixth Brandenburg Concerto drift soothingly over him.

Twenty minutes later, Candy re-appeared dressed in Winnie the Pooh pyjamas. She looked cute, and he pulled her down beside him and put his arms around her.

Candy gave a sigh of relief when she came down and saw Mason looking relaxed in front of the television. She had heard him tidying the room and been terrified he might have found evidence of what had happened there just a few minutes before.

A pang of guilt made her go to him and snuggle up on the old sofa, and she put her head on his shoulder, thinking how warm and familiar, how comfortable, he felt. His lingering cologne was one he'd worn ever since she had known him and newer more fashionable varieties bought as presents stood unopened in the bathroom cupboard. He had a very slightly larger waist line than when she'd first met him, but he'd aged well, with barely a grey hair among the dark ones. Apart from slightly deeper laughter lines, he looked very good for his forty-five years.

So, she asked herself for the hundredth time, why was she risking her home and family for an opportunistic swine like Nick? Excitement, and the chance to feel young and sexy again, she supposed were the driving force, and Nick was an exceptional lover who brought out the best – and the worst in her – in bed. With him she was uninhibited, and he adored her supple dancer's body. Nick had a vivid imagination which he used to full effect, taking her to heights she had hardly dreamed of, and she shivered with pleasure at the memories.

'Are you cold?' Mason asked her, clasping her more warmly in his arms.

'No, I'm not cold,' she murmured, knowing that there was a place inside her which was frozen with fear. Nick wanted to end the relationship, but Candy felt such despair and desolation at the very idea, she couldn't imagine how she would live without him. It couldn't be allowed, she vowed; she would do anything to keep him – absolutely anything.

'Are you in a better mood now?' Mason asked carefully.

'Yes, and I'm sorry I've been so horrible. I hated you being at rehearsal without me tonight, so I've decided that if I'm still welcome I'll come back and help out.'

'Of course you're still welcome,' he said with delight. 'And will you play Tabitha? There's no-one who would do it like you – or look so good in a leotard.'

'Okay. Yes, it will be fun.' In fact the idea appalled her, but Nick would be at most of the rehearsals. She knew her lover would be devastated if their affair became common knowledge, therefore a little blackmail might be in order, she decided. But in the meantime, until she could convince Nick that he couldn't live without her, she had to keep Mason sweet.

'Shall we go to bed?' asked Mason, stroking her cheek.

With a smile, she took his hand and led him upstairs.

Stage Struck

Saturday, 1st November

Lauren climbed out of bed at nine o'clock, wishing she hadn't agreed to help paint the set. It had been a hard week and she was tired.

Usually she worked from the offices of Green Ideas, a flourishing advertising agency in Sipton and loved her job, but one of their most important clients was showing an interest in a big campaign after Christmas. Her boss Gordon Green, known not surprisingly as Gee Gee, had given her the chance to work with him, planning their presentation - so this week had entailed three days travelling to London to discuss their requirements. Since Lauren hated trains and the city, it had been an ordeal. However, things had gone well and her own ideas had been incorporated into the scheme Gee Gee was offering. It would be a real *coup* for her if their presentation was accepted and she was nervously awaiting their decision, due on Monday. If it went well, she knew she was in line for promotion.

Lazily she stretched, and went downstairs to make a mug of tea in her tiny kitchen. Bugsy, her little bulldog emerged from his basket under the stairs and followed her as she filled the kettle, waiting for his morning biscuit.

Lauren gave him an affectionate pat and smiled as he crunched and dribbled bits of Boneo on the floor.

'Mucky pup,' she chided him. 'Out you go. Do what you have to do in the garden while I get ready. You can come with me and paint the set this morning. I'll tie a paintbrush to your stumpy old tail.' She laughed at the image and went back upstairs to run a deep hot bath with lots of bubbles.

Bugsy was the light of her life and went almost everywhere with her. Fortunately, Gee Gee was a softy who allowed the dog to come to the office and sit on a rug under Lauren's desk. In fact, he was so loved by everyone at the agency that Lauren suggested he should go on the payroll as company pet. His flat, wrinkled, brown and white face had even graced one or two adverts. No-one knew much about him although the vet thought he was about two years old when Lauren had adopted him after he followed her home from the park one day. He had been hungry and sick, and since no-one had claimed him he moved in and adored Lauren every day since then. He would sit and stare at her, a picture of contentment, as if he couldn't believe his luck.

An hour later Lauren and Bugsy set off for the church hall, picking up Rose on the way. Lauren wore a paint-covered sweater and jeans and Rose had elected to wear some old leggings with an aged shirt over a thick jumper.

'Don't we look glamorous?' said Rose. 'Hi, Bugsy.'

He wagged his tail in greeting, and ran up and down the rear seat of Lauren's old car, excited by the outing.

They opened the gate to the back car park at the church to find the men had already made a start on pulling out all the flats, which were still adorned with the remains of Professor Higgins's library from the last production.

Mason greeted them cheerfully as he fussed Bugsy, and Nick, emerging from the shed, dazzled them with a smile.

'Good morning, ladies. Paints are in the shed and new brushes in that bag. Everything needs a white undercoat, and then we can start painting the Magic Forest on those, and Warthogs Castle on those.' He indicated two different stacks. 'Lauren, your artistic skills are needed.' He showed her some drawings of the proposed sets while Rose grabbed a paint brush and went to help Mason.

'Clive and John are in the shed trying to make sense of the heap of rubbish that's accumulated,' Mason said. 'We can't put our lovely painted sets back in there unless they have room to dry properly.'

Just then a rat ran out of the old wooden building and Rose shrieked with fright as it scurried across her foot.

'My goodness, you're as white as a sheet,' said Mason, putting an arm around her, causing her already raised heart rate to soar even further. 'Sit on this bench a minute. Oh, look!' he exclaimed, pointing as Bugsy chased the rat into the bushes. 'What a hero!'

'Did you see that?' Clive came rushing out brandishing a large stick. 'Oh, well done, Bugsy.'

The dog emerged from the bushes with the rat limp in his mouth and proudly dropped it at Lauren's feet, where it gave one last twitch and lay still.

'Thank you, Bugs,' she said faintly and went to sit next to Rose. 'Did you bring a flask, Rosie? I need a coffee after that. Can't stand rodents – even dead ones.'

A moment later there was a crash and a shout of triumph from the shed and John emerged carrying another rat by the tail. 'It had a wife,' he grinned. 'There's a nest at the back, but the babies have gone. I hit it with a shovel,' he explained, pleased with himself.

The bodies were removed, coffee consumed and for the next two hours they painted diligently until all the flats were white and gleaming, ready for their new rôle; later, they'd be stacked carefully in the shed to dry. Rose gazed round at the accumulated treasures from dozens of previous productions. There was an Adam fireplace made of plywood, curtain rails, and enough bric-a-brac to stock an antique shop. Pictures, old carpets and an Aladdin's lamp, gleaming in the sunlight that filtered weakly through the dusty window. Rose picked it up and smiling, gave it a rub.

'What is your wish, Oh Mistress?' John bowed solemnly, his hands together. 'Your word is my command.'

'Nothing you could give me unfortunately, Genie.'

'I'll buy you a drink.'

'Done.'

'Right,' Nick said, 'that will do for today, we've made a good start.' He peeled off his overall to the accompaniment of *The Stripper* from those assembled. 'Hey, save the jokes for the production. Now who's for a pub lunch?'

'We're not exactly dressed for it,' said Rose, 'and Lauren's got paint in her hair.'

'Never mind. You can sit in the corner and we'll shield you from sight with our manly bodies.'

'Thanks, Mason. How gallant. Okay, come on, Rosie, we can wash the worst off in the Ladies and you can pick the white bits out of my hair. We'll see you guys at the pub in a while. Clive, can you take Bugsy?'

The girls went in to the building through the side door from the car park, past the Ministers' office, and across the foyer to the Ladies. Rose tried not to look to her left where florists were busy arranging flowers for a wedding in the main church. However, the overpowering scent of lilies caused her to cover her nose and rush into the toilets almost gagging. Weeping, she leaned over the sink, gasping for breath.

'That was unfortunate.' Lauren put her arm around her. 'I am sorry,' she said, and waited until Rose calmed down.

'I simply have to get over it. I feel such a fool. I can't go through my life having a panic attack every time I go in a church or smell lilies.'

'Maybe you should get some help?'

'You know I've tried that. My counselling lasted six weeks after it happened, but it didn't help. It just seemed to drag up the whole horrible business again, and I had to keep living it over and over. Explaining how I felt, why I felt that way. It was almost worse than the original trauma. No. If I'm going to get over it, I'll do it my way.' She took a deep, resolute breath. 'Right, now let's get the white splodges off your hair and go to the pub.'

***

Twenty minutes later, considerably cleaner, they slipped out of the church by another door and crossed the High Street to the Fox and Rabbit.

'Do you really like Clive?' Rose asked Lauren.

'Yes, he's lovely, but he has a lot of baggage - the divorce and so on. Judging by his face when he mentioned it the other evening, he's far from over it.'

'But you're going out with him anyway.'

'As a friend. We have a laugh, but he's not ready to get involved with anyone yet, and I don't want to risk being hurt. I should warn you, Rose, friendships develop during a production because we become a very close-knit group as the show progresses. Almost like a family. Sometimes it's good – sometimes things develop that shouldn't.'

Rose flushed, wondering whether her attraction to Mason was written on her face, and vowed to be extra careful. She would hate even Lauren to realise she had feelings for him. 'Sorry, I'd floated away... What did you say?'

'Oh, Rose – I've been asking you to come shopping with me for a dress for the dinner dance. You know what I'm like - I'll probably buy something grotesque.'

'I'd love to go with you! Tell you what, next Saturday we'll go to John Lewis, shop, and have lunch.'

'Deal.'

The pub was crowded, with a pleasant hum of chatter and Rose notice Lauren's eyes were only seeking one person.

They carefully made their way to where the others were sitting near the fire, and Mason rose to greet them. They asked for shandies and he went to order drinks, while Clive and John shuffled up a wooden settle to make room for them. Rose couldn't help noticing that Clive gently pulled Lauren to sit beside him, or that she flushed with pleasure and gave him a shy smile.

'Lunch, as promised, is my treat – you've all worked magnificently,' proclaimed Nick and everyone decided on the bangers and mash special which made ordering simpler.

'Why do you call wieners bangers?' John asked Rose, and she almost choked on her drink.

'Why do you call sausages wieners?' she chuckled. 'We sometimes call them bangers because if you don't pierce the skins before you cook them, they go bang.'

'Why didn't I think of that?' he smiled. 'So obvious.'

As they ate, Bugsy circulated around their legs and did rather well for titbits.

Stage Struck

'Are you doing anything this evening?' John asked Rose tentatively. 'I just wondered whether you liked Thai food? A new restaurant has opened in Walkers Way. Fancy giving it a try?'

'Well...'

'Please don't feel pressured. It was just a thought.'

'I don't feel pressured, John.' She smiled, noticing he looked embarrassed, and rather pink. 'And I love Thai food – thank you.'

'Great! Shall I pick you up?'

Rose gave him her address and realised that Lauren was watching her with raised eyebrows and a little smile. 'I need to go, Rosie, I have to feed Bugsy – he's still hungry, even if he's had more titbits than are good for him. And I've a week's ironing backed up.'

'Okay.' Rose wriggled out from behind the wooden table and joined her friend. They said their farewells and headed back to Lauren's car which was parked near the church.

'You got a date, girl?' asked Lauren.

'Just a Thai meal tonight. I only want him as a friend, and I promise I'll make sure he understands that.'

'Why? I mean, for Heaven's sake, Rose, he's lovely. And that accent...'

'I'm not ready for a big romance.'

'If you say so. But he'd be a lot better for you than Mason.'

'Mason? What are you talking about?'

'You fancy him.'

Rose gaped at her friend and was about to deny it, but on second thoughts she knew it would be pointless; and if Lauren had realised, who else might have picked up the vibrations?

'You don't miss much,' Rose said at last, 'but I would never do anything to encourage him or damage his marriage. Do you think he realises?'

'No, shouldn't think so. He's too pre-occupied with the show and his problems with Candy. Anyway, he's far too old for you. He's at least forty-two.'

'Yes, I know. But he is gorgeous.'

The girls laughed and set off for home with Bugsy barking for his dinner all the way.

Rose waved goodbye to Lauren and went into her little Edwardian house, intending to spend the afternoon catching up with the housework and ironing. But after a quick rush round with the vacuum and a duster, she abandoned the idea and sank into a chair by the fire with her script.

She had a pretty good idea of most of her lines already; learning had never been a problem for her. But the last few nights she had slept poorly. Since joining the drama group and being forced to go through the church, the nightmares had come back. At least once every night she woke with a shriek and then was too afraid to go back to sleep. But as she sat trying to focus on her lines, they began to get fuzzy and within a few minutes exhaustion overcame her; her eyes became impossibly heavy and with Min curled up warmly on her lap she fell asleep.

When she woke with a sudden start, it was dark and someone was knocking at her door.

'Oh, good Lord, its seven-thirty,' she gasped, gazing down in dismay at the grubby clothes she had been wearing to paint the sets. There was nothing for it but to answer the door and she was mortified to find John standing outside, a picture of sartorial elegance, and clutching a bunch of freesias.

He looked a little startled before breaking into a grin. 'You forgot, huh?'

'No, no John, I didn't forget – I haven't slept properly for a week and when I came home I crashed out in my chair. I'm so sorry. Please come in.' She shut the door and took the flowers. 'They're lovely, thank you.' Carrying the flowers into the kitchen, she added, 'I'll fix you a drink and be ready in ten minutes.'

John was entranced by the slightly unfocused, sleepy blue eyes and tousled hair of his date. She looked delightfully cuddly, and he would have happily volunteered to pop out for a takeaway to share on the sofa. But she was clearly embarrassed, so he accepted the offer of a black coffee while she pounded upstairs to shower and change.

While he waited, John took the opportunity to wander round Rose's pretty living room. It was intrinsically English, he thought; chintz, dark wood, a glorious Tibetan rug and some rather good water colours of seascapes on the wall. Classy. He then crossed to peer at pictures of the family on her small desk. There was a school photo of a young boy, and another of a family group including Rose with people he presumed were her parents, and possibly an older sister. He picked it up and was still speculating about that a few minutes later, when Rose re-entered the room.

He turned to admire the transformation. 'Wow, Cinderella, you *shall* go to the ball!'

Rose had changed into a classic little black dress which stopped just above her knees, accentuating her long shapely calves. She wore black court shoes, and a red velvet jacket was slung over an arm. She had swept her hair into a spiky knot and applied a touch of lipstick and mascara. She looked stunning.

He held out the framed photo. 'Your family?' he asked.

Stage Struck

'My parents, and cousin Samantha,' she told him. She gestured at the others. 'The school photo is Ben, Sam's son.'

He replaced it on the desk, taking a few seconds to calm his breathing. 'I booked a table for eight o'clock, so shall we go? I don't know about you, but I'm starving.'

Rose suddenly realised that she was too. With a nod and a smile, she allowed him to help her into her jacket. She locked the house, John opened the car door for her, and she slid into the seat of his smart but unpretentious BMW.

The restaurant was busy on Saturday night, and a smiling Thai waiter showed them to their table. John asked for a bottle of Chardonnay while they read the menu and then, being an expert on oriental food, he helped her to choose.

'So, Rose, why have you been losing sleep? You're not worrying about the pantomime, are you?' His dark eyes were kind, and she suddenly felt the awful pressure of tears close behind her own.

'No, no, nothing like that,' she murmured. 'Just things that come back to haunt me sometimes.'

'I guess we all have a few of those.'

'What are yours?' she asked, hoping to divert him.

'I was at Sendai airport in Japan on March 11th 2011 when the earthquake and Tsunami struck.'

'Oh, dear God.' She gazed at him in awe. 'What happened to you?'

'I survived by hanging onto a tree, but two friends were lost. I stayed to help for a month afterwards. It's not something you forget. I still wake up sweating sometimes.' He shrugged sadly. 'But, life goes on. Now, are you going to tell me about your demons?'

'They hardly bear comparison.' She paused, then with sudden resolution, decided to tell him the truth. 'My father was a vicar and I was brought up with strict rules of conduct and a very true - or at least I thought a very true - and real belief in God. But then two years ago my mother died in terrible agony from cancer.'

'I'm so sorry. Are you saying that shook your faith?'

'No, it didn't. I believed it was one of life's challenges I had to deal with. But a year later, my father went missing. The cleaning lady called me at the Nurses' Home at the hospital – she said she'd arrived to find the house in total disarray – like someone had gone on the rampage - but his bed hadn't been slept in. I rushed back to the Vicarage, and we called everyone we could think of but no-one had seen him. Then the verger came to ask for the keys to the church and we couldn't find those either.'

She paused and glanced at John.

'Go on, if you want to,' he said gently, reaching across the table and gripping her trembling hand.

She took a deep breath. 'I went with the verger across to the church and found the vestry door unlocked. While he was rummaging around in there for whatever he needed, I stepped into the main church…and …and…there was my father, sprawled in front of the altar. He was dead. He'd taken poison which must have caused an excruciating death. He was blue, with his tongue all swollen and sticking out, and his hands gripping his throat. He had pulled a huge arrangement of lilies over and fallen on them. As I looked at him, the smell from them was overpowering and even now they make me feel ill. We found a suicide note in his desk. He confessed that he had helped my mother to die and could no longer live either with her loss or his own guilt.'

John squeezed her hand. 'What a nightmare.'

'I don't know why that all came spilling out. It's not something I usually choose to talk about but, well, now I've told you I would be grateful if you kept it to yourself. Lauren knows, obviously, but I don't want the others in the group to…'

'Feel sorry for you?'

'Something like that.'

'Then it's between us. Here comes the food. I know spicy soup's your favourite, but I reckon this'll knock your socks off.'

He was right. They chatted easily over hot and sour soup, pineapple and fish curry and beef with bok choy with so many delicious side dishes that by the end Rose professed herself hardly able to move.

When they left the restaurant two hours later, she felt a lightening of the dark mood that had haunted her for several days and as the BMW pulled up outside her house she shyly asked John if he would like coffee. He accepted with a smile. 'But don't worry, Rose, your honour is safe; strictly coffee.'

Relieved, she opened the front door and they went into the warmth. John followed her into the little kitchen as she made coffee for him and Earl Grey tea for herself, and then they drifted back to the living room where it seemed quite natural to sit together on the sofa.

'I love your home. It's so welcoming and friendly.'

'Thank you. I bought it with the legacy from my parents. My mother would have liked it.'

'And your father?'

She shrugged. 'I don't really care what he might have thought about it.'

Changing the subject, John told her about his travels. He had a fund of stories from all over the world and she listened, fascinated. He didn't refer to the horror of the Tsunami again, and she didn't ask; she could imagine what it had been like and that was enough.

Finally, regretfully, he stood to leave.

'It's been a wonderful evening, Rose,' he said, taking her hand and raising it to his lips. His hand was firm and warm and his mouth soft against her fingers, and Rose felt a twinge of disappointment when he picked up his coat.

'I'll see you at rehearsal on Tuesday?'

'Yes…and thank you for dinner.' She opened the front door and after giving her the briefest kiss on the cheek he was gone.

Rose slept well that night; the demons, as John had called them, at bay; at least for a while.

John drove away in shock, knowing that he had fallen deeply, irrevocably and mind-blowingly in love.

Stage Struck

Tuesday, 4th November

Tuesday crept round very slowly for Candy. She had heard nothing from Nick, and she was angry and frustrated. Mason had tried to be loving, and obviously bitten his tongue a few times when she had shrugged off his attention, a fact which Lola had noticed with great apprehension.

'Mum – don't be such a cow,' she remonstrated with her, after listening to Candy snap a refusal at Mason when he offered to make dinner.

'Sorry, sorry,' Candy sighed. 'I don't know what's the matter with me.'

'I do.' Lola flounced out of the room, leaving her mother brooding over whether her daughter really did know about Nick. If so, she had an even bigger problem than she thought. Oh, if only she could put the wretched man out of her mind, but the obsession kept her awake at night and left her unable to concentrate during the day. As a result, she was weary and tearful and, what was worse, she looked a wreck. There were bags under her eyes, her skin seemed to have aged ten years and she'd put on three pounds from comfort eating.

She glanced at Mason as he sat moodily in front of a quiz show on television, his almost untouched dinner on a tray on his lap, and wondered for the thousandth time what was driving her to be so stupid. They made love the night after her last, stormy encounter with Nick, and to her surprise she was able to give herself enthusiastically, perhaps because she was feeling guilty, or perhaps as an absurd punishment to Nick. But since then she had sunk into a fit of gloom and despair, and spent her spare time plotting revenge on 'the bastard' as she mentally referred to her erstwhile lover.

At seven-thirty Mason dumped his tray in the kitchen and picked up his jacket. 'Are you coming to rehearsal or not?' he demanded.

'Yes, of course. I said I would, didn't I?'

'So you did,' he muttered. 'Lola, Leo. Ready to go?'

Lola pattered downstairs wearing leggings and a thick white sweater, her long hair in a plait which swung down her back. 'I'll come in my car,' she said, striding through the front door. 'I might be late.'

'You should come straight home afterwards and study,' Candy said tartly, accompanying her down the path. 'You've had too many late nights.'

'Look who's talking,' Lola snapped back as she swung her legs into her Golf. 'Leo, are you coming with me?'

'Oh, yes.' he replied gratefully and clambered into the passenger side.

Lola slammed her car door and drove down the road.

'Do you think they'll split?' asked Leo.

'No. Well, I hope not... but I need your help tonight.'

'What?'

'I'm seeing Alex after rehearsal. If they find out, they'll ground me. If they ask if you know where I am, say Caro and I were meeting up for a drink with some friends from school.'

'Which pub?'

'The Slug and Lettuce.'

'Okay, sis.'

'Thanks.' She smiled fondly at her younger brother, hoping he would cope if, as she feared, their parents' marriage fractured.

Candy and Mason drove to the church hall in silence, each wondering how they were going to get through the next few weeks.

Rose had arrived early and was helping Patsy put out the cups and saucers, when Lauren made an entrance which stopped everyone in their tracks. The door burst open and she posed, yelling 'Ta-Da – you are looking at the newly promoted junior partner who has just secured her first major contract.'

'Congratulations!' Clive and the rest of the cast surrounded her with affection, hugs, kisses and pats on the back, and Rose thought again how fortunate she was to be a part of this lovely group of people.

'How was your date?' Lauren asked, when she had calmed down and grabbed a cup of coffee.

'We had a lovely evening. He's sweet.'

'And?'

'And what?'

'Are you seeing him again?'

'If he asks me. I'll play it by ear. Look, here's Mason and Candy.'

'God, talk about thunder and lightning. I guess there's trouble at' mill.'

Rose picked up her cup and sat watching them. Mason's face was haggard and she had an irrational urge to go and give him a hug. He caught her eye and smilingly came over to her.

'Feeling more confident now, Rose? You're doing really well, especially for a first effort.'

'Thank you. Yes, I'm enjoying it now – though I can't imagine how I shall feel on the first night.'

'You'll wonder why you ever got involved until the audience start to laugh and cheer. And then you'll know. It's an unforgettable buzz.'

She glanced shyly into his dark eyes, wanting to touch the little crow's feet that formed when he smiled. 'I'll take your word for it. You look very tired. Can I get you a coffee?'

'Please. Black, no sugar.'

With a weary smile, he accepted a cup. 'You know, Rose, I think you're the first person to show me any care or concern all day.'

His words, combined with the appreciative glance at her legs, brought yet another flood of colour to her face.

'I'm sorry you're having a bad time,' she said softly, before turning to serve one of the dancers.

Across the room, Clive nudged John. 'Check out the body language over there. If I'm not mistaken our Rose is making eyes at the director.'

'I hope you *are* mistaken,' John replied quietly.

Clive turned to eye him sharply. 'Are you smitten, old man? You know, these things flare up during shows, and die away just as quickly afterwards. My advice is to keep whatever feelings you're brewing under a lock and key until after the show, when you can consider them more objectively.'

'I expect you're right, but I thought you liked Lauren.'

'I do,' he admitted ruefully. 'But I was seeing her before, and anyway I shall keep it pink and fluffy until the time is right. If it ever is.'

A few minutes later Mason called everyone to order and they began their rehearsal.

'Move down stage-left, Candy. You start your dance from there and lead the children round the trees in the Magic Forest.'

She nodded and did as he asked, all the time anxiously watching the door. Would Nick turn up this evening or not? Twice, latecomers arrived with apologies, and whenever the wretched door opened her heart turned over. By the time they broke for coffee, she was a nervous wreck and went to the Ladies to give herself space, use her inhaler, and calm her nerves. When she emerged five minutes later Nick had arrived and was talking and laughing with Mason. For a second she stood and stared at him. He gave a perfunctory nod and turned away.

Stage Struck

Taking a deep breath, she collected a coffee from Patsy and went to join the little group, positioning herself so close to Nick she could feel the warmth of his body. She brushed her hip against his as she leaned in front of him to put her cup on a table, and felt the usual tremor go through her, shaking her with an urgent desire to touch him. But he moved away to talk to Rose and Lauren, leaving Candy face-to-face with Mason.

In that second, the truth dawned on her husband. The sudden drooping of her shoulders, the bleak expression, the over-the shoulder glance at Nick, and the small sigh that escaped her lips, all told him quite clearly what the problem with Candy really was. And he wondered how he could have been so blind.

The rest of the evening passed in a bit of a blur for Mason. He felt as if he had switched to auto-pilot, but at last it was time to wind up rehearsal and people began to call their farewells and drift away. He watched as Nick made for the door, and his heart sank as Candy swiftly followed, almost pinning him in a corner before he could escape. He couldn't hear what was being said, but judging by the look on Nick's face her attention wasn't welcome. Nick glanced at Mason and taking in his expression spoke urgently to Candy, shook her hand from his arm and left abruptly.

She returned to Mason, trying to look nonchalant, but he could see the glint of tears in her eyes.

'What was all that about?' he asked.

'What?'

'Your conversation with Nick. It looked rather intense.'

'Intense? I don't know what you mean. I was just asking him about the props and lighting for the dance in the Magic Forest.'

'I see. All right, shall we go home?'

'Yes, I'm shattered. I'll go and change my shoes.'

She walked away, her heart pounding. How stupid could she be? To corner Nick like that in front of Mason had been crass and ridiculous, and now she was fearful Mason had made an unwelcome connection. She was going to have to be very careful indeed.

On the way home, Candy tried to make conversation. She forced herself to sound light-hearted, asking about Mason's feelings concerning the show, complimenting the way it was shaping up, and telling him she was glad now that she was involved.

He grunted replies to everything she said, and once through the front door he headed straight for the drinks cabinet, to pour himself a very large scotch. He didn't offer Candy a drink, but went to the sofa and turned on the TV, pretending to be engrossed in *Newsnight*.

Mason's mind was in a whirl, but now it seemed so obvious what had been going on. The late nights when she was supposed to be with Sarah; the turmoil in the living room the night he had come home, and she'd only been wearing a robe. Which meant, he thought, feeling quite sick, that Candy and Nick had sex on this very sofa, here in his own home, probably only a few minutes before he returned. And that night - the last time he'd made love with his wife - she had just been with another man.

The stark feeling of violation made him feel ill. With bile rising up in his throat, he stood unsteadily and rushed upstairs to the bathroom.

Stage Struck

Wednesday 12th November

For the next week or so Nick grew more and more concerned about Candy. There was no sign of a lessening of her obsession with him, and he was sick of fielding texts and phone calls, and getting home from work to find her parked outside his house. She tried pleading with him, producing endless tears, and he felt a heel. Perhaps she really was totally in love with him – but the time had come when that really was her problem, not his. Candy was getting right out of hand and, if she hadn't already, it was quite obvious she would soon let the cat out of the bag. Mason seemed cool with him at rehearsal, although he said nothing. Nick couldn't believe Mason was the sort of chap to stand by and say nothing if he knew about their affair.

Oh, shit, he cursed as he drove home. He was committed to stage managing the pantomime, and Candy had now agreed to play Tabitha, so there was no way they could avoid each other. Just now the wretched woman had pleaded with him not to end things – threatened that she was on the verge of a nervous breakdown. She was desperate to see him and she was quite sure Mason would find out soon because she was so unhappy at home, and imagine the scandal. She'd even made rather lewd suggestions about the things she would be prepared to do to him if only he gave her another chance, and his skin crawled at the idea. He wanted to be rid of her more than he could have imagined a few weeks ago – before he'd realised what a selfish, needy and manipulative woman she really was. Mason was a decent bloke, and on reflection Nick actually felt quite sorry for the poor devil.

The only way to minimise the damage, if Mason faced him with it, would be to say that Candy had blown a minor flirtation out of all proportion. He would apologise, and appear with another girlfriend as soon as possible. One he could parade in public, particularly at the dinner dance, now only five weeks away.

There was nobody in particular who took his fancy in his social circle, and even Nick had more sense than to try to pick up with anyone else in the group. So, he wondered as he arrived home, where to find a convenient woman?

Once indoors, he idly scanned the local paper, while waiting for a much needed coffee to brew. As he flipped through the pages, the personal column seemed to rise up to hit him between the eyes. Of course - an introduction agency! He picked out the adverts for respectable agencies which were interspersed with those for discreet massages, to 'let Mandy make your erotic dreams come true' and grimaced. All the adverts were rather puke-making, he decided, but *Meet Your Match*, sounded slightly less terrifying than some of the others. *We meet all our*

Stage Struck

clients in their own homes, the advert said; *to be sure they are free, single and special enough to meet YOU.*

Nick chuckled as he started to undress. Yeah, right. Well, *Meet Your Match*, you get the chance to make your pitch tomorrow, but tonight I sleep alone and, Candy, my flower, I'm afraid your pretty nose is going to be put painfully out of joint. Nobody blackmails me.

With a massive yawn, he fell into bed and was soon asleep. He dreamed of a blind date with a curvy blonde bombshell, who took off her clothes and turned to face him, having changed into Mason. He woke with a yell and banged his head on the bedside table.

Stage Struck

Thursday 13th November

The next morning, nursing a sore head and, on inspection in the bathroom mirror, a ridge of bruising round his eye, Nick picked up the phone and dialled the introduction agency. A crisp feminine voice answered and he explained that he was a lonely single, solvent male who needed some help in his busy life to find a soul mate.

'You've come to the right place,' said the woman who told him her name was Sandra Vine. 'We have a high success rate in matching executives. Two weddings already this month among our members,' she boasted, and Nick shuddered at the prospect. 'All of whom are in the social group A - like yourself.'

Nick stifled a chuckle and solemnly said that he'd love Sandra to come to see him. Would it be possible today as he had the morning free from his frantic work schedule? He was not surprised when she assured him she would personally visit him at eleven-thirty to discuss his requirements.

He rushed round tidying the living room and cleaning the toilet, before changing into smart linen trousers, an fcuk shirt and splashing on a liberal dose of posh aftershave Candy had given him for his birthday.

Promptly at eleven-thirty the doorbell rang and he opened the door to Miss Sandra Vine, proprietor of *Meet Your Match*, and cupid extraordinaire. That was how she laughingly introduced herself, and he took in the power dressing, deftly coiffed dark hair and immaculate make-up on this thirty-something apparition. He respectfully ushered her into the lounge and offered her a cup of coffee.

'Thank you, Nick, it will help us both relax,' she said, following him into the kitchen. He watched her cast a quick look round, mentally running a finger over the furniture, to see if he was A list enough to join her bloody agency. Already he was regretting the impulse to get involved, but it was too late now.

She smiled, leaning against the doorframe. 'Tell me something about yourself, Nick.'

'Well, I'm thirty-nine,' he lied, 'single – had a few close shaves but never found the right girl. I have my own PR agency, a good income, no excess baggage such as kids, criminal records or County Court Judgements. What else can I tell you?'

'Hobbies – interests, politics, religion?'

Stage Struck

'I belong to the local amdram group, I like dining out and travel. I'm not a rabid anything politically, and I go to weddings, christenings and funerals in church. I like jazz and classical music, can't stand pop and my favourite artist is Salvador Dali.'

'Really?' She smiled. 'A man after my own heart.'

Sandra accepted a cup of coffee and they retired to the lounge where she sat in an armchair and extracted a folder from her briefcase. 'This tells you about the agency but, as I explained on the phone, we're fussy about whom we take as members, so you need not worry we shall introduce you to gold diggers or desperate women.'

'Well, no offence intended, but surely you have to be quite desperate to join any agency?'

'Truthfully,' she replied, 'most of our clients are like you. They just find it hard to meet nice, normal people like themselves. They work all day, so how do they discover like-minded partners, especially single ones. I mean, any fool can get involved with a married person, and we all know the carnage that can cause.'

He nodded, trying to look shocked at the very idea. 'How soon might you get me my first date?'

'Well, first tell me what sort of person you want to meet. A non-smoker, someone without children, someone of another…er…ethnic origin, for example.'

'Hmm, I see. Yes to a non-smoker, I can't stand women who smell like an ashtray… Don't mind kids, if they're civilised, and I don't have a single prejudice about colour or religion.'

'Excellent. Well, we would be very happy to have you as a member, if you would like to join.'

'Perhaps I should think about it…' he stammered, suddenly nervous about making a rash decision. Besides which, she hadn't mentioned the cost yet.

'What is there to think about?' she asked. 'You have a problem – we can solve it.'

'You're right,' he conceded. 'Where do I sign?'

'Just here.' She gave him a form on which she had ticked the subjects they had discussed. 'And if you could let me have a cheque for five hundred pounds I will go back to the office and begin looking for your first introduction.'

He gasped. 'Five hundred pounds?'

'Nick, I am sure you know that you get what you pay for in this life. Remember that all our clients have paid the same amount, which shows their level of commitment to meeting someone special. If they want some old slag, they can look on the *internet*.' She spat out the last word, her lips curling in distaste.

'I see,' he said, politely.

'If you heard the stories I hear about the risks people take to meet a partner, your hair would curl,' she told him. 'No, this is definitely the way forward for someone like you. We'll change your life infinitely for the better. It's a small price to pay, I promise you. Now, I'll just take your photograph…it's strictly for our own use so we have a better memory of you when we're finding matches.'

'Do I have a chance to look at photos of possible dates?' he asked hopefully.

'Absolutely not. We know from experience that matches made by us work far better than letting you choose who you want to meet. Now don't get irritable with us if the first person you meet isn't Miss Right – it often takes a while to meet someone whose chemistry and values are lined up with yours. Patience is the name of the game, but I promise, we usually get there in the end.'

'Sandra,' he laughed. 'If you ever get fed up with your agency, I'll give you a job. You have to be the best saleswoman I ever met.'

She grinned cheekily at him. 'Thanks. But seriously, you won't regret this.'

He hoped she was right. She left, promising to call him within a day or two to offer him his first introduction, and he shook his head in amazement that he had just parted with five hundred pounds on a whim. 'Candy', he muttered, 'You were a very expensive mistake!'

By Thursday Lauren had a streaming cold. She arrived at rehearsal with a temperature and sat miserably at the side of the hall, away from the others, trying to keep her germs to herself, hunched into her shaggy coat. Her nose positively glowed and she could hardly speak.

'What are you doing here?' asked Clive moving over to her. 'You look awful.'

'Thanks,' she snuffled.

'I mean, you look as though you should be home in bed with a large whisky and a hot water bottle.'

'The show must go on. I can't let Mason down.'

John strolled over, took one look at Lauren and stepped behind Clive. 'You look awful, Lauren.'

'You're so kind.'

He laughed. 'Go home and sleep. Ah, here's Mason!'

They all regarded their director with concern as he joined them. He was pale, dressed in crumpled clothes, and was blinking and yawning as though he hadn't slept for days; which he hadn't.

Stage Struck

'You two look as ill as each other,' said Clive. 'Why don't we just cancel tonight and go home?'

'I'm fine, Clive, thanks. But Lauren, you look awful.'

'Thanks. If anyone else says that to me, I shall lose the will to live,' she grumbled. 'Someone bring me a coffee and I'll take some more aspirin. I'll be as lively as a spring lamb in half an hour, provided you all stop telling me I look as if I'm at death's door. I've got a cold, that's all.'

'Did Rose come with you?' John asked.

'No, she's coming in her own car tonight. I presume she didn't want to be in close contact with the plague.'

Clive dutifully went to fetch a drink from Patsy, and while she was pouring, Maureen Clarke came up to the hatchway.

'Maureen,' Patsy greeted her anxiously, 'did you see Winston lurking outside when you came in? I'm sure it was him, scuttling out of sight into Boots's doorway. I'm worried about him. He took it very badly, being left out of the show.'

'John and I saw him in the pub after rehearsal last week,' added Clive. 'He was very angry and quite drunk. He went into Sipton Wine Shop afterwards and came out loaded up with booze.'

'Silly old bugger,' muttered Maureen. 'I'll go out and see if I can find him. Mason doesn't need me for half an hour while he's working with the terrible twins.'

'Shall I go?' volunteered Clive.

'No, it's better if I do. I've known Winston for more years than I care to remember. He's lonely and he's a drunk, but underneath he's still a kind and generous man. Maybe I can persuade him to come in and have a coffee.' She picked up her fur coat and stepped outside, where it was foggy and close to freezing. The High Street looked deserted but she walked down the road past several shops, and noticed what looked like a tramp slumped in a doorway. She almost walked past, but a second glance caused her to gasp and run to the hunched figure.

'Winston! – Oh, for Heaven's sake, what's happened to you?' Her breath turned to ghostly vapour in the cold air. She crouched by him and shook his shoulder, but he didn't respond. His skin was waxy and luminescent in the streetlight.

'Wake up, you silly arse. Come on. It's me Maureen… Wake up!'

But Winston was out for the count and she feared he was getting colder by the minute.

Maureen ran back to the hall in a blind panic, breathless now in the thickening fog. 'Mobile – anyone got a mobile?

'I have,' said Candy, her brow creasing in puzzlement.

Stage Struck

'Call an ambulance quickly!'

'What's wrong?' asked Mason.

'Winston's out there unconscious on the pavement. If we don't get him inside he'll die of hypothermia.' Maureen gestured frantically. 'You chaps go and bring him in here, and Candy please call an ambulance. He's in the doorway at Holland and Barrett's.'

A couple of minutes later, Mason, Clive and John carried an inert Winston through the door and laid him on the floor. Seconds after them, Rose arrived and took in the situation immediately. She knelt by Winston's side and felt his pulse.

'He's very weak,' she said. 'And a weird colour. Does anyone know if he's had heart problems?'

'He's not drunk?'

'I don't think so.' She rolled Winston into the recovery position, put a coat under him with the help of the others, then covered him in a selection of coats and sweaters. She crouched by him, her finger still on his pulse. 'I hope the ambulance isn't too long.'

'Just a couple of minutes,' Candy said. 'That's what the girl told me.'

Rose eyed Winston anxiously. 'Let's hope she was right – he's not doing very well at all here.'

A minute or two later, Winston stopped breathing and Rose sprang into action. Rolling him onto his back she raised his chin and began mouth-to-mouth resuscitation. 'His heart has stopped!' she yelled, after she gulped in air. 'Can anyone else do CPR while I do chest compressions? We have to keep him going until the ambulance gets here.'

'I can,' volunteered John, and she moved to let him take over while she began external heart massage.

In the distance the nee-naw of the approaching ambulance broke the stunned silence.

'Come on, old chap – you can do this,' she implored Winston.

Two paramedics burst through the door. 'Well done, young lady, we'll take over now,' said the green-garbed man. 'What can you tell us about him?'

'His name is Winston; I think he had a heart attack and he's very cold.'

'Good spot.' Swiftly they tore open his shirt and attached electrodes from the defibrillator to his chest.

'It's like a scene from *Casualty*,' murmured an awed Clive.

It was only a few seconds, but seemed like an eternity before the shocks re-started Winston's heart and he began to breath on his own, at which point he threw up spectacularly. The

Stage Struck

paramedics wiped his mouth, lifted him onto a stretcher, and placed an oxygen mask over his face.

'You're going to be okay now, Winston,' one of them reassured him as they wheeled him towards the door. 'We're taking you off to St. Mary's for some TLC.'

'Can I come with him?' Maureen asked them. 'He has no-one else until we can get in touch with his children.'

'Yeah, of course, love. But hurry.'

Grabbing her coat, Maureen climbed into the ambulance which, blue lights flashing and siren wailing, disappeared into the fog.

'Rose, you just saved Winston's life,' said John, giving her a hug, and guiding her back into the relative warmth of the hall.

'I'm a nurse, John,' she reminded him. 'And you did magnificently too. Someone find me a mop and bucket and I'll clear up this mess,' she said, turning aside congratulations from Clive and Lauren.

'I think we'll abandon proceedings for tonight,' Mason decided. 'Lauren's ill anyway, and I don't know about anyone else, but after that I could do with a drink – and I certainly want to buy Rose one.'

So poor Lauren was packed off to her sick bed, Candy elected to go home saying that she felt ill after watching Winston throw up, and the remainder went to the Fox and Rabbit.

The cosiness of the pub, and a round of drinks, revived their spirits. John sat next to Rose and she turned and smiled at him, unaware of the devastating effect being close to her was having on him. Half an hour later, collectively feeling better, the group dispersed. John and Clive, who had come in Clive's car, said their farewells, leaving Mason and Rose the last to leave.

'Would you like a lift?' she asked. 'I presume Candy took the car.'

'That's very kind - if you're sure it's no trouble.'

'We're practically neighbours,' she reminded him.

'So we are.' He glanced at her as she climbed into the driver's seat and thought once again, how attractive she was. Her Titian hair gleamed, her long legs, encased in black jeans seemed to go on forever and her smile was always warm and genuine. He imagined being a sick patient and waking up in hospital to see her lovely face in front of him and decided he might never want to get well. And there was definitely some sort of buzz between them; nothing he could define, but she blushed when he spoke to her and seemed to go out of her way to please him at rehearsal. Mason, he told himself firmly, don't even go there. She's half your age. And two wrongs don't make a right.

He had been debating with himself whether to openly accuse Candy of having an affair with Nick, but so far had ducked it, knowing instinctively that it would be cataclysmic.

Theirs had always been a difficult match, he thought, but he had never really considered that Candy might cheat on him and he felt humiliated to the core. A couple of days of ruminating had made him realise that indeed humiliation was his strongest emotion, not fear of losing her love, for he'd long forgotten how it felt to be considered the centre of her world. But he did dread the children, the rest of the drama group and their other friends finding out what she had done. So he kept his counsel while deciding what – if anything – he should do.

Their relationship at home was becoming increasingly difficult. Candy tried being sweet to him, making his favourite dinner, asking his opinion about things and co-operating over the show. She had even cuddled up to him in bed, a rarity in recent times, but he'd yawned, made an excuse about being tired and rolled away from her, settling on the cold edge of the bed. She hadn't been out alone for two weeks and even he could see she was putting on weight; she seemed to be forever munching on some snack bar or other. Perhaps her sordid little affair was over?

He knew that any resolution of his relationship with his wife had to be put on hold until after the pantomime. Otherwise the work of a great many people striving to make the show a success would unravel. As for his feelings about Nick – they alternated between rage and indifference. He guessed Nick was a sexual opportunist, and Candy had been the opportunity.

Mason sighed deeply.

'That was a deep sigh,' Rose observed, glancing at him. 'I'm sure Winston will be fine once they stabilize him in hospital.'

'It wasn't Winston I was sighing about,' he heard himself say. Damn, that was a slip.

'Anything I can help with?'

'No, but thanks…er…you just missed my turning.'

'Oh dear, sorry. Never mind, we'll go past my house and take the next right.'

'Which is your house?'

'This one. The Edwardian semi with the white gate.' She slowed down so he could see.

'Would…would you like a coffee before you go home?'

'Yes, please, I'd love one.'

He followed her into the house, and was struck by the enfolding comfort of it. At her request he put a match to the fire, and sat beside it watching the flames grow, while she bustled into the kitchen.

Rose was wondering what on earth had possessed her to invite Mason into her home. But he had looked so wretched all evening, and he'd clearly been deeply shocked to see Winston at death's door.

She glanced through the doorway as the kettle heated. His head leaned back on the chair, eyes closed, and Min, her naughty Siamese cat, lay on his lap. He was absently massaging her ears, and she was purring in ecstasy. Rose watched his hands and had an irrational desire for them to be caressing her, but she shook the thought from her head, poured the water over the instant coffee and took the tray into the room, placing it on a small table next to him.

'Black, no sugar?'

'You remembered.' He smiled, and once again she was aware of colour flooding her face. 'Do you know how charming that is?' he asked softly. 'Watching you blush.'

'It's a curse – and with name like Rose I have always come in for a lot of ribbing; Rose Red being the usual taunt.

Mason smiled and took a few sips of coffee. He then glanced at his watch. 'I should go,' he said, replacing his cup on the table. 'I'll walk the rest of the way home; it's only a couple of minutes from here.'

Relieved, Rose led him to the front door. Having him in her house was a mistake and she wanted him gone before anything more intimate was said or done. But, as they found themselves face to face, she knew it was too late and froze, caught in the certain knowledge of what was about to happen. Standing so close to him, she could hardly breathe and, as she slowly raised her eyes to look at him, he suddenly gathered her in his arms, lowering his mouth to hers. If the fate of the universe had hung on it, there was no way she could have prevented herself from responding. As his kiss deepened, her lips parted, and she put her arms around his neck. And yet instinctively it didn't feel right and she tried to pull back.

'Rose, oh, Rose,' he gasped, as his hands moved down her, pulling her strongly against him. She could feel the strength of his desire, and it frightened her.

'No, no, please stop,' she gasped, struggling out of his arms. 'I can't do this.'

Mason instantly came to his senses and moved away with a groan. He covered his face with his hands. 'I'm so sorry – that was right out of order. I can't apologise enough.'

Stage Struck

Taking a deep breath, she too stepped back and opened the door. 'It never happened, Mason. It's been a stressful evening. Let's put it down to us both needing a little comfort. Now go home and get some rest, you look absolutely done in.'

As he walked away into the fog, she closed the door and leaned on it, waiting for her heart to return to its proper rhythm. She could still taste his kiss, recall the male smell of him, and she shivered. It's the edge of a slippery precipice, she told herself.

Her father would have said it was a path to pain and disgrace. But then, what had he known about anything?

Candy left rehearsal and went home to soak in a hot bath. She was cold through and through. She wondered how to keep up the façade of being nice to Mason, especially as he showed no signs of responding to her. He had even turned down her offer of sex the night before. She was afraid he might be suspicious, and she'd been on a knife edge for a week waiting for the axe to fall. But he had said nothing, and apart from essential conversations, he kept himself to himself.

The strain was beginning to tell. She felt permanently sick with anxiety and had an endless craving for carbohydrates, which had already increased her waistline by an inch.

Nick had not been at the abortive rehearsal that evening – he wasn't needed, so she'd been relieved not to have to see him. He was clearly outraged with her for trying to blackmail him, and she was afraid their affair was beyond hope – which made her sad and very angry. She had been so sure he was really in love with her but now her dreams were shattered, her heart ached, and the only way she knew she could recover was to wreak her revenge. It might take a while, she vowed, but sooner or later she would find a way to hurt him as much as he had hurt her. When he least expected it.

An hour later, Mason came home and she heard him downstairs in the kitchen. Putting on a robe, she stood at the top of the stairs. 'Any news of Winston?' she called.

'Not yet. I'll call Maureen in the morning.'

On an impulse Candy went down to Mason, put her arms around him and laid her head on his chest. She felt him tense, but he didn't push her away. 'It was really scary, wasn't it? I thought he was going to die right there. Rose was amazing.'

'Yes, she was.'

'Are you coming to bed now?'

'No, I'll be up later; don't wait for me.'

She drew back, realising her eyes were beginning to smart.

'Oh, God, where have you been?'

'To the pub – why?'

'You must have cat hairs on your sweater – look at my eyes – and my chest is tightening already.'

Recognising the symptoms, Mason rushed upstairs to find antihistamine tablets and her asthma inhaler, fuming about how ironic life could be. Candy had been having an affair for God knew how long and got away with it. He'd been to Rose's house once, done nothing worse than kiss her – and he'd given himself away because of a few cat hairs on his sweater.

By the time he got back downstairs, Candy's eyes were so swollen they had almost closed, and she was wheezing alarmingly. She took two puffs of Ventolin, swallowed a large dose of antihistamine, and breathed some oxygen from the emergency machine she kept at home.

'Where did you come up against a cat?' she asked at last.

'I have no idea,' he lied. 'I left my coat with a pile of others at the hall, perhaps I picked up some hairs which then got on to my sweater.'

'You didn't take your coat – remember, I reminded you and you said you didn't need it as you had your Aran sweater?'

'Then I have no idea. Maybe the hairs were blowing in the wind.' When you reach Australia, stop digging – and anyway, why should he have to defend himself? She was the one who was having an affair.

'Come on, let's get you into bed. You'll be fine by the morning.'

'Well, take off your sweater and put it in a bag for the dry cleaners – unless you're trying to kill me,' she wheezed at him.

He did as she asked before helping her upstairs and into bed. 'I'll sleep in Lola's room as she's staying over at Caroline's. You'll be more comfortable on your own.'

It was with enormous relief that he threw himself into his daughter's bed. At last, some time to think about the mess his life had slithered into, and try to work out how the hell to deal with it. But the pillow was lumpy and he couldn't get comfortable; there was something underneath. Curious, he withdrew a book and discovered he was holding Lola's diary in his hand. He turned it over, thinking how little he knew about Lola's life now that she was growing up. She wasn't exactly secretive but, he thought ruefully, neither was she Daddy's Little Girl any more.

He adored Lola and Leo, and he worried desperately what effect it would have on them if he and Candy were to split up. They were teenagers, but still vulnerable, still very needy, and he felt enormously protective of them. He held the book to his face, and he could smell Lola on it – now a more sophisticated perfume than the lovely baby powder and milk scent he used to love so much.

He stared at the diary, telling himself it would an absolute betrayal to read it, that there were no circumstances in which he would invade her privacy like that... But there are temptations and irresistible temptations. After a small hesitation as he struggled with his conscience, he flipped it open, expecting to see an entry about her sleepover tonight with Caroline. The book opened at where she had been writing the day before. 'I hope Thursday is going to be OK. Alex says it will be fine, and I don't have to do anything I don't want to – but I'm scared. I love him and I want to do it, but there are so many things I don't know. What if he thinks I'm a naïve fool? I mean here I am at eighteen, and still a virgin. I wish I could talk to Mum.'

Mason rolled onto his stomach and wept.

Lola was in a terrible state. She had never before really set out to deceive her parents but now she was planning to spend the night with Alex, a boy she had only known for six weeks, and with whom she was totally smitten. He was good-looking in a Brad Pitt sort of way as well as funny, caring and clever and what amazed her even more was the fact that he seemed to feel the same way about her.

She had managed to see him a few times without her parents' knowledge, usually on the pretext that she was spending the evening with Stella or Caroline, and had been stunned by the intensity of feeling between them. When he held her hand she trembled, when he kissed her she went weak at the knees, and when she had allowed his hands to explore a little further she had thought she would die of ecstasy. But Lola knew that with the stresses and strains at home, it was not a good idea to argue the case for a boyfriend. She was distraught at the possibility that her parents' marriage might break up, and since they had at least been united in telling her she could not have a boyfriend until after the exams, she was scared of defying them. But that was before she had met Alex and now he felt like the centre of her world.

So, battling her guilt, she had arranged to stay the night at his house while his parents were away in Derbyshire. It was the most daring and rebellious thing she had ever done, and as she drove through the gates of the large, Tudor-style house just outside town, her heart was in her mouth.

Alex opened the front door, helped her out of the car and picked up her small bag.

'You look pale and shaky,' he said closing the front door. 'Come in and have a drink and relax. Honestly, I'm not going to eat you.' He slipped an arm around her shoulders and led her into the big lounge. He put on some music and poured her a glass of white wine before coming to sit next to her on the sofa. 'Do you like chilli con carne?'

'Yes... Yes, I do. Why - are you cooking us dinner?'

'But of course. Mind you, it's the only thing I know how to make – but it's usually pretty good.'

Lola began to relax and take in her surroundings. The house was beautiful; expensively furnished with what she assumed were antiques and Persian rugs. She sipped her wine and followed Alex into the kitchen where he had set the pine table for a romantic dinner for two, including flowers and a candle.

'Sit down, *mademoiselle,* I shall wait upon you,' he commanded, pulling out her chair for her.

Smiling shyly, she did as he asked. So far, he had done nothing more than kiss her cheek when she arrived, for which she was grateful. She watched as he spooned rice onto plates, and then poured over the thick chilli sauce – adding an over-large sprig of parsley by way of garnish.

'It's not *cordon bleu,*' he said anxiously, 'but I hope you like it.'

Before long she'd eaten enough to quell her rumbling tummy, and laid down her fork. 'Can I have some more wine, please?'

He poured white wine and looked quizzically at her over his glass. 'Lola, if you're having second thoughts about tonight, I promise it won't change the way I feel about you.'

'No... No, I'm not, Alex. But I'm afraid...I mean... I'm very inexperienced.'

'Me too.'

Lola suddenly realised that Alex also was playing for time. He flushed slightly and she reached for his hand across the table. 'Are you telling me...?'

'Yes, it's the first time for me as well. So if you want to change your mind and wait for someone who knows what they're doing... '

'I find it hard to believe – with your looks, surely you could have had a dozen girls.'

'Well, thanks. But you see I watched friends at school winging from one girl to another, and bragging about it, which made the whole thing seem so naff and sordid. I just made a decision to wait until I found someone special with whom it would mean more than wham, bang, thank you, ma'am. Old fashioned or what? Anyway, look who's talking – you must have had a raft of blokes after you.'

'I know two girls who got pregnant and one who caught something nasty, all from boys they hardly knew, so I decided to be old-fashioned too. And to be honest I've just never felt...well, like this before; never really wanted to.'

'Are you positive you want to now?'

'Yes, Alex,' she whispered, moving her chair back. 'And I'm not hungry any more.'

He moved quickly around the table as she stood. He took her gently in his arms. 'Shall we go to my room?'

For Lola it was an unforgettable night of exploration, revelation and sweet passion, and as dawn broke she lay awake, her arms around a sleeping Alex, feeling incredibly protective. He had been gentle, and for someone who claimed to be inexperienced, an exciting and fulfilling lover. She was amazed and relieved that the whole experience had been fun; they had giggled endlessly, quite unembarrassed at their sometimes fumbled explorations of each other's bodies.

In the morning, Alex woke with Lola running her fingers softly through his hair and he stirred and smiled up at her.

'You're still here?'

'You want me to go?' she teased, well aware of the effect she was having on him.

'Never!' He smiled sleepily and began to caress her.

'That's nice,' she murmured then her eyes widened as she glanced at the clock. 'Oh, no, stop it, please...'

'What?'

She pointed at the time. 'We have to get to school or questions will be asked.'

'We could take a sicky.'

'No, Alex. If my parents find out I'll be in enough trouble. I was supposed to be studying Geography with Caro last night; I can't risk it. But as it's Friday I might be able to swing coming back here tonight.'

'How am I supposed to concentrate on my studies today with that prospect hanging in front of me?'

She kissed him and dashed into the shower, a huge smile on her face which stayed there all day.

Stage Struck

Friday, 7th November

Some time before dawn on Friday morning Winston slowly regained consciousness and wondered where he was. He had an oxygen mask over his face and he could hear the persistent beep-beep of a machine.

A nurse leaned over him and smiled. 'Welcome back, Winston. You're in St. Mary's Hospital but you're going to be fine.'

'What happened?' he asked groggily.

'You have a problem with your heart and because you got very cold, your blood got rather thicker than was good for you which caused a heart attack.'

'Will I die?'

'No, you've been very lucky this time, but the doctor will explain everything to you properly when he does his ward round. You have a friend waiting to see you. Do you feel up to saying hello – just for a moment?'

'Who is it?' he asked, puzzled.

'Maureen Clarke.'

'Oh.' He was surprised, having almost no recollection of his recent past. 'Yes, please, let her in, darling.'

A few moments later Maureen appeared by his bed and leaned over him with a frown. 'Hello, you silly old fool. What do you mean by giving us all a fright like that?'

'I'm sorry, Maureen,' he replied weakly. 'Didn't mean to be a nuisance.'

'Are you still in pain?'

'No. I just feel like I've been hit by a tank.'

'Well, you have to get some rest now, so I won't lecture you any more now.'

'I came to the church, didn't I? Is that where it happened? I vaguely remember feeling a pain in my chest, but after that it's all a bit of a blur.'

'Yes, Patsy had seen you lurking around like a dirty old man and got worried so I came to find you; but you were out for the count. We dragged you into the hall where young Rose and John saved your life when you stopped breathing and kept you going until the ambulance arrived. Everyone is worried about you. Can I now tell them you're likely to live to fight another day? Not that you deserve to.'

He nodded with the vestige of a smile. 'You're a hard woman.' He knew well enough that Maureen was simply continuing the banter they had shared for twenty years, and which he

Stage Struck

missed more than he could say after being left out of the show. 'Will you come and see me again soon... please?'

'I might,' she smiled, 'if you promise to behave yourself. And Jackie and Paul and their families are on their way from Scotland, they'll be here sometime tomorrow.'

'Ah... Did you have to?'

'Yes, of course I did. Do you think they would have ever forgiven me if you'd fallen off your perch and they hadn't made their peace with you? You've been given a chance to get well and sort your life out. Don't make a balls-up of it.'

She was gone, this old friend, with a swish of her fur coat and a clatter of high heels. Winston took a deep, reviving breath and knew she was right.

Nick drove to his office in Guildford, growling at the rush-hour traffic backed up on the A3, feeling thoroughly out of sorts. He had an important lunch date with a prospective client, plus at least ten phone calls to make before that. Public Relations was a demanding taskmaster and his fledgling business was growing so fast it was out-pacing the capacity of the existing staff to cope; the existing staff being himself, Gloria, his secretary stroke personal assistant, and Jeff, his partner.

Both Nick and Jeff were well known in their field and clients had sought them out when they left their respective companies to branch out together, knowing they would get innovative and exciting new ideas to promote their businesses. But the clients also knew their value to a new agency and were demanding and fussy.

Nick was tired and fraught when he finally pounded up the stairs into their small office suite, and mystified as to why Jeff was grinning from ear to ear as he spoke into the phone. 'He's just walked into the office. One moment, I'll hand you over...Sandra Vine.'

Nick slapped a hand to his head and turning away, tried to avoid taking the call.

But Jeff was having far too much fun to let him get away with that. 'It's the *Meet Your Match* Dating Agency,' he grinned, and stood, arms folded, leaning on the desk so that he could hear every word being said.

With an irritated grunt, Nick took the phone. 'Hello, Sandra, and before you say anything, can I ask you what happened to your confidentiality policy? Oh, did he, indeed; all right, I'm sorry, it was an understandable mistake... I see... You have? Really... and... uh huh.... hmm.' Jeff leaned closer to the phone until Nick pushed him away with a scowl. 'Right, if you give me the number I'll call her later.... I see... Yes, well thank you very much. Goodbye.'

He replaced the receiver and turned on his partner. 'You cheeky bugger. You let her think you were me. That's infringement of my …my…'

'Your what? You shouldn't have given her this number if you wanted to keep it a secret. Are you meeting someone, then?'

'Yes. But more than that is strictly my business...'

'Why do you need to use an agency? You normally have half a dozen women to choose from.'

'I want one with no links to my current social circle, and I desperately need someone to take to the drama annual bash.'

'Did the married one ditch you, then?' Jeff asked, perching on Nick's desk.

'I wish! No, I'm trying to get rid of her and she's being a silly girl. A new bit of fluff is what's needed to put her off the scent. It's all a bit messy.'

'You really are a bastard with women, Nick.'

'I can't help it. I just get nervous at the bong of wedding bells which is what they all seem to want sooner or later. Anyway, the one I'm phoning tonight sounds promising. She's from Cranleigh, so no-one will know her and she sounds attractive and intelligent. I'll give it a go. I've paid my five hundred quid, so I may as well get my money's worth.'

'Five hundred…'

'Right. Now, if you're quite done with prying into my private life, we have work to do.'

'Yes, sir' chuckled Jeff. '*Meet Your Match* Dating Agency…I don't believe it.'

It was late evening before Nick had a chance to make the call and he was irrationally nervous at the prospect. A blind date was something he had never had to resort to before. However, desperate times called for desperate measures, so, large gin and tonic in hand, he sat by the fire and dialled the number. It rang three times before a light feminine voice announced, 'Sam Jameson speaking.'

'Oh…er… Hello, my name is Nick. I was given your number by Sandra Vine.'

'Oh yes! Hi, thank you for making contact. It's so awkward, isn't it? I feel a real prat.'

'You, too?' He laughed. 'I've been trying to pluck up the courage all day.'

'Well, everyone thinks using an agency is the last resort of desperate people. I promise you, I'm not desperate but I don't have the chance to go out to meet people – fulltime job, eight year old son and hamster to deal with etcetera. How about you?'

Stage Struck

Nick had to think fast. He could hardly admit that he wanted a date with her to get him out of a sticky situation with a married woman. 'I'm busy too. I have my own business, and the rest of my life at present is taken up with stage managing a pantomime.'

'Really? I used to do a lot of amdram before I had Ben. I played the fairy in Cinderella once and fell off the stage when one of the pyrotechnics blew up behind me. Very ignominious. I tore my tights and broke my wand.' She laughed at the memory. 'But the man in the front row, in whose lap I landed, wanted to marry me.'

I want to marry you, thought Nick and then sprang to his feet in shock at the thought. Where the hell did that come from? He peered into his gin and tonic and wondered if he got the ratios the wrong way round. 'So, Sam, would you like to meet me? I would really like to see you and I wondered whether perhaps I could take you to dinner tomorrow?'

'Thank you. Yes, I would like that.'

Nick arranged to meet her at a restaurant in Cranleigh – about twenty miles away, since Sandra had given them both strict instructions to meet in a public place until they got to know each other. 'How will I know you?' he asked. 'I presume you won't be dressed as a Christmas fairy?'

'No, too chilly. How will you know me? Well, I'm blonde – oh, dear, here come the jokes – with brown eyes and I'll be wearing... let me see... what can I stun you with? Black trousers and red sweater.'

Nick gave her a brief description of himself and they said their farewells. He put the phone down and realised he could hardly wait to meet this lady with the lovely voice and delicious sense of humour.

***

When she got home that evening after school Lola found the house empty and with a relieved sigh she went up to her room.

Something was different. Her bed was made, but she had a sense that someone had been there. She turned back the bed covers and checked under her pillow. Her diary was still there but she could swear it wasn't exactly where she had left it. She always put it on the right, nearest the wall, but it was on the opposite side. She felt a lurch in her stomach. Her mother had been going through her room, invading her space, prying into her life – and probably reading her diary. And there was that fatal last entry which couldn't state more clearly that she intended to sleep with Alex, and had not been at Caro's the night before. Feeling sick and enraged she sat on the bed wondering what to do. Call her – that was the obvious thing.

Frantically, she dialled the number on her mobile phone.

'Caro it's me. Did anyone phone for me last night?'

'No. Why, should they?'

'Well, I was supposed to be sleeping over with you.'

'You were? It's nice to be told these things, you cheeky bitch. Are you going to tell me who you were with?'

'Alex, of course.'

'Lucky you. Did he come up to expectations?'

'Amazing. But I think someone's been reading my diary, so the earth might fall on my head when my parents get home.'

'They think you're still a sweet little virgin?'

Lola was not about to admit that until the previous night that had been the case. 'I let them think that – it makes life easier. Anyway, they've banned boyfriends until after the exams.'

'Well, you got lucky. No-one asked for you, Lola. Oh, and it's safer to keep your diary on the computer with a secret password.'

'I've never really had anything much to hide before.'

'Aren't you the goody-two-shoes? My mother would have a fit if she read my secrets. Keep me posted. Got to go and make myself beautiful – a crowd of us are going to Kiss Club tonight to boogie the night away. Do you want to come?'

'No, thanks. But I might say I am with you again if that's okay?'

'Can't get enough of him, huh? Yeah, it's fine by me. But don't forget my mum might answer the phone if someone calls.'

'Thanks, I'll risk it. 'Bye.'

Switching off her phone, Lola heard the front door open and close. Heart hammering, she took a deep breath before looking over the banister. Her mother was hanging up her coat.

'Hi, Mum.'

'Hello, sweetheart. Cup of tea and a biscuit?'

It was a daily ritual they always shared on days when there was no dance class. Lola blew out, counted to ten, and calmly went downstairs to put on the kettle.

'You all right, Mum?' she asked, placing a mug of tea in front of her.

Her mother seemed strained and on edge. ''Course. Good day? Lots of homework?'

'An essay and some research on the internet for a project, but I've got all weekend to do it.'

'Where's Leo?'

'He did tell you he'd be late. There's a football match at school. I promised to pick him up at six.'

'Oh...yes, of course.' Candy, who sounded vaguely distracted, was already into her fifth Hobnob biscuit. 'Your Dad won't be in 'til very late because he's dining with some clients. Perhaps we could go to the cinema or something – have a girls night out?'

'Um... Well, there's really nothing on that appeals to me, and some of my friends are going to the Kiss Club tonight. Do you mind if I join them and stay over at Caroline's?'

'Weren't you there last night?'

'Yes, but her mum doesn't mind and we have such a laugh. And we thought we might study all tomorrow to catch up. What do you say?'

'Oh, all right.'

'Thanks, Mum.'

Lola dashed back to her bedroom and phoned Alex. Suddenly she felt shy. She hadn't seen him all day at school and a quiver of fear went through her that now he had made a conquest of her he might not be interested any more.

'Hello, sweet pea. I've been thinking about you all day. When can I see you?'

'I'm supposed to be going out with my girlfriends and staying over at Caro's again.'

'Supposed to be?'

'Hmmm,' she smiled into the phone.

'How soon can you get here? My body's already in torment.'

'About seven. I have to pick up my baby brother from footie first.'

'Can't wait. 'Bye'

But then the front door opened and closed again. Alarmed, Lola went to look over the banister rail. 'Dad. I thought you were dining late with clients.'

'I cancelled.' He came up the stairs, went into the bedroom, closing the door with a bang, and Lola's stomach contracted again, making her feel quite sick. Her father always greeted her affectionately, but he had not met her eye, and had brushed past her without a hug or a kiss. She then realised with cold horror that it had not been her mother who had been reading her diary. She guessed he had slept in her bed to keep away from her mum and now he knew her secret.

After a few minutes he came out of the bedroom dressed in jeans and an old sweater. He looked exhausted and older, she thought, as unexpected tears filled her eyes.

'Daddy, can we talk?'

He stopped and looked at her, his heart aching at her beauty and the vulnerable soft mouth which was now trembling.

'Of course, Lola – shall I come to your room?'

She nodded and he followed her in and sat on her bed.

She perched on her computer chair. 'Did you sleep in here last night?'

'Yes. I'm sorry.'

'And you found my diary.'

'Yes. I shouldn't have even opened it – it was unforgivable.'

'Do you hate me?'

'Hate you? Good heavens, child, you and Leo are my reasons to live. Your mother had an asthma attack so she was more comfortable on her own. I didn't mean to pry.'

'You know about Alex.'

'Yes.'

'He's all right, Daddy. He didn't force, coerce or blackmail me into staying with him, and when I got there he had made us dinner. He gave me lots of opportunity to leave, but I didn't want to. I love him and nothing you can say or do can change that.'

'Well, angel, I suppose in these times you've done well to get to eighteen *virgo intacta*. You're probably a rare bird. So what can I say? Except, don't tell your mother yet, and make sure you keep up with your school work.'

'Are you very disappointed in me?'

'No – I'm immensely proud of both of you. And I'm so sorry things are obviously so difficult between your mum and me at the moment. Try not to worry about it too much – and don't get pregnant!' He rose and smiled sadly at her. 'Are you seeing him tonight?'

'Yes, but Mum thinks I'm staying over at Caro's again.'

'Then I should leave it like that. We don't want any more confrontations. We have enough to deal with, don't we?'

With a tearful sniff she snuggled into his arms, and for a long moment they held each other. He kissed her cheek before striding heavily downstairs to the drinks cabinet.

Stage Struck

Saturday 15th November

Rose was working for most of the weekend – which she was very glad of, as it kept her mind off what happened with Mason. Waves of guilt and shame kept washing over her. She could almost hear a burst of outrage from her father. So what? She'd never rebelled against him when he was alive and he could hardly hold her to account now he was dead, could he? If she *had* decided to have an affair with Mason, what the hell did it have to do with her precious father? Hypocritical bastard.

She sat drinking coffee in the nurses' room, once again fighting down the pangs of hatred and rage. She could never predict when these emotions would flood back to haunt her. When they did, she no longer seemed to have any recourse to her Christian belief, to prayer or forgiveness; her father had robbed her of those when he took his own life. But contemplating an affair with a married man was still totally alien to her and, even in rebel mode, she knew she could never have done it. But now it would be so awkward seeing him at rehearsal. Damn – it's ruined everything.

After finishing her shift at four o'clock, she decided to pop into the cardiac ward to see how Winston was getting along, with some anxiety, because she had only met him once before the fateful night of his heart attack.

He was lying with his eyes closed as she approached his bed and she was about to tiptoe away when the afternoon tea trolley rattled past and he jolted awake.

'What the...? Oh, hello, darling, have I died and gone to Heaven?' he asked, blinking owlishly.

'Winston, you won't remember me but…'

'I have a bad heart, not amnesia,' he said. 'Of course I remember you. You were at the audition, and I'm told you had the courage to give me the kiss of life the other night.'

'You gave us all quite a fright.'

'Please sit down for a moment, or are you on duty? I don't want to get you into trouble.'

'I just finished my shift. I'm on my way home. How are you feeling?'

'I'm not in pain, but they're going to do something called an angiogram…a balloon in the artery to unblock it…is that right?'

'More or less. It's a simple life-saver,' she reassured him.

'I'm not sure what the point is, really. I don't want to sound ungracious, but you would have done me a favour if you'd just let me go.'

'Don't say that. Life is precious – every minute of it - and you've been given yours back.'

Stage Struck

'But for what? I'm sorry, it isn't your problem, but...'

'You're depressed, understandably. Look, if you want to talk to me as a friend – a new friend – I promise you I'll keep it in complete confidence.'

He looked very pathetic lying there – nothing like the brash man who had made such a fool of himself at the audition, and she suddenly felt overwhelmingly sorry for him.

'I appreciate your kindness, Rose, but you're so young; what can you possibly know about pain, about loss, about wanting to find solace in the bottom of a glass?'

'More than you might think,' she murmured. 'Maybe I'll tell you one day. But right now, you're the one who needs to get his life back on track. Have your family been to see you?'

He scowled. 'Yes, my son and daughter came with their families yesterday. They live in Scotland.' He paused, trying to control a sudden rush of tears to his eyes. 'They were positively rubbing their hands together, seeing me like this. "The old buzzard is on the way out – we're a bit nearer to inheriting the family fortune".'

Shocked, Rose asked, 'Why do you believe that?'

'When my Peggy died, I thought I would too. I wish I had… But that's beside the point. The children kept pressuring me to move to Scotland. They wanted me to sell my home and give them the money so they could buy larger properties. Wanted me to move in with them, spending three months with one and three months with the other. What sort of life would that have been? When I told them what they could do with that idea, they abandoned me. Three years – I hadn't seen either of them since, until yesterday.'

'Winston, I'm so sorry. But you know you do have friends in the drama group. Lots of people who care about you - and they're very concerned for you now.'

'They'll soon forget me. I have nothing left to give now, have I? Too old and decrepit to play the dame – I forgot half my lines in *Pygmalion*. Why should they have any interest in me? Anyway, my dear, you must go. I'm suddenly very tired. Why is it, in hospital they wake you up to give you a sleeping tablet, then they're all clattering around serving breakfast at half past six when you can't even prise your eyes open? I thought one came into hospital to get well – not suffer an endurance test.'

Rose laughed and on impulse leaned over and kissed his cheek.

He grabbed her hand and raised it to his lips. 'Thank you for coming to see me. Will you come again?'

'I promise. Get some rest now.'

He watched her walk away, wishing his own cold-hearted daughter could be more like Rose.

Stage Struck

Rose arrived home, fed Min and made herself pasta before flopping in front of the fire with her script and a glass of white wine. But she couldn't settle. She was concerned about how Mason would view her at rehearsal on the coming Tuesday and she blushed at the memory of how she had responded to his kiss until common sense had taken a hand. In spite of the way she rejected his advances, she couldn't resist speculating what it might have been like to make love with Mason. But she did know how she would have felt afterwards.

Her previous boyfriend, Phil, had been her first lover and something of a disappointment in bed. Probably, Rose conceded, that was her fault as much as his, because she knew how her father would have reacted if he'd known that she'd lost her virginity before marriage. She'd only been to bed with Phil three or four times, and frankly wondered what all the fuss was about. When she had been hit by the trauma of her father's death, Phil was unable to handle her distress and faded out of her life. Since then she never mustered the mental energy to consider another relationship and spent the past year concentrating on buying and decorating her house. She'd been thrilled to find just the house she wanted so near to Lauren, her closest friend, who was always there when needed – even on one wretched night, rushing round in her pyjamas at three in the morning to minister tea and sympathy. Rose wondered how she would have coped without her.

She sat sipping her wine, so deep in thought that she didn't hear the first knock at her door. The second louder rapping caused her to leap out of her chair and rush to open it. She was stunned to find Mason standing on the doorstep, his collar turned up, either as protection from the cold wind, or partially to hide his face from sight.

'May I come in, Rose, just for a moment?' Wordlessly, she stepped back and allowed him in. 'I'm sorry – I just had to come to see you before the next rehearsal. I haven't slept since Thursday night and I just…' he sank into a chair and sat with his elbows on his knees and hands covering his face. He looked the picture of misery, and for a moment Rose ached to go and put her arms around him. Instead, she poured him a glass of wine which he accepted gratefully. She then sat in the chair opposite.

'Does Candy know you're here?'

'No – although as she is wondering where I came in contact with a cat as she had an acute asthma attack when I got home the other night. I must stay away from your lovely Siamese this time.'

'She's asleep on my bed…'

He glanced at her and grinned sheepishly. 'Well, that's safely out of bounds then. Rose, I came to see if you were still happy to be in the show after my awful lapse the other night. I don't know what came over me. I'm so embarrassed.'

'I'm sure I'm to blame as much as you are. Please don't let's say any more about it because I don't want to drop out of the show. I'm enjoying it. Lauren warned me that things can flare up during the rehearsal period when people get very close, and that it all fades away afterwards. We're grownups – we can deal with this, can't we?'

'I can if you can. I suppose it's obvious to everyone that Candy and I are in crisis?'

'Yes, it is, but we're your friends and we'll all support you through it if we can.'

'Candy is having an affair with Nick.'

Rose stared at him stunned, uncertain what she was supposed to do with this knowledge. 'Are you sure?'

'Yes.'

'Does she know that you know?'

'No.'

'Then you must be feeling very vulnerable. No wonder you were in need of …well, what happened between us.'

'Rose, believe me, I didn't plan for it – but when you looked at me with those huge blue eyes, something inside me melted. I couldn't help myself.'

'If we're honest, Mason, the same thing happened to me,' she said softly. 'I wanted you to kiss me.'

'What are you saying to me, Rose? That you want to have an affair with me? Because, my dear girl, that is all it could ever be. I am married – however unhappily - and I have two expensive children who are still very needy. And I'm much too old for you.'

'I know you're right. It would be a disaster and we couldn't…I couldn't do it. But just for a moment the other night, my defences were down and so were yours, so I was just as much to blame as you were.'

He stood, took her hands and pulled her to her feet. 'Rose, I'm more flattered than I can possibly tell you that you might even have considered it. You're beautiful, utterly desirable and it's taking every ounce of control I possess to walk away. But if I don't, ultimately you will get hurt, and you really don't deserve that.'

'I expect you're right. Thank you for being so thoughtful – most men would have taken advantage of me.'

'Believe me, Rose, in any other circumstances... Will you be at rehearsal on Tuesday?'

'Of course.' She smiled wanly at him as she opened the front door, and watched as he walked rapidly down the road.

A short while later there was another knock at her door. Wearily, she got up to answer it.

'It's the net-twitcher from down the road,' announced Lauren. 'I saw Mason come and then go, and I wanted to check you had your virtue intact.'

'Oh, yes, you don't need to worry.' Rose led her friend into the warmth of the living room. 'Glass of wine? Might as well finish the bottle now.'

'Please. Are you all right?'

'No. Well, you might as well know as long as it's a state secret between us.' And because they had always shared everything, she told her about 'the kiss' and the fact that Candy was having an affair with Nick.

'I'm not surprised,' Lauren mused, 'she can't keep her eyes off him when they're in the same room. I think Lola has cottoned on too. Oh, dear, we really don't need this with the show only six weeks away. As for you and Mason...'

'I told you, there is no me and Mason. I just had a schoolgirl crush and he picked up on the signals. Already I feel foolish and want to forget the whole business.'

'Good – what a relief. Spend time with John and have some fun. He's obviously smitten. I'm going out with Clive tomorrow.'

'Your life is so uncomplicated, Lauren.'

'You know it isn't really, but I don't suppose anyone's life is.'

'You haven't talked about it for ages. Have you thought any more about trying to find your natural mother?'

'It's fairly pointless, isn't it? She left me on a metaphorical doorstep aged two weeks, and as far as I know she's never tried to trace me since. But then I was a really ugly kid.'

'Oh, Lauren!' Rose moved to sit beside her friend and gave her a hug. 'I expect she was going through hell – things were less easy for unmarried mothers then. She probably thinks about you every day but assumes you wouldn't want to see her now.'

'Yeah, well, maybe I don't.' A flash of intense pain crossed Lauren's face, and she downed the rest of her glass of wine in a gulp.

'Maybe you should talk to someone about it. Someone who can advise you; help you to make up your mind.'

'A shrink?'

'No, you dope. But there are agencies that put people in touch, having made sure that's what both parties want.'

'Like I said, what's the point? She abandoned me. She won't want me now. Anyway, apart from that I have a great life, a new promotion, so I don't dwell on it. I had several sets of kind foster parents, I put myself through college and I have my own home, a job I love and friends like you; so it could have been worse. A lot worse.'

But Rose knew that inside Lauren ached to know her real mother, and her eyes filled with tears as she remembered her own.

Nick prepared for his date with Sam with more than a touch of anxiety. He had a haircut, carefully ironed his new white shirt and navy trousers, shaved and even took the car for a wash and polish.

What is the matter with me? I'm behaving like a fifteen year old going on a first date. Ridiculous – not my style at all, he thought ruefully. But then I've never had to resort to a blind date before.

Nevertheless, when he walked into the restaurant, his heart was beating a little faster and his palms were sweaty. So attractive, he thought, wiping them on a handkerchief. She'll be bowled over if she gets a clammy handshake.

Calming himself, he glanced around, wondering if she had arrived before him. There was no blonde wearing a red sweater and black trousers, so he made his way to the bar and ordered a gin and tonic, keeping a weather eye on the door. Just when he'd begun to think that she had changed her mind, a gentle hand was laid on his arm.

'Are you Nick?'

He turned to gaze down into a pair of twinkling green eyes, set in a heart-shaped face, framed, not by blonde, but golden-red shoulder-length hair. And she was wearing a green dress.

'Samantha?' He was taken aback.

She smiled. 'Who else were you expecting?'

'Well, a blonde in a red sweater, for starters.' He laughed. 'Is that a wig?'

'No. It's just that I wanted to take a look at you before committing myself. If I hadn't liked what I saw, I could have slipped away without you knowing who I was.'

'Very clever. Do I take it that you have decided I'm presentable?'

'Yes – and I'm sorry. But I've been on a couple of these dates before and you would be amazed at what turns up. One chap told me he was a Sean Bean look-alike when he was more like Mr. Bean. The other was wearing cowboy boots.'

'Well, I'm glad I pass muster on first appraisal.' Nick grinned at her. 'May I say you look delightful and I am *not* about to make an excuse and do a runner. What would you like to drink?'

She asked for a white wine spritzer and they went to sit in the lounge where the waiter brought them menus.

'Sandra told me you have a PR company – that must be fun.'

'Hard work, because my partner and I only set it up six months ago, although we've both been in the industry for years; but yes, I love it. What about you?'

'Less exciting. I'm an infant teacher. But I enjoy it, and of course with the school holidays it fits in around my little boy.'

'You said his name is Ben?'

'That's right – good memory. He's eight, well nearly nine and the light of my life. I have to tell you now, we come as a package.'

'I usually get on well with kids. Does he like football?'

'Is the Pope a Catholic?'

'Well, as long as he doesn't support Wolves, we should have a lot in common.'

'Manchester United, and now Real Madrid since half his team seems to have emigrated to Spain. Personally, I prefer rugby.'

He looked at her in astonishment. 'You're a very surprising lady. What else do you do?'

'Yoga on Wednesday and French classes on Monday. I lead such an exciting life.'

They chose from the menu and handed it back to the waiter.

'Just to get the question out of the way, Nick, is it true you're single? I know lots of people tell an agency that they are, when they have a lot of messy baggage in the background. I couldn't risk being in that situation because of Ben – so before we go any further, I want the honest truth.'

'I've never been married, Samantha, and that *is* the honest truth. I have been a selfish bachelor who has enjoyed the freedom of living life my way. But now, at the tender age of thirty-nine…okay, forty-five… I long to find someone special – maybe someone to settle down with.'

He realised with an enormous shock that he meant it. The end of his affair with Candy had finally brought it home to him that his age was catching up with him. He no longer had the energy to go through that again. Someone warm and loving to come home to every night suddenly seemed rather appealing.

'Tell me about your situation,' he asked.

'I was widowed when Ben was two. It was a car accident. We were driving through town when we were rammed by a drunken kid in a stolen Mercedes. Josh died before they could get him out, and I broke my pelvis. Fortunately, Ben was with my parents who were babysitting.'

'How awful.'

'It was a long time ago and Ben doesn't remember Josh, which makes me sad because he was a wonderful person. But life, eventually, goes on.'

'And since then?'

'I had a few dates, but frankly a woman with a young child is a difficult proposition for most men. I know I may never find someone I can love and trust like Josh, and I'm not prepared to make compromises. But that doesn't mean I can't try, does it?'

'Not at all,' he replied carefully.

The delicate watercress soup, followed by salmon in a champagne sauce, was delicious. Nick was relieved to find Samantha so easy to be with and the evening flew by far too quickly. It was half past ten when she finally laid down her spoon with a contented sigh. 'That was the most divine trifle I have ever tasted.'

'It's lovely to be out with someone who isn't on a diet. Not that you need to,' he added hastily.

Samantha threw her head back and laughed. 'Oh, Nick, stop treading on eggshells with me. I'm size twelve – just – and like every other woman I know I'd love to lose ten pounds. But at thirty-seven I'm not likely to regain my size ten figure without making myself miserable - and I can live with that.'

'I think you look lovely – I never went for stick insects anyway.'

'Thank you,' she smiled at him. 'I've really enjoyed this evening, but I do have to go because my neighbour, Mrs Evans, is babysitting.'

'Can I see you again?' Nick asked, signalling for the bill.

'Yes. I would like that.'

'Next week?'

'What about next Saturday – maybe we could go to the theatre or the cinema?'

'That's a great idea. Have you seen *Mama Mia*?'

'In London? No, but I would love to. I doubt we would get tickets at such short notice.'

'Leave that to me. I have low friends in high places.' He grinned, tapping the side of his nose.

'I like you more all the time,' she smiled.

'I live in hope, Sam. Oh, and just to reserve a date a bit ahead, the drama group I belong to are having their pre-Christmas dinner dance on December the tenth. It fell to me to organise it this year, so I'm hoping it goes well. I would love you to accompany me.'

'I'd like that – but what will you tell your friends about me?'

'You mean that we met through a dating agency? Well, I suppose we'd become an interesting topic of conversation, so I suggest we just say we met through mutual friends.'

'Good idea. I can arrange for Ben to stay with my parents for the weekend, which gives me a late pass.'

Nick helped her into her coat and walked with her to the car park. She turned and smiled up at him, and he stooped and tentatively kissed her cheek. She looked at him quizzically as he stood with his hands resting lightly on her shoulders.

'Could we try that again?' she asked softly.

'With pleasure,' he smiled and, drawing her into his arms, gently kissed her soft mouth.

'Mmm.' She smiled up at him. 'That was as nice as I thought it would be.'

A burst of fireworks went off close by, making them both jump, and then laugh.

'That must have been some kiss. I'll see you next Saturday.'

'Can I call you before then?' he asked, surprising himself.

'Yes.' She climbed into her little red Ka and, with a wave, was gone.

Well, thank you very much, Sandra, he thought. A great first date. She's lovely, and just the ticket to put Candy's nose well and truly out of joint. I wouldn't mind seeing her for a while… In fact, I'd like to see her again very soon. He supposed her son might be a complication, but this time at least there was no irate husband lurking in the background. Yes, this one could be fun.

He drove home, singing along to the radio. But as he turned into his road, his heart sank. Candy was parked at his kerb, waiting for him.

He leapt out of his car, slammed the door ferociously and stormed over to her. 'What do you think you're playing at?' he demanded. 'Are you trying to wreck all our lives?'

'I missed you. Where have you been? You're all dressed up.'

'A business meeting.' Why on earth am I lying to her? he wondered.

'On Saturday?'

'Go home, Candy. Just leave me alone. We have nothing else to say to each other.'

To his relief, she started the car and drove away.

But he was left feeling uneasy. The joy of the evening had evaporated.

Tuesday 18th November

Rose arrived early for the Tuesday rehearsal and was helping Patsy get the coffee cups out when John and Clive arrived.

'Have you heard how Winston is?' John asked.

She told him about her visit. 'He's very depressed and he misses being a part of this so much. We have to do something to include him when he's had his operation.'

'We'll think of something. Come for a drink with me after rehearsal – just the two of us?'

'Okay,' she agreed.

Mason and Candy arrived together. Rose glanced at Mason and smiled before turning to talk to Lauren and Clive, and sensed his relief when she paid him no further attention.

'Right, chaps,' he summoned his cast, 'let's get started. We're doing the whole of Act One tonight, no scripts and with all the songs and dances – so beginners on stage, please.'

John, wearing his batik skirt, launched into his opening routine with Clive and the first two or three scenes went reasonably well. Candy, wearing a leotard and tights to aid her movement, was finally showing some personality as Tabitha, the witch's cat, whilst Maureen Clarke as Verruca brought boos and hisses from those watching. When Rose finally walked on stage wearing leggings under some thigh length boots which Patsy had found in the company wardrobe, there were roars of approval and she instantly forgot her lines.

'I'm so ... so sorry...' she stammered.

'Don't ever apologise if you dry up,' Mason told her. 'You just wait for a prompt and carry on.'

'Sorry...I mean...sorry.'

'Shall we start that scene again?'

The second time she got through it with several prompts and Mason made them do the scene a third time, at which point she couldn't remember what day it was, let alone a word of her script, and was close to tears.

'All right, I think we'll stop for coffee,' said their exasperated director. 'Rose, can I have a word with you, please?'

She followed him to a quiet corner, expecting a few sharp words, but he said to her, 'I apologise about that; I shouldn't have been so hard on you. Tonight must be as difficult for you as it is for me. It's probably my fault you're a bit wobbly, so please don't let it shake your confidence. You're going to be just fine.'

Stage Struck

'Thanks. I'll do my best. Nick has just walked in. How are you going to deal with that?'

'He's my Stage Manager. I can't do the show without him, so I just have to bite the bullet, don't I? Anyway, it takes two to tango. Have some coffee and then we'll carry on.'

Rose bit her lip, feeling both sorry for Mason and anxious about the fault line which seemed to be gathering strength in the group. A bit more pressure and there would be a full scale earthquake. She watched as Candy glanced at Nick under her eyelashes, trying to catch his attention. He ignored her totally and a flash of fury crossed her face, quite frightening in its intensity. Rose crossed to her and tried to divert her by asking for help with the simple dance routine she had with Lady Marian.

'Can we just go over it while everyone is finishing coffee please, Candy? I can't remember my lines tonight and my feet certainly can't remember the steps.'

'Yes, of course. Where's Lola?' She summoned her daughter who, Rose decided, had a definite glow about her. She was in a sunny mood and beamed happily when asked to practise her routine. By the time they had gone through it again, Rose was more confident and went back on stage feeling relatively cheerful.

The dance went well, and to her eternal relief she remembered her lines, earning her a wink of approval from Mason.

'You should relax more, Rose,' said Lola. 'Have a bit more confidence. Smile. You're going to be very good.'

'Thanks. You seem to be doing rather a lot of smiling yourself tonight, young lady.'

'It isn't a sin to be happy, is it? Except in our house of course. But,' she whispered, 'I have to tell you that I have a lovely reason to be happy.'

'I'm glad,' replied Rose. 'Is he nice?'

'He's divine. My dad has found out and caved in about it. I was amazed that he wasn't more cross. But my problem is that Mum doesn't know and she'll go ape. They've both forbidden boyfriends until after the exams, but Daddy was quite sweet about it. He's told me not to tell Mum for now and I won't – but if she finds out that he already knew there'll be yet another bust up.'

Rose began to feel awkward, wondering what the young girl would think if she knew she was confiding in someone who had almost become involved with her father.

'It's all so difficult,' Lola continued, 'and spoiling what should be such a happy time for me. I mean – Alex, well, he's nice, Rose, really he is. He's handsome, clever and thoughtful…and when I look at some of my friends' boyfriends, he's a real diamond.'

'And you love him?' Rose asked when Lola finally paused for breath.

'I adore him. And because I'm so afraid of Mum finding out, I worry all the time and can't concentrate on my schoolwork. It's so hypocritical. It isn't as if she's an angel... I mean, well, parents can be very confusing.' She shrugged and smiled a little tearfully at Rose. 'Sorry, it isn't your problem. But did your parents let you have boyfriends when you were doing your 'A' levels?'

'My dad was a vicar.'

'They're supposed to be good listeners. You must take after him. Maybe that's why I felt the urge to tell you?'

'Perhaps,' Rose said. Lola's comment surprised her. She hurried on: 'I was brought up very strictly, and they too would have gone ape, as you put it, if I'd gone behind their backs. So I do sympathise. Perhaps if you introduce him gently and don't push to be out late every night, your mother may come round to the idea.'

'You reckon?'

'Sometimes it's difficult for mothers to accept that their daughters are grown up; that they are sexual beings. They feel threatened...and old.'

'Old - my mum? Well, she is forty-something. I suppose that *is* old really.'

Thinking that both Lola's parents had more things to worry about than their daughter's love life, she gave the girl a gentle hug. 'Are you taking him to the dinner dance?'

'I suppose I could. Do you think that would be a good idea?'

'Yes. It's a chance for them to meet him on neutral ground. If he turns up looking smart and they can see he's a decent bloke, it might break the ice very nicely.'

'You know, Rose, I think that's a brilliant idea. I was going to take my boring brother, but I'll ask Alex if he'll go. I expect Leo will want to be with Gillian anyway.'

Mason called his daughter to rehearse a dance with the children who had arrived for their run-through and Rose thought how sweet and tender Lola was with them. She gently coached them how to follow her routine, and they responded, fierce concentration on their small faces as they hopped and twirled on chubby feet, to the music of *The Teddy Bears' Picnic*.

Rose leaned on the hatchway, watching. 'She's a lovely girl, isn't she?' she said to Patsy who was washing the coffee cups.

'She is,' replied Patsy. 'I've known her since she was shorter than me of course – and Leo. They used to be a happy family. Unfortunately, things look rather less cosy at the moment. I'm not gossiping, but it would be hard to miss, wouldn't it?'

Rose wondered if Patsy was giving her a veiled warning – whether she too had noticed Rose's attraction to Mason. 'Let's hope they resolve it.'

'Indeed. Right, I must go and be a teddy bear for Scaliban. Wait till you see my costume. It's almost finished. Oh, and while I think of it, could you pop round to my house to try on the outfit I'm making for you? I found some fishnet tights in the Fancy Dress Shop and the boots look good on you, how lucky they fit – but the green tunic probably needs a few alterations.'

'It sounds wonderful. You are clever, I can't get a button to stay on.' Rose watched as the little lady pottered off to rehearse.

Half an hour later Mason called an end to proceedings for the evening, and between them the cast restored the church hall to its former order.

'Anyone for the pub?' he asked.

John glanced at Rose and she smiled and declined Mason's suggestion. Clive and Lauren left together, and everyone else seemed to have somewhere to go. 'What about you, Candy?' he finally asked his wife. To his obvious amazement, she agreed, smiled brilliantly at him, taking his arm as they wandered across the road.

'Wonders will never cease!' Patsy exclaimed as she climbed into her specially converted car. 'Let's hope it isn't the calm before the storm.'

***

Rose and John had agreed to drive separately to The George, a pub just outside Sipton, and since he'd arrived first, John ordered two soft drinks. He sat watching for Rose to come in, wishing his heart wouldn't thump quite so hard at the idea of being alone with her; if you could call a crowded pub alone. He was desperately afraid of seeming too eager because there was a reserve about her which told him that she wasn't ready for a relationship. For now, he knew he would have to settle for being her friend and, hopefully, confidante. He'd been touched that she'd felt able to share her traumatic story with him. It was a privilege and he had told no-one, not even Clive, about the tragedy that still haunted Rose.

She came through the door, looking around, then spotted where he'd bagged a table in a corner. She'd loosened the cascade of corkscrew curls after rehearsal so that her hair now fell shimmering onto her shoulders. Having changed back into those figure hugging jeans, she'd topped them with a thigh-length, cuddly sweater. As she crossed the lounge bar every head turned to look at her, but she seemed totally unaware of that – or of how proud John was when she sat beside him.

'Gosh, I'm glad that rehearsal is over,' she said with feeling. 'It was a nightmare – my lines just vanished into the ether. Couldn't remember my name.'

'Clive says everyone has a rehearsal like that. It's apparently unlucky to get to the first night without a bad rehearsal.'

'Well, I'll take your word for it. Now, what are we going to do about poor old Winston? I know he's a lush, but he is so lonely without the group, and he has a sad story too. His children sound abysmal. Will you come with me to see him tomorrow?'

John was delighted she had asked him. 'Perhaps we could have supper somewhere afterwards?' he dared to ask, and she smilingly accepted. 'When is he having his operation?'

'I spoke to the Sister on his ward this morning and he may have had the procedure this afternoon if he was in a stable enough condition. The sooner, the better. If so, then he should be out of hospital in a few days. We need to convince him he's still a valued member of the group. He's embarrassed by his behaviour at the audition and thinks everyone despises him now.'

'We'll work something out when he's well again. In the meantime,' John suggested, 'perhaps you and I can take him under our wing?'

'I think that's a lovely idea.'

A while later they left the pub and John walked with Rose to her Skoda.

'Shall I pick you up to go visit Winston tomorrow?'

'No, I'll just be coming off duty at seven, so I'll see you on the ward. I'm afraid I'll be all dressed up as a nurse.'

John laughed. 'Gee whiz Ma'am, and wad'ya expect me to say to that?' he drawled.

She wagged a finger at him, 'Behave!' and then, reaching up, kissed him lightly on the lips before jumping in her car and driving away.

He stood, smiling like an idiot, as he watched the lights of her car fade into the distance.

***

Nick left the rehearsal feeling relieved. Candy had done no more than glare at him, but he had been on edge all evening, dreading she might to do something stupid. Now, at last, he was able to go home and make a late call to Sam. He had called her every night since Saturday and she seemed to like his attention. He found he had so much to say to her and their phone calls were usually at least an hour long.

She answered the phone on the first ring and her soft voice caused his body to stir.

'I can't stop thinking about you,' were his first words. 'Do we really have to wait until Saturday to meet again?'

'Come to supper tomorrow. You can meet Ben, but you must promise not to give him the idea you might be more than a friend. It's much too soon.'

'I give you my word.'

'Six-thirty then? He goes to bed at eight.'

'I'll look forward to it, Sam. And I promise I won't rush you, either.'

'Thank you,' she said solemnly.

They talked for a while until she wished him goodnight and hung up. He fell into bed at midnight and tried to read a book, but all he could think about was Sam. Her warm smile, the twinkle in her eyes and the way she made him laugh. He tried not to let his imagination run wild, but the idea of taking her to bed, which seemed a fairly distant prospect, made sleep impossible.

Then his thoughts turned to her son. What if Ben hated him on sight, was a monster, a horror with three sixes hidden under his hair? What if he was violently jealous of his mother having a boyfriend? They came as a team; that much he was sure of, so he had to make friends with this child at all costs. Should he get a present for Ben? But that would be buying his friendship and he felt sure they would both instantly see through that ploy. No, he decided, just be cool - whatever cool meant in this situation.

Finally, at three in the morning he fell asleep and woke with the alarm at seven, his whole body feeling like lead. He took a shower and had just emerged with a towel wrapped round his waist when the phone rang. Hoping it might be Sam, he grabbed it, only to find Candy on the other end.

'Candy, why on earth are you calling at this hour? Mason will hear you.'

'He left half an hour ago – an early meeting.'

'Okay – but I still want to know why you're calling me.'

'I want to come round and spend the morning in bed with you, to remind you what I can do for you – and you for me. Please, darling, don't keep on like this, I can't bear it.'

'Don't be ridiculous. Candy, it's over. Sooner or later you have to accept that. I've moved on and so must you.'

'What do you mean, you've moved on? Are you telling me you're already seeing someone else?' she demanded furiously.

'Yes, if you must know - I am.'

'You bastard! How could you.'

'Candy, we had an affair. It was a mistake…'

'*A mistake?*' she screamed.

'Because you're married and anyway you're just too needy for me. I can't be there for you all the time – you wear me out. Now I want you to go back to being a friend and stop risking the happiness of your family chasing something you can't have! You're being very selfish.'

'*I'm* being selfish!' she exploded.

'And' he continued, 'I wish to God I had never got involved with you in the first place. Now leave me alone, or…'

'Or what, Nick? You'll tell Mason about us?'

'The man has eyes in his head, Candy. He probably knows already.'

'No, of course he doesn't!'

'Then don't push your luck. You'll lose everything, including the respect of everyone in the group. Look, we had a good time – a great time – but I don't want you any more, Candy. I really don't want you.' And he put the phone down with a great sense of foreboding.

Stage Struck

Wednesday 19th November

Maureen Clarke visited Winston that afternoon and was shocked to find him lying apparently lifeless with a nurse leaning over him.

She rushed over. 'Is he all right?'

'Are you a relative?'

'The closest thing he has in real terms, yes.'

'He had his angiogram this morning, so he's still groggy. But it went well and he should feel a great deal better by tomorrow. With luck, he can go home at the weekend.'

'What a relief. Thank you.'

The nurse left them and Maureen leaned over Winston, a tight lump in her throat. His wretched children should have been here for him, she thought – to encourage him when he woke up and make him feel cared for. 'Hello, you silly old bugger,' she said softly as Winston opened his eyes.

'The Wicked Witch of the East,' he croaked. 'I died, then?'

'Yes, you did. Funny how Hell looks just like the cardiac ward at St. Mary's, isn't it?'

'It's a close call. The food has to be better down there - at least it would be hot.'

'How do you feel?'

'I can see two of you at present…but otherwise not too bad.'

'You get kicked out of here in a couple of days, so you'd better make the most of it. Are the children staying to look after you?'

'No, my dear Maureen. Having been assured by my doctor that I am likely to survive, they cleared off back to Scotland, and good riddance.'

'I'm sorry. Peggy would be disgusted with them.'

'Yes,' he sighed deeply.

'Well, I have more bad news. I plan to move in with you for at least a week.'

'Really?' he turned his head and stared at her. 'Why should you do that? There's no need to feel sorry for me, I can hire a nurse to stay for a couple of nights.'

'Are you worried about what the neighbours might say, then?'

'Maureen, I don't give a hoot what anyone might say. I'm grateful, really, I am…but...'

'Then that's settled. Give me your keys and I'll stock the fridge and make up the spare bed. Sorry to disappoint you, but I'm not planning to sleep with you.'

'You'd be pretty safe if you did…' His voice broke. 'But what about your job?'

Stage Struck

Maureen leaned over and dropped a kiss on the top of his head. 'The school can run for a week without its headmistress. Must go – behave yourself with those pretty nurses.'

He watched her walk through the double doors at the end of the ward and gave in to tears of weakness and anguish. The children had been almost hostile when they realised he would recover. Jackie had been back yesterday and tried again to persuade him to sell the flat and move to Scotland on the basis they had discussed three years before.

'You can't stay on your own now, Dad, and you can't expect us to keep running to and from Scotland every time you have a crisis. We have lives and businesses to run. It's totally unreasonable. You could live with us for three months and then with Paul and Sharon for three months. That way we both keep some privacy and semblance of normal life.'

'And you get my money before I die...'

'We could buy another property before prices go any higher, yes. I mean it's coming to us anyway, so why not have it now when we can use it? It's ridiculous to put us in this position.'

'I don't know what I did to deserve such cold-hearted children. Your mother was a warm and caring person.'

'Oh, Dad, don't be like that! We want what's best for you.'

'Really? Perhaps we were given the wrong babies in the hospital...'

Her face hardened at that.

'Get out,' he said brusquely, 'go back to Scotland and you can wait for your money until I keel over.'

Jackie remonstrated with him until the heart monitor by his bed switched into overdrive, beeping rapidly, causing the staff to arrive at his bedside at a run. Jackie was ordered out of the ward, but the episode had brought the decision to operate on him with all speed, which they had, the following morning.

He gazed around the alcove of four beds of which his was one, and sadly wondered whether perhaps he should have simply given in, sold his flat, moved to Scotland and hoped God wouldn't keep him waiting too long to be called. If only that young Rose had let him die, he thought with frustration, everybody could get on with their lives without him being a nuisance.

Now Maureen felt she had to move in to look after him. And in truth he had no idea how he would manage without her. He supposed sadly, his former friends in the drama group would also probably pay lip service to caring what happened to him.

'Life's a bitch,' he sighed, 'and then you die.'

***

Stage Struck

Rose finished her shift at seven and as promised, went straight to the cardiac ward. John was waiting for her by the door, carrying a large bunch of flowers.

'I thought they might cheer him up,' he smiled, wishing his own heart would stop doing such leaps and jumps at the sight of her. She wore her hair piled under a nurses' cap, still a feature of St. Mary's, and a dark blue dress denoting her status as Sister. Dark tights and lace-up shoes completed the ensemble, making her appear very efficient, he thought. And he could suddenly understand the obsession some men had with nurses' uniforms. 'Shall we go in?'

'Yes.' She smiled and nodded. 'Are you all right about this? You look a bit uncomfortable.'

'Sure, I'm okay. Just a bit out of my comfort zone, that's all. I mean, I got his part in the show. If I hadn't, none of this might have occurred.'

'You didn't clog up his arteries. This could have happened at any time.'

'I guess. Come on, then – let's go see him.'

Winston gaped when he realised the two visitors walking down the ward were for him. His eyes filled again with tears when John laid a large bunch of flowers on his bed. He picked them up and buried his nose in the fragrance.

'Tha... thank you,' he stammered. 'Thank you.'

'You look better,' Rose told him. 'I popped in this afternoon when you were still out of it after your operation.'

'You did? That was kind,' he said gruffly, 'but I don't want to be a bother to anyone.'

'Are...er...are you in pain?' asked John.

'Not really. A bit sore, but they seem to think I'll live. At least for now.' He regarded John for a moment, recalling that this was the man who had robbed him of his role as dame. He was young, handsome and charismatic, and Winston knew in his heart that John would steal the show. 'How is it going – the pantomime?' he asked, leaning back on his pillows.

'It has its moments. Some rehearsals are better than others. I'm getting very nervous about it now.'

'Humph... Never been nervous on stage in my life. Confidence, that's what you need...confidence.'

For several minutes he regaled them with stories of his long career on the amateur stage until he suddenly became tired and laid back, his eyes becoming droopy.

'They tell me you can go home the day after tomorrow,' Rose said. 'How will you manage? I mean, can we help?'

87

'Maureen is moving in for a few days. Good of her.'

'I'm so glad.' Rose took his hand gently and he squeezed her fingers. 'We'll come and see you at your flat in a day or two - if that's all right?'

'Yes. Yes, please.' He realised that, apart from odd visits from Maureen, it would be the first time anyone had ever seen the inside of his flat.

Rose and John left the hospital and drove back separately to her house so that she could change.

'I'm exhausted,' said Rose as they went into the hallway where Min was waiting to be fed. 'Do you mind if I just throw some scrambled eggs together rather than go out?'

'I'll cook,' John volunteered. 'You go and change.'

'You like to cook?'

'Yes, ma'am,' he said proudly. 'I'm pretty damn good, too.'

'Then be my guest. There are eggs and ...'

'Go upstairs, Rose, I'll find my way around your kitchen.'

'Okay, could you give Min her food - it's in the cupboard?'

'Sure. Come on Min, you can show me where...' and the pair of them disappeared into the little kitchen, the cat meowing loudly at his heels.

Rose took a shower, pulled on a comfortable pair of jogging pants and T-shirt, and twenty minutes later went downstairs to find John had set the small dining table in the corner of her living room. He'd even found wine glasses and a candle. He ushered her to a seat, opened a bottle of red wine and, after filling the glasses, vanished into the kitchen. He reappeared a few seconds later, triumphantly carrying his creation on two plates.

'Fluffy mushroom omelettes, salad and sautéed potatoes, madam!'

'What a star!' she gasped. 'Thank you.'

'Cheers,' he smiled, raising his glass to her.

'Hey, this is good vino. I hope I didn't open a treasured bottle. It was in the cupboard.'

'Supermarket special offer,' she reassured him.

As they ate, John regarded her across the table. 'Are you sleeping better now? I think you still look very tired.'

'I didn't sleep well last night,' she confessed. 'The nightmares came back – the whole awful thing replayed in my head and when I woke I swear I could still smell lilies.'

'How do you feel about your father now?' he asked, refilling her glass.

'Indifferent.' She lowered her eyes and twisted her napkin around her fingers.

'I don't believe you.'

'I try not to think about him.'

'I still don't believe you. Sorry, it's none of my business.'

'I can't cope with thinking about him too much,' she told him at last. 'I get in such a state... I feel hate, rage, betrayal... everything except grief or love. He killed my mother and then he killed himself and left me to deal with the aftermath. I despise him and I expect God does too.'

'My God would understand.'

'Are you religious?' she asked, surprised.

'Not in any formal way. He and I have a casual relationship. I knock on His door in times of trouble. "Hey there, give me a hand with this, would you, Lord?" and he seems happy enough with that. More often than not I find a solution to my problem. I must say I have no time for organised religion. Sorry, I know you're devout.'

'No, I'm not,' she interrupted sharply. 'My father preached love, forgiveness, the sanctity of life and I thought he believed in it. But he was a sham.'

'He was only human.'

'What did you feel about God after the Tsunami?'

'I had some pretty sharp words with Him. But I don't buy into the Heaven and Hell thing. I don't believe God necessarily has a duty to step in and stop bad things happening, either. He didn't stop the Tsunami. But look how much love and help was poured in afterwards to those poor people who survived. That's where my God was, in the hearts of those who came to help. I think we all have a free choice about which side we decide to be on.' He picked up their empty plates and moved through to the kitchen. Rose followed and watched as he neatly stacked them in the sink.

'So what about Heaven and Hell?' she asked, fascinated. 'Are you saying you don't believe in them?'

'No. I have an open mind on re-incarnation, but Heaven as described in the Bible as some sort of paradise, with harps and fluffy clouds, sounds a boring place. I mean, if you don't have a challenge, what point is there in living – in this world or the next? Coffee?'

She shook her head and, warming to his theme, he continued, 'I don't believe God lets us gain all the knowledge we accumulate during our lives only to stick us in some sterile environment where we can't use it when we die. Equally, the concept of fire and brimstone seems a useless exercise. Sending someone back to try again, to lead a better life – now that, I think I can relate to.'

'If and when you feel the need – who do you pray to?'

'Whoever's listening?' he smiled. 'Don't know, really – but someone sure tunes in when I need him.'

'Then, do you think Heaven and Hell are here – on earth?'

'Can you imagine anything worse than the things we see everyday on the news?' he asked sadly.

'So where is my father now?'

He came to her and gently enfolded her in his arms, her head resting on his shoulder. 'He's not burning in Hell, Rose, of that I *am* sure.'

'I feel guilty because I get so incredibly angry with him that I can't mourn for him – when I know he must have gone through a year of mental torture after he helped Mum to die.' Tears trickled down her face. 'He must have suffered terribly.'

'Anger is a type of grief. One day you will line it all up in your head and feel better – but that may not be for a while. In the meantime, you have to accept how you feel now, and wait for it to pass. And it will.'

Releasing her, he refilled her wine glass and led her to the sofa where he sat with an arm draped around her shoulders. It felt comfortable as she rested her head against him.

'Sorry for pontificating at you,' he murmured into her hair.

'No, you gave me food for thought.'

After a short silence John stood up. 'I'll do the dishes and leave you in peace.'

'You will not,' she exclaimed, rising to face him. 'Do the dishes, I mean. I have a free morning tomorrow and it's my housework day.'

He kissed her lightly on the cheek and she returned the compliment by brushing her lips across his – the merest whisper of a kiss before she stepped back and looked at him, a confused expression in her blue eyes.

'I'll see you at rehearsal tomorrow, then?'

'Yes… John…'

'What?' Just for a second he had the heart-stopping notion that she was going to ask him to stay.

'Nothing – I'll see you tomorrow.'

He left and sat in his car outside for a minute or two, watching as Rose's bedroom light came on. She waved to him as she drew the curtains, and he blew her a kiss. 'Sleep well, my darling,' he murmured as he started the engine.

Pulling the edge of the curtain aside, Rose watched John's car disappear down the road.

Stage Struck

Perhaps it was the wine, but an unfamiliar longing had awakened inside her, and as she let the curtain fall back into place she realised how close she had been to asking him to stay.

***

Wednesday afternoon passed slowly and Candy was in a rage. She snapped at two small girls in her dance class, reducing them to tears. Their irate mothers said that the children would not be coming back.

Now the heavy traffic amplified her bad mood. She cursed and mouthed obscenities at another driver who had taken a while to move away at the traffic lights. Predictably, as she recklessly overtook him in the High Street, he gave her the time-honoured crude gesture and she was so incensed she barely stopped in time at a pedestrian crossing where a mother and two children were crossing. The woman shook her fist at Candy and hurried her children across the road to safety.

Heart pounding, Candy pulled over and lowered her head on her arms on the steering wheel. She was horrified at what could so easily have happened. Her breathing was becoming difficult; the shock had triggered her asthma. 'Serve's you right, you silly bitch,' she muttered to herself, searching in her bag for the inhaler.

When she calmed down, she re-started the engine and drove very carefully to *Waitrose* where she shopped without really thinking what she was buying. How could she be so stupid? Why did she feel so angry and out of control?

Nick had humiliated her, and it was the first time in her life she had been dumped. The boyfriends before Mason had been shed at a time of her choosing, but Nick had unceremoniously used her and then insulted her by saying, 'It's just an affair – I don't want you anymore.' How dare he, she fumed.

By the time she reached home she was feeling a little more in control, but dismayed to find Mason had arrived early from the office. He helped her bring in the shopping and she chatted brightly to him, wishing the children were around, but both were spending the night with friends after going to the cinema. So, she decided, perhaps this was the time to dispel any suspicions Mason might have about her affair; she was scared what might happen if they had a row and one of them brought up the subject. She had a feeling their marriage would instantly be over, which would be very inconvenient, to say the least.

For the past week she'd been trying to be nice to him, keeping things calm and hoping he would come to believe that she had just been having a bad spell with her hormones. But he'd been cool and polite in return and made no attempt to touch her with affection.

Through the kitchen doorway she studied her husband, as he sat with a scotch in front of the television while she cooked dinner, and wished he was more exciting. Where had the romance gone, the inventive sex, the little love tokens?

Truculently, she tried to make an effort over the meal and set the table with candles and a bottle of plonk. Afterwards, wearing the scraps of lacy underwear Nick had given her, she sat on Mason's lap, running her fingers through his hair and kissing him passionately.

'Darling,' she whispered, 'I know I've been horrible, and we've had a bad time recently...but I want to put things right. Please, please will you make love to me?'

Mason was taken aback and fleetingly wondered what her agenda was; it had been a long time since she'd made such an effort and he supposed she was doing her best to put their marriage back on track.

But he didn't want her.

She dragged him upstairs and began to undress him with apparent eagerness and he did his best to respond, but in his heart he knew the whole evening was a contrivance.

To his chagrin, when it came to it, the only way he could make love to his wife was to imagine she was Rose.

***

That evening, Nick left work early to give himself time to shower and change before making the twenty mile trip to Sam's house. He was surprised to find he could hardly wait to see her again. What was is about this woman? Telling himself he was too old and wise to get emotionally involved with someone he'd only just met, he set off to Cranleigh just before six o'clock with flowers for her and a football magazine for Ben.

Thanks to Sam's very precise directions, he found the house easily, and arrived exactly on time. He wondered whether he should wait a few moments. He didn't want to appear over eager.

The front door was flung open and a small boy stood watching him.

Feeling nervous - not something he was accustomed to - he gathered his small gifts from the back of the Land Rover, locked it, and strode up the garden path.

'Hello,' Nick greeted the child. 'You must be Ben. My name is Nick.'

'I know. Come in, Mummy won't be a minute. She's changing out of her jeans. She said she didn't want you to see her looking like a tramp.'

Nick laughed and ruffled the boy's short brown hair. 'Your mum would look good dressed in a bin liner.'

Stage Struck

'Yeah – she has great legs, hasn't she?'

'Ben, you're a man after my own heart. I bought flowers for your mum, but I heard you're a football fan and thought you might like this.' He handed over the magazine and Ben took it with a wide grin.

'Do you like MU too?'

'Yes…though you will think I'm really sad because my favourite team is Chelsea.'

'Mummy likes rugby, but I don't understand it. Are you going out with her?' he asked candidly.

'Would you mind?'

'No. She needs a boyfriend and that sex stuff.'

'Ben!' Samantha stood in the doorway, her face aflame and eyes sparkling with laughter.

Nick coughed to cover a hoot of mirth, and Ben looked slightly bemused, as if wondering what he had said that was so funny. 'Well that's what Brian's mum said when I went round to tea…' he explained stoutly.

'I'll talk to *her* tomorrow,' Sam chuckled. 'Nick, what a welcome. Can I get you a drink?'

'A beer would be great,' he said, finally getting control of himself before following Sam into the kitchen where she went to the fridge for a can of lager.

He studied her neat house and loved the homeliness of it. Ben's paintings were plastered over the walls and fridge, a half-made model of a dinosaur sat on the kitchen table and in the living room a table in the corner held a collection of puzzles, books and the inevitable Play Station.

'Can you play Walter Whizz-bang?' asked Ben.

'Can I what?'

'It's a computer game,' Sam explained. 'There are two controls for this contraption and you have to chase little imps through the forest and zap them into green goo.'

'Well, Ben, I'll have a go if you show me what to do.'

Within a few minutes he had more or less mastered the control buttons and they began their first game. Ben scored two million points and Nick lost spectacularly with five hundred. The second game went rather better and he only lost by a million. The third went to Nick by a whisker.

'Now play Mum!' He grinned. 'She always beats me.'

'Supper is ready…but okay, just one game,' she said, frowning with concentration, as she took the controls. It was a cutthroat match, but Sam won with a whoop of glee.

They ate supper together, a simple meal of lasagne and salad, but delicious, and Ben was allowed to watch the Disney Channel for half an hour before bed while Nick and Sam washed up.

Nick smiled. 'He's a great little boy. You must be very proud of him.'

'I am. It hasn't always been easy for him, having no Dad, but fortunately he has a positive personality and often it's been Ben who pulled me through the bad times.'

Ben didn't protest when told it was bedtime and sleepily said goodnight before disappearing upstairs. Sam went to tuck him in while Nick made coffee. He chose a CD and waited for Sam to re-appear, which she did a few moments later.

'Oh, this is nice,' she sighed, picking up her coffee mug and curling up on the sofa. Nick went to sit beside her and was aware that while upstairs she had freshened her lipstick and sprayed on flowery cologne. 'Tell me about your friends in the drama group. If I'm to meet them, I ought to know who is who.'

'They're a friendly crowd,' he said. 'Lots of them are involved in the pantomime, so look out for the girl playing Robin Hood. She has the longest legs I've ever seen and there's her somewhat eccentric friend Lauren... and the new guys are John, who, rumour has it, is sweet on Rose, and Clive, who is apparently dating Lauren. You can't miss Patsy, even though she's only four foot tall...and then there's the warring couple Mason and...Candy. Mason is the director.'

'And Candy?'

'Choreographer. She plays the witch's cat. I have to tell you she's well cast, so take no notice of her if she's spiteful.'

'Why should she be spiteful to me? Is she likely to be jealous?'

Good Lord, thought Nick, women had a train of thought that men could never match. How did she get to that? 'No, of course not. She just has a caustic tongue. There's one in every group I've ever belonged to.'

'Where is the party to be held?'

'The Glen Eagles Hotel, a few miles outside Sipton.'

'Yes, I know it. We had a family dinner there a couple of years ago.'

'It's dinner jackets,' he continued, 'but usually it's just a fun evening. People do their party pieces after dinner before the disco starts, so if you have a favourite story or monologue we'd love to hear it.'

'I'll think about it... It's a long time since I did anything like that. In fact, Nick, it's a long time since I did a lot of things. I'm afraid you might find me rather mundane – a boring single mum and all that.' She raised troubled eyes to him.

He responded with an emphatic shake of his head. 'Never.'

He felt her relax against him. Unable to resist any longer, he pulled her even more closely into his arms and kissed her. She tensed for a second, but then wound her arms around his neck and kissed him back. The soft warmth of her mouth, her breasts pressed against his chest and the curve of her body in his arms had a rapid and predictable effect on him, and an alarm bell rang in his head. Reluctantly, he released her.

'I've wanted to do that ever since I set eyes on you. In fact, ever since I spoke to you on the phone. But I promise we'll take things at your speed, Sam. I just want you to know that I'm bowled over by you. I think we could have something very special but if you don't think you can ever feel the same, I'd rather you told me now.'

'I like you too, Nick, and I won't deliberately hurt you,' she murmured. 'I told you that things between us can only be right if Ben is happy. '

'I don't have much experience with children, but I hope he and I can be friends.'

Sam nodded. 'Then let's see where this journey takes us.'

He stroked her cheek and she turned her face into the warmth of his palm, closing her eyes. He tangled his fingers in her red-gold hair and gently kissed her eyes, nose and mouth. When she opened her eyes to look at him, there was no doubt that she wanted him too.

'I think I should go now,' he said, gruffly.

'Yes,' she smiled and, easing herself out of his arms, rose and pulled him to his feet. 'I don't want you to think I'm some cheap tart who drags you up to bed on a second date.'

'I think you're delicious, gorgeous, feminine and divinely sexy. I want you right now more than I can tell you. But you know that. However, I'm going home for a cold shower and an early night, because I think it's too soon for you to cross that line.'

She rose on tiptoe to kiss him and he held her tightly. Then, taking a deep breath he stepped back. 'Goodnight, flower. I'll talk to you tomorrow.'

His arm around her, they moved to the hallway where he dropped a kiss on her nose. ''Bye.'

''Bye,' she replied softly, letting him out.

He walked resolutely down the path, turning as he opened the car door. She was leaning against the doorframe smiling. After a second, she blew him a kiss and disappeared inside.

Stage Struck

'What is going on here?' he wondered aloud. This was meant to be a convenient girlfriend – someone to help him get rid of Candy. He had not come to it with the slightest intention of - what? Falling in love? Ludicrous. Impossible. And yet, as he started the car and pulled away, feeling ridiculously happy, he was certain that he was on the edge of the most important relationship of his life.

Already he knew in his heart that to lose Sam would be a catastrophe, and as he drove home he debated whether it would be a mistake to take her to the drama dinner dance. He wasn't sure he wanted to share her yet. But surely this was the whole reason for finding himself a new girlfriend in the first place? To displace Candy as painlessly as possible - and to divert Mason's suspicions about Nick's affair with his wife. Suddenly, he didn't really care what Mason, Candy, or anyone else thought about him. All he wanted was to spend the rest of his life with Sam.

And the very idea astonished him.

Stage Struck

Friday 21st November

Lauren breathed in the stale air of the waiting room, desperate to open a window. Desperate to turn and run. Restlessly she walked up and down, occasionally glancing at the glass-panelled door, barely resisting the urge to bolt. But she had come this far in the search for her birth mother, it would be ridiculous not to see it through. She thought that she'd rarely been so scared in her whole life.

The elderly receptionist shuffled her paperwork and smiled encouragingly. 'Shouldn't be long, lovey. Why don't you sit down?'

Reluctantly, Lauren sank into a red plastic chair, her knees jammed together to stop her legs shaking, her fingers tightly entwined.

This was a bad idea. Better to leave now.

Resolutely, she sprang to her feet and was moving towards the exit when the office door opened and it was too late. 'Lauren? Please come through. My name's Jane Gladstone.'

Taking a deep breath, she followed Mrs. Jane Gladstone, a cosy-looking, middle-aged lady in a bobbly green wool cardigan. The office was quite cluttered. Tutting, Jane cleared a mountain of files from a chair for Lauren.

'What a mess! Just relax, my dear, you're as white as a sheet. I promise you, nothing we say or do today is going to be life-changing. Now then, we have your birth certificate and notes from the social services made at the time you were left.'

'Abandoned.'

Jane peered over her bifocals. 'That's a very emotive word, Lauren.'

'I feel pretty emotional about it.'

'Understandably. Anyway, it seems there was nothing left with you except a note to say you had been born on the fourteenth of August, in the Queen Elizabeth Hospital; that your mother had named you Lauren, and that she was sorry, but she couldn't look after you.'

'It isn't much to go on, is it?'

'Well, we have sources that checked the records at the QE and the only girl born that day was to a Mary Crane. The others, strangely, were all boys. We have a very old address for her and we'll try writing to that. The letter will simply ask her to get in touch with us and come in for a meeting without giving any details. If she has moved – got married perhaps and changed her name - it will be hard to trace her. Maybe someone living there will remember her and forward the letter.' Jane smiled, holding up a document. 'The hospital notes of the delivery record her date of birth, blood type and a few medical details. The Registry of Births and Deaths has thrown up a Mary Deborah Crane with that birth date, and she came from Brighton.'

'Brighton?' Lauren mused. 'I've been there on holidays as a child. And I never knew...'

'No, life's full of odd little coincidences, my dear. All we know so far is that her family used to run a restaurant there, but they have also gone. There is still work to be done. Shall I ask Kirsty to bring us some tea? Maybe a biscuit?' she offered gently.

Lauren shook her head. 'How old was she – when she had me?'

'Sixteen. You see how hard it would have been for her, especially back then?'

'And with me not exactly being a thing of beauty.'

Ignoring this comment, Jane added, 'And if her family refused to support her...'

'Yes. Yes, I appreciate that. There's no mention of who my father might have been?'

'I'm afraid not.'

'Well, thank you.' Lauren rose and made for the door.

'Please wait.' Jane came quickly around the desk and gently took her arm. 'Don't run away now. You obviously need to resolve this, because it's causing a blockage in your life. You need to move on, but you can't.' She persuaded Lauren back into the chair.

'I'm so frightened of what we may discover.'

'I know you are. Just ask yourself why you need to know. If it's an important reason, you have to pursue it.'

'It's important.'

'So we go ahead?' Jane asked, sitting behind her desk again.

'Yes. Yes, we go on.'

'Right.' Jane shuffled her papers and pulled out a form. 'Just in case we do find her, Lauren, we will need some information about you. Something we can tell your mother about your life; hobbies, interests and so on. And a photograph. It will make you seem a real person to her and help her get over what will probably be a huge shock.'

'It all sounds rather unlikely doesn't it?'

'We're still investigating. We have lots of resources, especially now with facilities on the internet. But I'm afraid we have no way of knowing when new information may come to light.'

'I understand. I know it's a slim chance you'll trace her.

'Lauren, don't give up hope.'

'I don't know how I'll deal with it if you do find her.'

'Let's face that when we come to it. If we find her, we'll help both of you any way we can. Don't hate her. The poor little thing was no more than a child herself.'

'And I was a two-week old baby.' Self-pity was not usually in Lauren's nature, but with tears pouring down her cheeks, she sobbed helplessly. Jane reached for a box of tissues and came to stand beside her, placing an arm around her shoulders.

'Why now?' Lauren gasped at last. 'Why, when I have lived my life accepting my past – why now does it suddenly matter?'

'Maybe because something important is going on in your own life? Often people come to us when they reach a crossroad - perhaps when they get into an important relationship or are pregnant themselves. You'd be amazed at how many pregnant women suddenly want to find their birth mothers.'

'Well, I'm certainly not pregnant.' Lauren smiled shakily. 'There's absolutely no chance of that. I'm sorry to weep all over you. I'm grateful for your kindness, really.'

'We'll let you know the minute we hear anything.'

Lauren filled in a form giving the details Jane had asked for, and promised to send a photograph.

She walked back to her car, reflecting that the information she had just provided about herself gave no indication of the pain of rejection, the fear of trusting anyone totally, that had stalked her all her life. With a knot of anxiety twisting at her stomach, she drove home, wishing she had followed her instincts to let this particular sleeping dog lie.

Stage Struck

Thursday 27th November

That evening rehearsal proved to be a tense and touchy affair. Nick had to attend as by now, with so few weeks to go, there were a lot of details he needed to check with the rest of the technical team; lighting, music, which pyrotechnics to order for the flashes that would accompany every entrance by Verruca, and not least, how to shepherd around the actors and lots of noisy children backstage, ensuring they were in the right place at the right time.

Maureen Clarke was in a foul mood having again slept badly in the spare room at Winston's flat.

Two of the small dancers had fallen out and were wailing loudly to their mothers who were now arguing with each other.

The lighting expert called in to say he had flu' and the start of the rehearsal was delayed even further because Patsy brought along a pile of costumes for the cast to try on.

Not surprisingly, Mason was in a grouch and Candy seemed not to be talking to anyone in a civilized tone.

Rose sat watching the proceedings with a frown. Her own costume fitted and looked sensational. The green tunic emphasised her bosom and slim waist and the fishnet tights were scratchy but incredibly sexy. And as for the boots…

Lauren stood back in mock amazement. 'The rest of us might as well go home, Rosie,' she laughed. 'You'll stop the show when you walk on in that outfit. We won't get a look in.'

'I'm nervous enough already, thanks, so don't tease me,' she grumbled.

'Oh, stop growling. Come and help me make the coffee while Patsy's busy with the costumes.'

They switched on the water heater and put out the cups. 'Cheer me up,' Rose said, 'and tell me how are things going with Clive?'

'He's lovely,' Lauren replied with a sad smile. 'But we're just friends. I'm not sleeping with him, if that's what you're asking. What about you and John?'

Rose blushed. 'I almost asked him to stay with me the other night,' she confessed.

'Why didn't you?'

'I don't know.'

'Mason?'

'I told you – there's nothing between us.'

'Right.'

'Lauren, there isn't.'

'Lauren, there isn't what?' said a voice from the hatchway.

'Oh, hi, Mason....er...there isn't any sugar in the cupboard,' Lauren improvised.

'That's because it's in the company box of stuff on top of the fridge. Is there hot water yet for a black coffee? I'm parched and fed up with twiddling my thumbs waiting for people to finish with Patsy. I must say, Rose, you're going to stop the show.'

'If anyone else tells me that, I shall emigrate,' she smiled. 'What is it about fishnet tights that make men go wobbly at the knees?'

'I'll take Patsy a coffee,' volunteered Lauren. 'Can you serve the others, Rose?' she added, moving out of earshot.

'How are you?' Rose asked quietly. 'I mean...well, you know...'

'Yes, I know, my sweet,' he replied with a grimace. 'I'm just hanging on in there till after the show, and then I shall have to make some decisions. I'll be glad to get this damned dinner dance out of the way. It's going to be a difficult evening. Thank you for caring – and I'm glad I can still talk to you.'

'Me, too,' she replied, handing him a black coffee. 'Ah, Nick. Coffee?'

'One with a double dose of caffeine please, Rose.' He yawned as he approached the hatchway. 'I hate rehearsals like this. Nothing seems to get done and we don't have the time to waste. Mason, I've ordered all the lighting gels we need and the lorry to take the set to the theatre is booked, so we're more or less organised back stage.'

'Good. Thanks.' Mason moved quickly away to talk to Barbara, the pianist, who was also getting edgy with a few chorus members who seemed unable to sing in key.

Nick stood by the serving hatch watching Candy, a speculative and wary expression on his face. He wondered whether he should try to sooth her feelings. He had been angry and frustrated that she wouldn't accept the end of their affair, but nevertheless, he felt a twinge of guilt that he had been so brutally honest with her. And Hell hath no furie...

She glanced at him, feeling his eyes upon her and turned away to help a small dancer into a frilly dress.

He returned his cup to Rose and, trying to appear casual, went up to Candy and murmured in her ear.

Stage Struck

Mason, who was also watching Candy, noticed his wife smile provocatively at Nick as he whispered to her. They left the hall separately by the back door of the hall which led into a alleyway to the High Street.

Taking his time, Mason opened the door a crack and peered outside. Candy was talking animatedly to Nick but he could only catch the odd word. Then his wife put her arms around Nick's neck and pulled his face down to hers. Mason shut the door with a bang, overwhelmed by a wave of anguish and humiliation. Two-faced cow! He fled to the Gents and shut himself in a cubicle, retching and coughing. How could she?

It was after nine o'clock when the rehearsal finally got underway, and by that time tempers were frayed, lines forgotten and children over-tired. Mason called a halt half an hour later to address the cast and crew.

'Sorry, but tonight has been a waste of time.' His lips were colourless and his face quite grim. 'At the moment, this show is a complete shambles. When we resume next Tuesday, with only four weeks – that's *eight* rehearsals - to go to the first night, I want lines learnt, cues to be spot on, songs and dances to be perfect, and lots of energy from everyone.' Arms akimbo, he glared at everyone in turn. 'Otherwise, you can find another damned director.'

With that, he slammed out of the hall, leaving a stunned silence behind him.

Saturday 13th December
The Day of the Dinner Dance

The day dawned grey and freezing cold with the threat of snow, and Nick hauled himself out of bed with a groan. He made breakfast, but then couldn't eat it. Sipping an extra strong cup of coffee he fell to thinking again about the last confrontation with Candy ten days ago. He didn't know whether to be relieved or suspicious that he hadn't heard from her since. He'd asked her to meet him briefly outside so that he could apologise for being so blunt with her, and to ask her to try to preserve their friendship, but he realised, as she appeared beside him in the dark alley behind the hall, that he'd made another mistake. Her eyes held a triumphant glint in them as she sashayed up to him and ran a hand up his leg to his groin, causing him to jump backwards.

'Please, don't do that, Candy, I just wanted to speak to you calmly about our relationship, before this damned dinner dance.'

He had tried telling her the things he hoped might soothe her ego – that she was lovely and sexy and that he wished things could be different, but that playing with fire with a married woman was not a long term part of his life plan. He told her he was sorry for saying such unkind things to her, admitted he had behaved like a first class bastard, grovelled and pleaded with her to understand. But she simply dissolved into tears and flung her arms round his neck, saying she couldn't bear life without him. He told her sharply that if she didn't pull herself together she'd ruin her marriage and hurt her children.

'We must put the affair behind us - for everyone's sake,' he ended.

'You already have, you swine – you told me you're already seeing someone else! Tell me that isn't true.'

'Well, yes I am - but not seriously. I mean, I thought if I brought someone else to the dance it would stop people speculating about you and me.'

'So it's just a date?'

'Well, yes…but...'

'All right, then, I accept that it's probably a good cover, but don't expect me to just give up on us, because you're too important to me, Nick. I seriously can't bear to be without you.'

'You're going to have to grow up, Candy, and get over it sooner or later. For everyone's sake, make it sooner.' And he had stormed away from her and driven home in a rage.

Now, as he contemplated the cold, curling toast and lukewarm coffee in front of him, he dreaded the coming evening. He had seen Sam half a dozen times in the preceding few weeks – *Mama Mia!* Had been a great success - and he dared to hope that she was beginning to feel as deeply for him as he did for her. He had taken her and Ben out to Thorpe Park and he truly liked the little boy, who showed no sign of jealousy about Nick's relationship with his mother. In fact, he seemed positively to encourage it.

The dinner dance loomed as a possible disaster zone and he wished he could find a reason to duck it. But Sam would want to know why he didn't want her to meet his friends, so he had to hope that Candy would behave herself. Surely even she wouldn't embarrass herself and make a scene in front of the entire company?

He wished he could come clean to Sam about the whole sordid business. But he was mortally afraid she would decide that someone who slept with his friend's wife was not to be trusted -and certainly not a fit person to have around her son. So there was nothing else for it, he decided, he had to face it out, keep Sam firmly by his side all evening, and make sure he was never caught face to face with Mason and Candy.

Nick had promised to go to the hotel early in the evening to check everything was organised, give them the table plan and pay over the money he'd collected with great difficulty from nearly a hundred people. He wondered once again where all these so-called members were when one needed an extra hand backstage or front-of-house. Yet miraculously they could always be counted on to turn up for a social occasion. However, dinner and a disco was what they had ordered and that was what they would get.

***

Rose and Lauren spent a girly day enjoying a massage and manicure, having their hair done and lunching at a very expensive restaurant.

It was over lunch that Rose became certain there was something Lauren wasn't telling her, as she kept drifting away, a glazed expression in her eyes. Rose waved a hand in front of her face 'Hello...ship to shore...'

'Sorry.'

'Tell.'

'What?'

'Whatever it is you're thinking about so deeply. Is it Clive?'

'No.' She paused for a moment and Rose was concerned to see her friend's eyes suddenly fill with tears. 'I set the process in motion, Rose - to find my mother.'

Stage Struck

'Oh, Lauren…' she said, taking her friend's hand. She searched her face. 'Well, I think it was the right thing to do,' Rose said firmly. 'You've been thinking about it for so long and it's been eating away at you. Perhaps now you can resolve it and have some peace. And who knows, maybe a wonderful relationship with your mother.'

'But what if it's a Pandora's Box?'

'I assume you have been to an agency which specialises in these things?'

'Yes.'

'So, they're going to lead you by the hand and make sure – if indeed they find her – that the relationship is likely to work. It will be one step at a time, Lauren, so don't panic. What finally prompted you to make this move?' she asked curiously, signalling to the waiter for the bill.

'The fact that I have no-one of my own. Maybe I never will. You see I really like Clive a lot, but I feel I'm keeping him at arm's length a bit and I wonder if it's my fault we're still…well…just friends. He's fine about it - in fact, he seems to prefer it that way, but I feel sort of starved. I want to be loved, but I'm not sure I can love wholeheartedly in return.'

'You're afraid of making a commitment to someone who might hurt you – abandon you, like your mother did? Is that the problem?'

'I suppose so,' Lauren agreed, pushing away her coffee cup. 'And I thought if I could find her and discover the truth about why she did that, maybe I would feel more able to get close to Clive. I suppose I feel incomplete.'

'Lauren, you're the most balanced, lovable and complete person I know.'

'On the surface. Anyway – it's our secret, Rosie.'

'Of course. Now let's go to your house, feed poor Bugsy and have a rest before the bun fight tonight.'

'Right, let's,' laughed Lauren. 'I have a feeling there'll be some interesting dynamics this evening.'

***

When John and Clive arrived to collect her and Lauren, Rose had been almost overcome with shyness – because John, in dinner dress, looked like a matinee idol. She could tell from the look in his eyes that he was equally impressed with her, and she was glad to have lashed out on a swirly, gold Monsoon dress which showed off her Titian hair to perfection.

'You'll both need warm coats, girls, it's starting to snow,' John advised as they stepped shivering into Lauren's house.

***

Stage Struck

The day had begun badly for Candy. Her car wouldn't start and proved to have burst something vital because she'd neglected to fill the radiator with anti-freeze. 'How was I supposed to know about that?' she stormed at Mason. 'I don't *do* car mechanics.'

Mason ignored her and called the AA who arrived promptly and towed the car away.

'I need to get to the hairdresser, Mason – so I'll have to borrow your car.'

'Sorry, I have things to do. You'll have to call a taxi.'

With no further explanation he left her on the pavement, climbed into his car and drove off.

Lola had already gone out so Candy had no choice but to call a taxi which arrived half an hour later. This meant her hairdresser couldn't fit her in until later in the morning, so she had been forced to wander round the shops to fill in time and had spent a small fortune on the red dress which, in her heart, she knew was far too young for her. But what the hell, she grumbled to herself, I have the legs and the face so, by God, I'll show Nick what he's missing out on.

Now, waiting in the hallway, Mason was visibly shocked when she emerged from the bedroom and descended the stairs.

'Like it?' she asked, swaying her hips at him.

'No – but it's too late to change now, we're late. And tonight, Candy, you'll do me a favour and behave yourself.'

'Just precisely what do you mean by that?'

'I think you know what I mean,' he replied tersely. 'You've dressed like a tart – don't add to my embarrassment by behaving like one.'

'What's wrong with you, Mason?'

'Oh, nothing. Just get in the car and let's get this over with.'

Candy was at a loss as to why Mason should be so on edge with her. She'd seduced him a few nights before and he seemed to have enjoyed that; she'd been really loving and considerate and extremely careful not to be caught trying to contact Nick. In fact, the only time she had spoken to him in several days was when the bastard lured her outside at rehearsal.

Mason was behaving out of character, she decided and there had to be a reason.

As they arrived at The Glen Eagles, a light dusting of snow began to fall. They crossed the car park and she took Mason's hand, which was cold and unyielding.

'I'm sorry if I've upset you, darling. Let's just try to have a nice evening with our friends. You look a dish in your dinner jacket and I don't really look too bad, do I?'

'No, Candy; I'm sorry,' he said moodily. 'You look amazing.'

***

Stage Struck

The Glen Eagles Hotel was about three miles outside the village, a Victorian pile in extensive grounds which had once belonged to one of the captains of industry in the late 1800s. Tastefully extended, it offered sixty bedrooms and a couple of large function rooms, but still retained its charm and olde world atmosphere with the aid of roaring log fires in all the receptions rooms, dark oak panelling and rumours of a ghost. Nick suspected the ghost was the product of some wily advertising agency; but she was now quite famous and people came from far and wide in the hope of seeing her.

Nick parked his Land Rover and walked across the chilly tarmac to the grand entrance of the hotel. At the reception desk he asked to see the Event Manager, who took him through to the Burns Rooms where the tables were laid out. There were six tables, each seating ten and Nick went round them putting place names at the settings, making sure that he and Sam would be at a table on the opposite side of the room to Mason and Candy. Satisfied, he went into the bar for a much needed gin and tonic while he waited for Sam to arrive. She had said she'd be there at seven-thirty and he could hardly wait to see her.

'Weather report's not too promising, sir,' said the barman, handing him his drink.

'Indeed? Well, let's hope it holds off till the morning,' grimaced Nick. 'I hate snow. One day I shall move to Spain and never come back.'

'Really? Well, don't go without me,' said a soft voice behind him.

He turned and pulled Sam into his arms, giving her a crushing hug. 'I'm so glad to see you.'

'I can tell,' she laughed, smoothing her dress. 'Mine's a glass of white wine, please,' she said to the barman. 'Nick, I feel as nervous as a kitten and ready to run.'

'Let's both run. If we leave now, everything's in place; they can have a great evening and I can have you to myself.'

'No fear. I spent a week's wages on this dress – and anyway, I'd like to meet your friends. Just don't leave me alone until I find my feet. It's a long time since I went to a party like this.'

'I'll stick to you like glue, I promise,' he told her, leading her to a table in a darkened alcove. 'You look stunning, Sam. I'm so proud to be with you.'

'And you look like James Bond in your dickey bow.'

'How's Ben?'

'Looking forward to being spoilt by my parents for a whole weekend.'

'A whole weekend?'

'Yes.' She glanced mischievously at him from under her lashes.

'My imagination has gone into overdrive.'

'Let's just see how things go, Nick. No promises.'

Other new arrivals wandered into the bar, and Nick took Sam's hand across the table. 'I can hear Lauren and Clive over there, so let's go and say hello. Are we sticking to the story that we met through mutual friends?'

'A dating agency sounds rather naff, doesn't it? You know, I'd almost forgotten that *Meet Your Match* ever had anything to do with us! It seems an age since we had that first awkward meeting at the restaurant.'

'Yes, it does. But I'll always be grateful to them.' He led her by the hand to where Lauren was perched on a bar stool, laughing at some quip of Clive's. She was wearing a blue, layered chiffon dress, high heels and sparkly things in her hair.

'Lauren, you look astonishing,' grinned Nick.

'I look like a bloody Christmas Fairy, but I couldn't let the side down, could I? Hello, I'm Lauren,' she smiled at Sam, holding out her hand.

'I'm Sam…'

'Do I know you from somewhere?' asked Lauren, a puzzled expression on her face. 'You look so familiar.'

'I don't think we've met. I'm sure I would have remembered.'

'Anyway, now we know Nick's big secret. He wouldn't tell anyone who he was bringing tonight. This is Clive…and ah, here are our friends, Rose and John.'

'Rose!' Sam gasped and laughed aloud. 'So much for keeping a secret round here,' she whispered to Nick. 'Rose is my cousin.'

'Sam!' Rose rushed to give her a hug and introduced John. 'But what are you doing here?'

'I came with Nick.'

'Nick - did you really? Well… it's a small world, isn't it? And how is darling Ben?'

'He's wonderful – staying with doting grandparents this weekend.'

'Now I know where I've seen you before, Sam,' piped up Lauren. 'Your photo is on Rose's mantel shelf.'

Nick stood back for a second before joining in the conversation. This was not a complication he could have anticipated and he was shaken. He realised now why Sam had looked vaguely familiar to him on their first meeting; her hair colour was so similar to Rose's and they had a familial look when one saw them together. But now he felt awkward and fervently wished he had followed his instinct not to bring Sam.

To his relief, the conversation around the bar was very general, although he sensed that Rose was not making direct eye contact with him.

Other arrivals brought a gust of icy air through the bar and Maureen announced that it had begun to snow in earnest.

As Rose talked to others who were arriving, Sam slipped back to Nick's side and took his hand. He pressed a quick kiss against her hair.

'What a coincidence,' she giggled. 'It just shows how hard it must be to keep an illicit affair really secret. You never know who you might bump into, do you? As it is, Rose is now dying to know all the details, so I promised lunch next weekend. Wow, look at that couple.'

Nick's heart lurched as Candy and Mason walked in, hand-in-hand. She was wearing a little red dress which barely covered the essentials and brought wolf whistles from Clive and John, causing her to smirk with pleasure. Her hair was swept over to one side of her face, falling in a tumble of gold curls. Her make-up was flamboyantly bright, and the silver high heels did great justice to her shapely legs. But, thought Nick, although it would have looked sensational on a woman of twenty-five, it looked a little over-the-top – a bit tarty - on Candy. Clearly, she was making a statement and Mason seemed faintly embarrassed. Candy's eyes searched the crowd until she spotted Nick and flashed him a look of pure contempt.

'That's Mason, the director,' he said, his mouth dry. 'And his wife, Candy.' He gulped at his drink.

'She makes me feel a real frump,' muttered Sam, but Nick whispered in her ear that she looked classy and beautiful, and she smiled happily up at him.

'Oh, that's interesting... See that pretty blonde?' Nick murmured, pointing to a young girl who had just come in with a rather handsome young man.

'Hands off,' Sam chuckled, 'she's too young for you.'

'She's Mason and Candy's daughter.'

'And she looks very uncomfortable, doesn't she?'

The warmth of the hotel enveloped Candy and Mason and half a dozen people called a greeting as they moved from Reception into the bar. It was then that Candy spotted Nick and Sam and her heart almost leapt out of her chest. Sam, dressed in a green silk dress which showed off her glorious Titian colouring, looked classy and elegant. And she didn't look like a casual date; the way she and Nick glanced at each other was intimate and highly charged, and Candy wanted to go up to him and throw a drink in his face.

Fortunately, an inner voice screamed at her to keep her dignity and she had just brought her temper under control when Lola arrived with her boyfriend. One look at the two of them told her that this was not a casual relationship either. Their hands were firmly joined and the young

Stage Struck

man looked rather nervous until Lola reached up and whispered something in his ear, causing him to give her a quite devastating smile.

There was a small silence as Lola rather self-consciously led her new boyfriend to the edge of the crowd at the bar. Candy's eyes widened at the sight of her daughter, dressed simply in a black mini dress and low court shoes, as she blushingly introduced Alex.

'Um, Daddy, Mummy, this is my boyfriend, Alex Johnson.'

Mason recovered first and, taking a deep breath, held out his hand to the young man. 'Pleased to meet you, Alex. Will you have a drink?'

'Thank you, sir. A cola would be great – I'm driving.'

'Me too, please Daddy.' Lola flashed him a grateful smile and turned to her mother.

Candy stood with narrowed eyes, trying to quell a rush of jealousy as she regarded the good-looking young couple. 'Well, young lady, you kept this a secret,' she smiled coolly, holding out an immaculately manicured hand. 'How do you do, Alex,' she said to the young man who, she was instantly certain, had already robbed Lola of her virginity.

'We met at college,' Lola said. 'Alex is hoping for a place at Cambridge, studying Law.'

'Then I hope you don't take up too much of his time before the exams,' said Candy, pointedly.

'We're both taking our exams seriously, Mummy.'

'Yes, well, now is not the time or place to discuss this.' Candy turned to gaze in disbelief at the ghastly creature on the arm of her beloved son. 'Ah, there's Leo and Gillian – whatever is the girl wearing?' And Candy floated away to get a better look at the apparition in white on Leo's arm.

Gillian was wearing a long white, clingy dress which looked as though it had been sprayed on; she had gothic make-up, her dark hair gelled and spiked. There was more than a glint of amusement in her eyes as Candy approached them and, after a second of wide-eyed appraisal, turned on her heel and walked away. She overheard the girl laugh and tell Leo that she'd achieved her ambition – to leave Candy Fairfax speechless for once in her life.

Nick breathed a sigh of relief, realising that Candy's attention had been diverted from him and Sam. The bar was filling up with people desperate to get warm and grab a drink before moving in to dinner. Nick led Sam back to their alcove, away from the mêlée and took her hand across the table, thinking how lovely she looked in the soft lighting.

'Sam, this may be a strange time and place to say this, but it's very important to me that you know that I love you.'

'You hardly know me, Nick,' she said softly, curling her fingers around his.

'I know. But please believe me when I tell you that I never knew I could feel like this about anyone. It's a complete revelation.'

'There must have been lots of other women...'

'A few, but I have always avoided commitment. I didn't think I would be very good at it.'

'I see.'

'What does that mean?'

'I don't know, Nick. I just want to take this one step at a time, because of Ben. I'm really very scared of getting hurt – and worse, of Ben getting hurt. I do like you a lot, I really do. In fact, it would be very easy for me to say I love you, too...'

'I'm not asking you to, Sam. I just want you to know that I desperately want our relationship to develop into something rich and meaningful.'

'Then let's see where it takes us.'

A shadow fell across them and to Nick's discomfort Candy stood beside their table.

'Hello, Nick.' She smiled icily, glancing at their entwined fingers. 'Are you going to introduce me to your...date?'

'Yes, of course.' He rose to his feet and made the introductions.

'Candy, you look sensational,' smiled Sam. 'I wish I could wear a dress like that. Nick tells me you're a dancer.'

'Yes. But he told us nothing about you, Sam.'

'Sam and I met through mutual friends, Candy. There's nothing else to tell, really,' Nick said mildly. 'Come along, Sam, I think it's time to move people into dinner before they all get too drunk to find their places.'

***

It had been a monumental shock to discover, on arrival at the hotel, that her cousin Sam was dating King Rat, as Rose had mentally dubbed Nick. And what was worse, she looked incredibly happy and totally smitten. As did Nick. A glance at Candy's face confirmed her fears that she was shell shocked, and Mason looked anxious and ill at ease.

'Candy's gone a bit over the top, hasn't she?' whispered Lauren. 'What a dreadful outfit. I sense strong undercurrents in these dark and dangerous waters.'

'Me too,' replied Rose, unhappily, 'And my poor cousin could be right in the middle of all this.'

Stage Struck

'What are you two plotting?' asked Clive, bringing their drinks.

'Nothing – I do hope dinner won't be long,' grumbled Lauren, rubbing her tummy. 'Lunch seems an aeon away.'

'No, it's all right, you won't starve. I think Nick is shepherding everyone into the Burns Rooms – bring your drink with you.'

With Sam by his side, Nick moved into the throng and ushered the noisy crowd through into the Burns Room where they consulted his large table seating plan. Gradually, everyone found their places, pulling the Christmas crackers on each table, donning silly hats as they did so.

Nick had deliberately placed himself and Sam on a table with members of the group whom he hardly knew, and who would therefore not be too curious about Sam. It also meant he could sit with her and chat quietly without intrusion.

He watched the waiters serving the first course wondering whether he would be able to eat at all as his stomach was in such a knot. He picked nervously at the melon and Parma ham in front of him, but as the evening progressed, he began to relax.

'It's a nightmare, organising something like this, isn't it?' commented Sam a while later, tucking into her Christmas pudding. 'It's bad enough being asked to do the PTA charity night at school, and that's only a buffet. But you can wind down now, Nick – everything is fine, the meal was delicious and everyone is having a good time.' Sam took his hand under the table and he lifted her fingers to his lips and kissed them gently.

'You don't miss much do you, flower?'

'You looked completely stressed out when I arrived. Even more so when you discovered Rose and I are cousins.'

'It was just so unexpected. Are you very close?'

'Yes – though we haven't seen each other for a while as we both lead such busy lives. Her mother and mine were twins, but she lost her Mum a while ago to cancer and her Dad a few months after that.'

'Poor Rose. She's a great girl.'

'Yes, she is.'

Rose, John, Clive, Lauren, Patsy and Maureen Clarke were to share a table with Mason and Candy. As they sat down, laughing and donning paper hats from the crackers, Rose noticed Candy's eyes repeatedly searching across the room for Nick and Sam.

'She's gorgeous, your cousin Sam,' enthused Clive. 'Lucky old Nick! I wonder where he met *her,* the dark horse.'

'Through mutual friends, or so he said. Where does she live, Rose?' asked Candy, sweetly.

'In Cranleigh, with her little boy, Ben. She's a teacher.'

'A little boy? Divorced?'

'Widowed, some years ago, in a car crash.'

'That's sad. How long have they been seeing each other?'

'I don't know, Candy. I haven't seen Sam for several weeks.' Rose glanced uncomfortably at Mason who was studiously buttering a roll. 'Mason, are you happier now, with the show? You seemed very stressed about it when we had that awful rehearsal back in November,' she said, trying desperately to change the subject.

'It's going to be fine, Rose.' He smiled and shrugged. 'It certainly was a lousy rehearsal that evening, but there's always a few of those. It's improved a bit since then and it will be all right on the night, as they say.'

'I finished your costume last night, John,' piped up Patsy. 'Four layers of stiff petticoats and a patchwork dress. They'll look great with the striped rugby socks and glittery boots. And I've ordered your bright pink, curly wig.'

'I can hardly wait, Patsy. I sure wish my Mom could see me!'

'And for me?' asked Clive.

'A jester's outfit, complete with a hat with three points and bells on them,' she chuckled. 'You'll have it on Tuesday.'

They talked light-heartedly through the rest of the meal, and when coffee was served the DJ changed the tempo of the music he had been playing quietly during dinner, drawing several couples onto the small dance floor. John led Rose, and Clive, taking his cue from John, gently pulled Lauren to her feet. The four of them amused the rest of the group by adapting a dance they had together in the show to fit to the current number one hit.

'I like it better like that,' chuckled Mason. 'I think we'll keep it in.'

'Would you like to dance?' Nick asked Sam.

'Yes, but I warn you, I'm not very good at jigging about. I prefer a slow dance because I have no sense of rhythm. Are you a good dancer?'

'Dreadful,' he lied, leading her onto the small crowded floor and taking her into his arms.

Patsy and Maureen, who had come together, decided to call it a night as the weather was getting worse, and slipped away, leaving Mason and Candy at the table.

'Aren't you going to ask me to dance, darling?' she asked him plaintively, as the tempo changed to a slow and smoochy ballad.

Reluctantly, he got up and followed her out onto the floor, where Sam and Nick were dancing closely. Mason noticed that Sam and Nick almost immediately left the floor and went into the bar; he also noticed the tight-lipped expression on Candy's face as she watched them go.

The evening was proving to be absolute torture and he wished they could leave. But there was to be a short cabaret and he had been inveigled into reading a monologue by Stanley Holloway – appropriately, *Old Sam's Christmas Pudding*. As quickly as he decently could, he led Candy back to the table where Lola and Alex were waiting for them.

'Daddy, this isn't really our thing,' Lola said, 'so we're leaving now with Leo and Gillian and going on to the Kiss Club in town.'

'All right kids, take care and I expect to see you at breakfast in the morning.' Mason smiled at Lola who came up and kissed his cheek, whispering a thank you in his ear.

'You shouldn't let them go.'

'Oh, don't be so sour, Candy. Let them have fun. He's a nice young man and we can't realistically expect her not to have a boyfriend till she's finished her exams.'

'You've changed your tune.'

'Well, frankly, since you make their lives – and mine - such a misery these days, I feel happier knowing she has a decent chap as a boyfriend. She could be getting into all sorts of trouble.'

'What do you mean, I make your life a misery?'

'Oh, forget it,' he snapped. 'It isn't the time or place, is it?'

Sensing danger, Candy picked up her bag and retired to the Ladies, shutting herself in a cubicle while she fought back tears of rage and frustration. She heard the main door open and close and assuming there was no-one at the wash basins, she came out, only to come face-to-face with Sam, who was renewing her lips-gloss.

'Oh, hello. Candy, isn't it? I've met so many people here tonight that I'm having trouble with names.'

'Yes, I'm Candy. So how long have you been seeing Mr. Wonderful?'

Sam looked at her quizzically. 'A while,' she replied carefully.

Stage Struck

'Oh.'

'Is that a problem for you, Candy?'

'For me? Good heavens, no. Whatever made you think that? I just can't keep up with Nick's girlfriends. He seems to have a new one every week.'

'Is that right?'

'I'm afraid so. But enjoy him while you can.'

Just then the door opened and Rose came in, stopping short with a small gasp when she saw Candy and Sam talking. Diplomatically, she moved into the space between them. 'Hello girls. Are you having a good evening?'

'Yes, Rose – I loved your dance routine,' laughed Sam. 'I'm longing to see this show.'

'Wait till you see me in fishnets and John in a patchwork dress. He's a riot even before he puts on a costume. He's going to steal the show.'

'He seems lovely,' smiled Sam.

Candy having been effectively sidelined, stalked out. Sam and Rose glanced at each other and gave a sigh of relief.

'Is she really as vitriolic as she seems?'

'She's going through a bad time.'

'Nick told me she might be spiteful.'

'Just ignore her, Sam. Come on – the cabaret is about to start and we can't miss John and Clive's interpretation of Laurel and Hardy.'

The cabaret was a great success and, having done their various acts, many of the guests either decided to leave, or retired to the bar. Nick had one last dance with Sam before checking on the weather outside and deciding it was definitely time to go. He looked at her little Ka, sitting almost up to its hub caps in snow and knew she would be unlikely to get through the deepening drifts in that.

Returning to where she was saying farewell to Rose in the foyer, he took her aside and told her the news. 'I know it sounds like a set up, Sam, but the lanes from here are going to be treacherous. Why not leave your car here till the morning and come back to my place. My four-by-four will get through most things, but I'm afraid your little one might not. I promise to be on my best behaviour if that's what you want - the bed's made up in the spare room.'

'Nick,' she said, smiling shyly at him. 'I don't think I want to sleep in the spare room.'

'Then let's go, flower, while we still can.'

Stage Struck

Candy watching this exchange from a distance, raged at the intimate look which passed between them. She watched them get into Nick's Land Rover, remembering a couple of passionate encounters she and Nick had enjoyed on the back seat and felt physically sick at the prospect of him making love to someone else - either in the car – or anywhere else. He won't get away with this, I swear it, she muttered to herself, before pinning on a bright smile and returning to where Mason was propping up the bar, looking rather worse for wear.

'Mason, how much have you had to drink?' she demanded. 'You know I hate driving in this sort of weather.'

'Then maybe we should stay here for the night, my darling wife; a romantic night in a hotel with a ghost – how about that?'

'We may not have a choice. I'll go and see if they have a room,' she snapped, and went to the desk, where the receptionist was talking on the phone. Tapping her foot in irritation, Candy soon realised that the conversation was about the fact that all the surrounding roads were blocked by snow, and there had also been an accident. Maybe, she thought maliciously, Nick and his floozy had crashed their car. Serve them right.

'Excuse me, madam,' said the male receptionist, 'I'll be back in a moment, but I have to inform everyone that there is no way out on the local roads tonight. They're either blocked by snow drifts or closed by the police. Everyone will have to stay here.'

'Then please can you reserve me a double room?'

'Certainly – give me your name and I'll make sure you're first on the list.'

The receptionist then sought out the DJ and asked him to make the announcement and went around telling everyone in the bar.

There were forty people effectively stranded, including Lauren, Clive, Rose, John, Candy and Mason.

'Well, at least we don't have to worry about drinking and driving,' smiled John. 'Rose, I'll go and reserve two rooms, shall I?'

'Yes – thanks. I'll, um, order some more wine, shall I?' She watched as he joined the short queue of people waiting at the desk, her heart pounding, because she suddenly knew that the last thing she really wanted that night was to sleep alone in a hotel room. Throughout the evening, she had danced with him closely; enjoying the feel of his athletic body and loving the way he seemed unable to keep his eyes off her.

It felt as though something had changed, something was different and suddenly she urgently wanted to tell him that two single rooms were not what she wanted at all. It was a liberating and

Stage Struck

joyful feeling, and she was moving to catch him up when Mason stepped in front of her and took her hand. Shocked, she tried gently to withdraw it, but he held on tightly and turned her towards him.

'You look so lovely tonight, Rose,' he said, slurring his words very slightly.

'Thank you, Mason. Now I think it would be a good idea to sit down over there until Candy comes back and takes you up to bed.'

'Rose, you know perfectly well that I don't want to go to bed with Candy – I want to go to bed with you. I've wanted to ever since the first time I saw you. And you said you wanted me too – that night at your house – you know you did.'

'Did she indeed?' Candy stood, white with shock, a couple of yards away having heard the whole exchange.

'Mason! For God's sake, stop it.' Rose was almost beside herself with panic. 'What are you talking about?'

'She did, you know. She said she wanted to have an affair with me.'

'I didn't, truly, Candy, I didn't. He's drunk and talking nonsense.'

'Is he? Tell me, Rose, do you by any chance have a cat?' demanded Candy.

'A cat? Yes, I do. What the hell has that got to do with anything?'

'Nothing, except I'm violently allergic to them.'

Rose blanched, remembering her conversation with Mason. 'Candy, there is nothing between me and Mason, I promise you. He's just rambling because he's had too much to drink. I'm in love with John.'

John, now standing a few feet behind Rose, caught his breath. What a way to hear the words he longed for her to say to his face – but did she mean them? He moved forward and put his arm protectively around Rose, who was shaking with shock and mortification.

'Come along, honey, let's remove ourselves from this undignified little scene and go to our room. I've ordered champagne to be sent upstairs as you suggested.' And he led her away and into the lift, leaving Mason and Candy facing each other in what promised to be a row of earth-shattering proportions.

But as the lift doors closed on Rose and John, the main hotel door opened, ushering in a gust of icy wind and a very distressed Nick and Sam. Nick went quickly to Mason and beckoned Candy to come closer.

'There's been a terrible accident, Mason. I'm so sorry but it was the car with your children and their partners.'

Stage Struck

A stunned silence fell over the gathering and then Candy screamed. Mason gasped as though someone had thrown a bucket of cold water in his face and sat down abruptly in a chair.

Sam rushed over to Candy and put her arm around her. 'Let's get your coats, and then we'll take you both to the hospital.'

'Are they badly hurt?' croaked Mason.

'We don't know how seriously injured they are. I think we were the first on the scene – the roads are terrible and they had probably been there some time.'

'I saw the kids leave here about three quarters of an hour ago,' murmured Clive.

'We called the emergency services,' continued Nick, 'which arrived a few minutes ago and they're now all on their way to hospital. It seems the car skidded into a tree and rolled over into a ditch. It was only by chance we saw it at all in the blizzard.'

Sam added, 'Fortunately, it didn't catch fire.'

'They rarely do,' Nick said, 'except in movies. A fire-fighter said they were all wearing safety belts, so with luck they may have been saved from the worst.'

'Nick, will you take us now?' pleaded Mason, who suddenly seemed to be stone cold sober.

'Of course.'

Someone had brought their coats and Sam helped Candy into hers and led her to the Land Rover while Nick guided Mason by the arm.

'Was her face damaged...was Lola disfigured?' Candy asked in a whisper. 'And did you talk to Leo?'

'Truly, I don't know,' answered Nick. 'It was an unlit road and snowing hard. I really can't tell you anything of any use.'

The snow had lessened but the roads were a nightmare of sheet ice and snow drifts. Waved through by the police, Nick drove slowly through the lanes and when they reached the crash site – now lit by spotlights from the recovery vehicle, Candy began to cry. The car was a total wreck – barely recognisable, and it wasn't hard to imagine what might have happened to the passengers.

'I'm so sorry you had to see that,' Nick muttered, negotiating a slippery bend, 'but we'll be at the hospital soon.'

It took nearly an hour. Even after they joined the main road, there were traffic jams and abandoned cars littering the verges. By the time they entered the warmth of the chaotic emergency department at St. Mary's hospital, Candy had gone beyond hysteria into a near catatonic state of shock. The others sat her on a chair and converged on the reception desk.

'Four young people were brought in after a car crash within the last hour,' Nick told the nurse on duty. 'The parents of two of them are here.'

Eventually, a harassed-looking doctor approached them. 'Mr. and Mrs. Fairfax? Come this way, please,' and Nick and Sam watched as Candy and Mason were led to an interview room.

It was then that Sam suddenly went to pieces and clung to Nick, sobbing her heart out.

'This is how it was when Josh died,' she wept. 'Everything about that night is replaying like a film in my head - especially seeing the car like that. Only then I was in agony too. Oh those poor parents, what they must be going through.'

'I'll get you out of here soon, Sam, I promise.'

'No, Nick. We need to stay to see what we can do to help. I'm sorry about that outburst, I'm just being silly,' she said sniffing and mopping at her eyes with Nick's handkerchief. 'Could you find us some coffee?'

He went in search of a coffee machine and Sam turned to watch as two more distraught parents were escorted into the department by the police; obviously Gillian's family, as she heard them asking about their daughter.

Candy and Mason emerged from their interview room with the doctor and before they disappeared down a corridor, Mason came over to Sam, his eyes red and anguished.

'What news?' she asked as Nick rejoined them.

'They're still doing tests and things. But Leo is unconscious – probably has a fractured skull; Lola has come round and may have escaped with concussion and a dislocated shoulder. They think Alex has a couple of broken ribs and Gillian may need an operation for some internal bleeding.'

'Thanks for letting us know, Mason. Shall we stay?'

'No, we'll be here for the rest of the night. But thank you for everything you did. If you hadn't spotted them, they'd all have died of hypothermia, if nothing else.'

He left them and returned to an ashen-faced Candy before being led away to see their children.

Nick took Sam by the hand and helped her into the Land Rover. It took almost another hour to get to his house, by which time the snow had stopped and the landscape was still, white and eerie. They went inside and Nick poured them both a large brandy and turned on the gas fire. Sam sat on the floor in front of it, gazing into the flames, and he came to join her.

'Are you all right?'

'Yes. I've calmed down now. Sorry I reacted so badly.'

'It's hardly surprising.'

Stage Struck

'I try not to think about that night, but sometimes I have to confront it. I can still see Josh, dying beside me in the car and relive the horror of being unable to do anything. I feel my own pain and remember wondering whether I might die too and leave Ben with no-one. I still feel so guilty that Josh died and I survived. Anyway,' she smiled tearfully at Nick, 'tonight we should be thinking about those poor young people and hoping and praying they'll be all right – not dwelling on the past.'

'This is not how I had hoped our first night together would turn out,' he told her gently.

She put down her glass and turned into his arms, giving a long, shuddering sigh. 'I'm all right now. I'm so glad you were there – for all of us. Can we take these drinks to bed? I'm utterly drained and exhausted. But, if you don't mind, I'd like to be with you tonight – just to be close and comforted.'

He helped her to her feet and led her to his room. He found her one of his T-shirts to sleep in and when she emerged from the bathroom wearing it, he knew he would have to keep himself firmly under control. She climbed shyly into bed beside him and snuggled into his arms, where within a couple of moments she fell soundly asleep.

Nick lay awake for a while, thinking what a strange turn events this evening had taken before he too drifted into an uneasy sleep.

***

Rose and John's lift arrived at the third floor and John unlocked his room. 'I have the key to your room down the corridor, but come and have a drink first; you look as if you need one.'

Rose nodded. 'Yes, all right.' He ushered her in and shut the door.

Crossing the room, he said, 'I'll see what's in the mini-bar. Take a seat.'

She sank into a chintz armchair and John brought her a tumbler and a miniature brandy bottle, and poured one for himself. 'What in the name of O'Henry was all that about down there?'

'It was nothing really. Mason being silly after a few drinks too many.' She poured the drink and took a gulp which made her cough.

'I heard what he said, Rose – that you wanted to have an affair with him.' John came to sit on the bed facing her. 'Is it true?'

'No.' Rose felt the usual flood of colour to her cheeks and decided there was nothing for it but to tell John everything. 'I suppose when I first met him I had a bit of a crush. One night I gave him a lift home and he came into my house for a coffee. It was just one of those mad moments…'

'You went to bed with him?' asked John quietly.

'Oh, no!' She gasped, horrified he might believe that. 'Truly I didn't, but as he was leaving he suddenly kissed me. I suppose I must have invited it, but it never went further than that. He came back and apologised the next day and told me that he did care about me, but that an affair would be a big mistake and anyway I had already decided that for myself.'

John took a swig of brandy and sat on the edge of the bed, his elbows on his knees, staring at the floor. Rose felt panic rising in her throat. She was going to lose him and the prospect was unbearable.

'We parted friends,' she continued, her voice high pitched and strained, 'and now we are – or at least I thought we were – over it and comfortable with each other again. He had recently found out Candy is having an affair and I suppose he just needed someone to console him.'

'I see. Well, I can sympathise with him for wanting you, and I guess he did the decent thing, but that doesn't tell me how you now feel about him.'

'I don't feel anything for him, John.' She moved quickly to sit beside him on the bed and shyly took his hand.

'Are you sure? I know we have kept our friendship on a platonic basis so far, but you must know how I really feel about you.'

'Whatever the attraction was – it just evaporated.'

'Really?'

Rose was silent for a moment and then, her heart beating wildly, she put her arms round his neck. 'Will you please make love to me?'

He looked quizzically into her eyes for a second then tentatively brushed her lips with his. Her mouth was soft and responsive and as her arms tightened, he kissed her deeply, pulling her down to lie beside him on the bed's coverlet. But then she felt him draw away.

For a few seconds he stared at her, as if making a decision, and then scrambled to his feet. Picking up her room key from the bedside table, he held it out to her. 'I think you'd better go, honey, or I shan't be responsible for my actions.'

'I don't want to go, John,' she said, giving him a shaky smile. 'Please don't send me away.'

He put the key down and took her back into his arms. 'Oh, Rose,' he said urgently, 'tonight is not the time. I need to be very sure before this goes any further. It's too important.'

'You're right; there is no reason why you should trust me,' she murmured. 'I'll see you in the morning.' And, snatching up the key, she ran from the room, hardly able to see through tear-filled eyes.

***

Stage Struck

Lauren and Clive watched in dismay as Mason and Candy left with Sam and Nick to go to the hospital.

'I wish we could do something to help,' said Lauren. 'This is just awful. What a terrible end to the evening.'

'Come on, let's get some coffee. I don't know about you, but I could manage a nightcap to go with it?'

She nodded. 'Cognac, please.'

He ordered from the barman and returned to Lauren who was searching in her bag for a tissue to wipe her eyes.

He gave her a handkerchief. 'Perhaps the kids won't be too badly hurt, after all, so try not to worry.' Clive gently led Lauren into the now deserted bar and ushered her to a table.

The waiter brought their order and Lauren sipped her cognac and then picked up the teaspoon, absently stirring the coffee.

Clive moved to sit beside her and put an arm around her.

She rested her head comfortably on his shoulder. 'I've known Lola and Leo for years,' she said. 'I can't believe they could both be badly injured – or worse. It must be awful being a parent at a time like this.'

'I agree. I can't imagine having to cope with the loss of a child. Thank God Wendy and I never had any.

'Do you want children one day?'

'I don't know. What about you?'

'Yes, I do, but I'd probably be a lousy mother.' There was a tremor in her voice and, concerned, Clive pulled her round to face him.

'Why do you say that? I think you'd be great with kids. I mean, you're so full of life and optimistic. I've never met anyone who makes me laugh like you do. What was your family life like? You've never really talked about it.'

'It was okay, I suppose,' she shrugged.

'Where do your parents live?'

Lauren considered for a moment, still stirring her coffee until he gently took her hand and stilled it.

'You're going to wear a hole in the bottom of the cup. I'm sorry if I asked an unwelcome question. Please, let's just forget it.'

She smiled sadly and wound her fingers around his. 'I had a series of foster parents. I never knew my mother because she abandoned me at a police station when I was about two weeks old.'

'My God, I had no idea.'

'How could you? It isn't something I usually talk about. Among my friends, Rose is the only one who knows.'

'It isn't something to be ashamed of, sweetie.'

'I suppose not, but I just didn't want people with real families to feel sorry for me. I suppose I feel a bit of a freak. Little Orphan Annie, raised by the State. It's not much of a pedigree, is it?'

'You were never adopted?'

'No, I was an ugly little blighter. I had a hare lip and cleft palate – so you see I wasn't much to look at when I was small. Maybe that put people off. But I was lucky, I had good people to look after me and I'm still in touch with the last ones who are quite old now.' She paused, remembering with gratitude the kindness of Hetty and Bert. 'I was also very fortunate to have one of the top surgeons fix my face. I only have a small scar which I hide with make-up,' she said, touching her upper lip.

'I never even noticed it. It certainly doesn't make you any less kissable.' After proving the point, he continued. 'Do you know anything about your mother?'

'No. Absolutely nothing. My name is all she left me.' She took another large sip of cognac.

'Didn't the authorities try to find her?'

'I suppose so, but she never surfaced. Maybe she emigrated. Who knows?'

'It's none of my business - except that I care about you. Have you never tried to find her?'

Lauren fell silent for a moment, fighting the urge to withdraw into herself, but at last she took a deep breath and told Clive, 'Yes, just a few weeks ago. I've thought about it for so long, but it's a big step to take. It could be a totally negative thing to do – maybe she still wouldn't want to see me and even if she did I might not like her.' She twisted her fingers together. 'I'm terrified about what I may have started. Terrified.'

'I can understand that.' Taking the handkerchief from her, he gently wiped a tear which was threatening to drip off her chin. 'You must be very angry about being left like that?'

'I think I might be even angrier if I found her and discovered how much I'd been deprived of. I mean, well, my life's been a real struggle. I never had a secure home, enough money or close relationships. I worked as a waitress to see myself through art school and I more or less had to find everything out for myself the hard way, all through life. But I survived and I'm really quite proud of that.'

'And so you should be. And promoted into a partnership as well. I'm proud of you,' Clive said firmly. Then he gave her a slight frown. 'I sense there's a "but"...'

She nodded. 'There's a piece missing. Something inside me wants to know why - why she dumped me, what is she like, do I have brothers and sisters, is my father alive, do they look like me...all sorts of things. And there's a small part of me that wants to say to her, "Look, I survived and made a go of my life in spite of you, you rotten cow." I mean, if someone just dumped you and disappeared, how would you feel?'

'Someone did, Lauren. My wife.'

'Oh, Christ, I'm so sorry! That was crass of me.' She squeezed his hand. 'Tell me about her.'

'When Wendy vanished I just couldn't understand why. We had what I thought was a normal, happy marriage. We had our rows and disagreements, like anyone else, but I had absolutely no idea there was any sort of problem.'

'She left you for another man?'

'No – she left me for another woman.'

'Ah... That must have been even more difficult.'

'I don't know whether it was or not. I came to the conclusion she really couldn't help her sexual preferences. But I felt such a fool for not guessing. She was a feminine, bubbly girl and I adored her. Then she joined a tennis club, where she used to go several times a week. I couldn't hit a ball if my life depended on it, so I was happy for her to be having fun, and of course that's where she met Ronda. But it's history now, and after so long I wish her well.'

'Can I ask you something rather...personal?'

'Of course. This seems to be a night for disclosures and revelations, doesn't it?'

Lauren picked up her spoon and began to stir her cold coffee again, while Clive sat watching her, waiting, holding his breath.

At last, she raised troubled eyes to him. 'I hardly know how to say this, but I was always afraid to get too close to any of my former boyfriends. It was all strictly for fun and in the end they all drifted away. I suppose it was just impossible for me to trust anyone completely. Is that how you feel, too?'

'Yes. Yes, it is. But it's a rather sterile existence, and one I want to leave behind.'

'Perhaps you can understand now why I probably seem to have been keeping you at arms' length. It's only because I'm afraid of getting hurt.'

'Lauren, I was afraid to get too close to you as well. We're both members of the same reject club, aren't we?'

She nodded, embarrassed. 'I wondered whether it was me giving you the wrong signals; whether I had just become cold and unlovable. The truth is… that's what has finally prompted me to look into my past - to try to lay those ghosts so that I can move on. It's a cliché, but I really need to know who I am. Until I met you, it didn't seem so important.'

'Dare I ask you why it's important now?'

'Use your imagination,' she whispered.

A wide grin lit up his face. 'Sweetheart, I'm so glad we said all this, because I feel exactly the same. I've wanted you from the moment I laid eyes on you, but I've been desperately afraid to make a move in case you ran a mile. Dare I ask if the barriers are down now?'

'Yes.'

'Then, darling Lauren, will you stay with me tonight?'

'Yes,' she smiled.

***

Mason and Candy sat next to Leo, willing him to open his eyes, but he lay in a coma, his face swollen and bruised.

At last an exhausted-looking young doctor came and ushered them into a small side room.

'I'm Dr Chang,' he told them. 'There is good news and bad, I'm afraid. Fortunately, there's no depressed fracture of the skull, but the MRI scan shows a nasty hair-line crack and the trauma has caused serious swelling. Until nature takes care of that and the swelling reduces, he's likely to remain unconscious, and we shan't know if there's any residual damage until he wakes up.'

'How long will that take?' asked Candy, tightly clutching Mason's hand.

'It's hard to say, but probably at least twenty-four hours - maybe longer. There doesn't seem to be any bleeding in the brain, so there's no need to operate. Just talk to him, let him know you're there, because he can probably hear even though he appears to be asleep.'

'Have you finished checking over Lola?' asked Mason.

Dr Chang nodded. 'Yes. She's very sore, as we had to manipulate her shoulder, and she has some punishing bruises, but she'll be hobbling around in a day or two. Gillian is in theatre for some internal bleeding but it's not major surgery– a keyhole laparoscopy - and Alex has a couple of broken ribs and contusions. They're all young and should recover quite quickly. It's so fortunate they were wearing seatbelts or we would be looking at a much greater tragedy.' He turned to the door. 'I'm afraid we have had a lot of accident victims tonight, so if you will excuse me...'

'Yes, of course, doctor,' Mason said, nodding absently. 'Thanks.'

Candy and Mason returned to Leo's bedside and sat watching the regular blip of a light on a monitor.

'The doctor said we should talk to him,' whispered Candy, 'but I don't know what to say. I've never felt so inadequate in my life.'

Mason took his son's hand and leaned over him. 'You're going to be fine, old chap,' he told Leo firmly. 'You're safe in hospital and you've had a bang on the head. Don't worry that you can't speak or respond, because that's normal. When your brain gets over the shock, you'll be able to wake up properly. The others are all going to be fine, too. We're going to see Lola now – but we'll be back soon.'

Lola was in a ward, and they hardly recognised her at first. She had some stitches on her hairline; her cheek was puffy and turning purple and her left arm was in a sling. Candy gently put her arms around her, weeping loudly.

'Shut up, Mum, you'll wake the other patients,' Lola pleaded with her. 'How is Leo?'

'Still unconscious,' Mason told her, 'but they say he isn't likely to come round for some time. What happened, baby?'

'Alex was driving and he was being very careful, honestly. We were just going very slowly but the road was downhill and twisty. I think he braked too hard and lost control. We hit a tree and the next thing I remember is being lifted out of the car by the ambulance people.'

'Have you seen Alex?'

'Yes, he's in the next ward, but they brought him in a wheelchair to see me because we were both so upset. Gillian's having an operation, isn't she? Her parents were here a while ago.'

'Yes, but I think it's just keyhole surgery to make sure she isn't still bleeding inside. It's supposed to be pretty minor stuff,' Mason said. 'What about Alex's parents?'

'They're in Barbados. He hasn't told them about the accident.' Tears ran down her cheeks and she brushed them away impatiently. 'Poor Leo... Do you think he'll be all right?'

'He'll be fine. Now try to get some rest. If there's any change, I promise we'll come straight back and let you know.'

'Thanks, Daddy. Give him a kiss for me.'

Candy and Mason sat by their son all night watching as he lay oblivious to the world.

'He looks so like you,' whispered Candy. 'You were only his age when we first met, do you remember?'

'Yes. I wonder whether he will stay the course with Gillian?'

'I hope not. Horrible creature.'

'Candy, she's just a kid. You wore the weirdest clothes when I first met you. Flared trousers, for God's sake. My mother wasn't too impressed with you, either, I seem to remember. Gillian's okay – she's a good lass.'

'If you say so.'

It was four in the morning when Mason, dozily holding his son's hand, felt Leo's fingers twitch. He leaned forward to take a closer look. Leo's head moved and his eyelids began to flicker.

'He's coming round!' he called urgently to Candy, who was also half asleep in a chair. With a gasp she came to stare and then went running for a nurse.

The nurse came quickly to Leo's side. 'It's a good sign,' she told them. 'He's beginning to float to the surface. Now go and get something to eat and then try to catch a nap in these two chairs, otherwise, I'll have two more patients.'

They left the ward almost too exhausted to speak and were soon sitting opposite each other over bacon rolls and steaming coffee.

Mason ate automatically, without tasting the roll. He ate because his body simply needed food. Candy nibbled at her roll and looked everywhere but at him. He sought for something to say to his wife. She looked done in and incongruous in her silly red dress. With her hair now collapsed into a tangle, her mascara smudged, and her face blotchy from crying, she suddenly looked very pathetic. He reached for her hand and she held his gratefully.

'I'm sorry,' she whispered and bit her lip to try to hold back a fresh bout of tears.

'For anything in particular?' he asked.

'Just everything. I never thought I could feel so terrified, so helpless.'

'I know. But tonight we are wrung out and it isn't a good time to talk about things is it?'

'No. But I want to, Mason,' she pleaded.

'But not now. Let's just get through this crisis, shall we? It isn't a time for heart-searching. All I can think about is Leo lying there.'

'What if he's brain-damaged, what if he's physically disabled?' she whimpered. 'I don't think I could cope.'

'You'll damn well have to, Candy, and so will I. He'll need us both more than he ever has before, God forbid, if that is the case.'

She nodded. 'I know he will… I didn't mean I would shirk that…but I'm frightened.'

'Let's go back. I can't sit here any longer.'

He strode away from her, back to the Intensive Care room.

Leo lay so still and pale with wires and tubes attaching him to machines and drips.

'Come on, son, come back to us. Please,' Mason wept. 'Come back.'

They took turns to sit by Leo and watched the clock endlessly ticking the hours away. But at nine o'clock Leo slowly opened his eyes. He blinked in confusion for a few seconds, and then, to their eternal relief, turned to look at his parents.

Stage Struck

The Morning after the Night Before

Rose slept badly, tossing and turning in a strange bed, frequently waking and then drifting off into a dream where she endlessly replayed the embarrassment of John's rejection. She wondered how she would ever face him again – or any of the others in the group who now thought she'd tried to persuade Mason into an affair. All the fun will have gone out of the show now, she thought miserably. Everything is in ruins. And John must think I'm some sort of sex-maniac to boot.

With a loud groan, she swung her legs out of bed and padded to the window to see what prospect there was of escaping the hotel before anyone saw her. In typical British fashion, the weather had changed dramatically overnight and a steady rain was falling, melting the snow and turning it to slush.

Stripping off the silk slip she'd slept in, she took a quick shower and brushed her teeth with the hotel's complimentary disposable brush.

She was zipping up her gold dress when the phone rang. Rose jumped and stared at the infernal machine for a while before plucking up the courage to answer it.

'Hi, Rose - I've ordered room service breakfast for the two of us. Come on over to my place.' John sounded up-beat and very normal. She feared that he was just being his usual courteous self and was probably hoping she would refuse.

'Thanks, but I'm really not hungry,' she said stiffly. 'I want to get home as soon as possible. Min will be starving and I have a hundred things to do today, so I'll get Reception to call me a taxi.'

'Rose, just stop it. Now come here this minute before I drag you. I'm pouring the coffee and there are scrambled eggs, bacon and hot rolls to go with it. Be a shame to waste it.'

'Well...I...'

'Cream and sugar?'

'Yes, okay.'

'I'll leave the door ajar.'

She walked slowly down the corridor to John's room. As promised, the door was unlatched and she popped her head round.

He was wearing a robe and serving food onto two plates from a trolley. 'Hi! This looks great – I'm ravenous!' he said. 'Come on. Sit here next to me and we can eat on our laps and be comfortable. Did you sleep okay?'

'Yes, thank you,' she lied. 'And you?' She sat on the bed.

'Sure.' He handed her a plate and she balanced it on her knees. He placed her coffee on a side table by the bed. 'Rose, if I hurt you last night, I'm real sorry.'

'No... yes... Well, I expect I asked for it and I'm sorry too. I can't imagine what you thought, overhearing Mason like that.'

'I know he was drunk and I believe everything you told me. I do trust you, but last night was not the right time to spend the night together. If you'd regretted it afterwards, there might have been no way back for us – and I didn't want to risk that.'

'You're right.'

'So am I forgiven?'

She mustered a smile. 'You're forgiven.'

'Good, let's eat up before the egg goes hard. And then we'd better go feed that hungry moggy of yours.'

Fifteen minutes later they went downstairs together and met Clive and Lauren in Reception settling their bill. Rose noticed their fingers were linked, but they seemed tense and anxious. 'Good morning,' she greeted them. 'Is everything all right?'

Lauren frowned. 'You didn't hear about the accident?'

'No – what...?'

'Leo and Lola and their partners were in a car accident last night,' Clive explained. 'Nick and Sam came back here to take Mason and Candy to the hospital.'

'That's terrible,' John said. 'Have you heard from them?'

'No. We're going to the hospital now. Do you want to come?'

'Of course we do,' said Rose. 'How awful.'

They hurried to their car and after a few wheel spins in the slushy snow, managed to travel slowly to St. Mary's.

'Wait here,' Rose told the others as they made their way into the Emergency Department. 'I'll go and find out what's happening.'

A few moments later, she quietly slipped into Intensive Care, where Leo was still attached to a variety of monitors; Mason was sitting beside him, dozing in a chair.

'Mason...' She touched him gently on the shoulder and he woke with a start before rubbing his eyes and rising to face her.

'Rose... how'd you get here?'

'John, Lauren and Clive are downstairs, but I pulled rank to come in to see how the kids are doing. How is Leo?'

Mason nodded and glanced at his son. 'He has a hairline skull fracture, but he's improving slowly. He recognised us early this morning and he can move everything, so we're hopeful he'll recover fully.'

'Thank God. And the others - Lola?'

'Generally battered, but nothing life-threatening.'

'What a relief.' She looked around. 'Where's Candy?'

He ran hands down his face; he looked so drawn. 'Gone home for a shower and a rest – then she'll come back and relieve me soon.' He grimaced. 'I seem to remember I caused you enormous embarrassment last night. How can I ever apologise?'

'Just forget it. It was unfortunate, but you were the worse for wear. I don't want to talk about it any more.'

'All right… And will you still be in the show?'

'Yes, the show must go on, isn't that what they say? You'll have to replace poor Leo, I presume. It takes a while to get over an injury like that.'

'It's the least of my problems.'

'Well, I'll leave you in peace. I'll pop in to see Leo and Lola tomorrow – I'm on a late shift from four o'clock until eleven.'

'Thanks.' He looked so dispirited and weary that she felt her annoyance with him melting away. She flashed him a warm smile and turned to go. But her heart sank as she came face-to-face with Candy at the door.

Although looking pale and stressed, Candy had changed into tight jeans and a strawberry pink sweater, pulled her hair into a pony tail and put on some make-up. She was clutching a small plastic tray of takeaway coffee cups and a paper bag of food. 'What are you doing here – or need I ask?'

'I'm the deputation with the door pass; I came to find out how Leo and the others are.'

'I see.' She stood back, indicating to the open door. 'Well, now you can go and tell everyone, can't you?'

Wordlessly, Rose left and returned to John and the others in the waiting room. 'They're going to be all right,' she told them. 'Leo is recovering slowly from a head injury.'

'Thank God,' breathed Lauren.

'Candy came in just now,' said John quietly. 'Did you see Mason upstairs?'

'Yes, briefly, and he's mortified at his behaviour last night.'

'So he should be. Well, there's nothing to be done here, so let's go feed the cat, shall we?' She nodded and he eyed Clive and Lauren. 'Coming?' They agreed that they could do nothing there.

John took Rose's arm as the four of them trailed back to the car, their evening finery now wilted and crushed in the grey drizzle.

***

Sam woke as Nick came into the bedroom with toast, marmalade and coffee on a tray. 'Good morning, flower. I'm sorry not to be presenting you with Eggs Benedict and champagne – but I hope this will do for now.'

'Wonderful – thank you.' She struggled to sit up, adjusting the T-shirt. He propped a pillow behind her and she said, 'This must be shattering your illusions. I look like the wreck of the Hesperus in the mornings.'

'You look cute,' he grinned. 'Your hair is a tangle and you have a couple of smudges under your eyes, but I'm still having trouble keeping my hands off you.'

She regarded him over the rim of her coffee cup and then slowly replaced it on the tray. 'I wonder how the youngsters are?'

'I phoned a few minutes ago and spoke to Mason. Leo is surfacing and the others are recovering.'

'Thank God.'

'Sam, do you have to rush home?'

'No. Ben will be fine with my parents until this evening. But I need a shower…'

'Help yourself – there are towels over the radiator.'

She slipped out of bed and disappeared into his elegant *en suite* shower room. Soon he heard the water running and Sam humming a tune. She'd left the door ajar and a cloud of perfumed steam was escaping into the bedroom. He crossed to look out of the window. Rain was falling and the snow was becoming patchy and grey. But he hardly noticed, so aware was he of Sam and his feelings for her which were quite beyond his control. It was exciting, frightening, awe inspiring and completely overwhelming.

When she re-appeared, wrapped in a large towel with another wound like a turban around her hair, and stood in the doorway looking at him, he was totally unable to resist moving quickly to her and taking her in his arms.

'I'm not sure I can bear this any longer. I'll wait for you downstairs.' He was about to turn away but her arms tightened around him and she pulled his mouth to within an inch of her own.

Stage Struck

'No, don't, that isn't what I want, either.' The towel around her dropped in a damp heap to the floor and he removed the other from her head, allowing her hair to fall in a glorious, scented cascade around her shoulders. 'Love me, Nick. Please, just love me…'

He needed no second bidding.

Candy watched Rose walk away and let the door swing shut. She put the tray down then handed a coffee and bacon sandwich to Mason. Without acknowledging her, he put the cup on the bedside table and bit into his sandwich.

'What's going on between you and her?' she asked, sipping her coffee.

He nearly choked on the sandwich. 'Between me - *and Rose*?'

'You said last night you wanted to go to bed with her, and that she wanted you too. You seemed pretty certain about it then.'

'I was drunk and fantasising; I'm sorry to disappoint you.'

'Disappoint me?'

'Well, it would give you a chance to justify your affair with Nick.'

'My what? Don't be ridiculous, you can see for yourself he's madly in love with the new girlfriend.'

'And you are beside yourself with jealousy.'

She stared at her husband in horror. 'What are you talking about?'

'I saw you a couple of weeks ago – in the alleyway behind the church.'

Candy gasped and her eyes widened. 'But, Mason…'

'It's pointless to deny it, Candy – it's written all over you. You must think I'm a fool.'

'Let me explain…'

'Look, I don't want to talk about it now. I assume he's dumped you, judging by the moods and tantrums recently, so somehow we have to get through the next few weeks until the show is over. I'm not abandoning the work of so many people because of you. And now over a thousand tickets have been sold, so there's no way back. But don't you dare make insinuations about me and Rose.'

'I'm sorry...'

Discarding half his sandwich on the cabinet, he said, 'I'm going to see Lola and then home for a couple of hours.' He stood and gulped his coffee. 'Call me on my mobile if there's any change.' And he stormed out, just as Leo opened his eyes.

'Oh, Leo!' she sobbed, grabbing his hand. But he pulled it free and turned his head away.

Stage Struck

Candy was stunned. Mason really had known for weeks, but never said a word, and she suddenly realised she was furious about that; surely most men would shout and scream and threaten the lover with castration. Mason had just taken it on the chin because he didn't want anything to upset the preparations for the damned pantomime. She was fuming. Was that how little he really cared about her? Did it truly not matter to him that his wife was having an affair? It was the worst slap in the face she could have received and she was devastated.

She sat beside Leo, tears streaming down her face, a sick knot in her stomach and a slow burning hatred of Nick gathering pace in her heart.

***

John dropped Lauren and Clive at Lauren's house, and then went on to Rose's a few doors down the road.

'Shall we go and see Winston again later?' he asked.

She nodded, relieved that he was going to give her space to collect her thoughts alone after the traumas of the last twenty-four hours. 'This evening? And then perhaps I can take you out for dinner – you're always treating me.'

He smiled and kissed her gently on the mouth. 'Mmm... That would be nice. I'll pick you up at seven?'

'Okay.'

She watched his car disappear round the corner and let herself in, to find a frantic Min yowling for food. 'I'm so sorry, Minny,' she soothed. 'Brunch for you and a cup of tea for me. What a night!'

She spooned cat food into Min's bowl and went upstairs to change into jeans and a sweater before settling on the sofa with an enormous cup of Earl Grey while the fire crackled into life. She was tired and disturbed at the changes in the group and even more worried about Sam, who looked so happy to be with King Rat. It was a long time since she'd seen her cousin with such a glow. After Josh's death she'd been almost suicidal. Now Sam could be a pawn in a very nasty game, and Rose knew there was nothing she could do to protect her. Either way, Sam was going to get hurt.

The doorbell rang, and Rose dragged herself off the sofa, expecting to see Lauren, but it was a bedraggled and distressed Mason who stood on her doorstep.

She stared at him, confused and wondering what was expected of her.

'You'd better come in.' She stepped back allowing him to walk past her into the living room.

'I had to see you, Rose,' he said. 'I just wanted to tell you that Candy knows that I know about Nick. She made insinuations about you and I'm afraid I let rip – so she is liable to be in a very vitriolic mood.'

'What are you going to do?'

'Nothing for the moment. We have enough problems with two injured children and the sodding pantomime to deal with. Afterwards… well, we'll have to see. I'm just so sorry I got you into this mess. Has it ruined things for you and John?'

'No, I don't think so.'

'You said last night that you were in love with him. Is that true?'

She blushed and shrugged. 'I don't want to discuss that with you. Now I think it would be better if you left.'

He nodded and they both walked to the front door. He opened it then turned to rest a hand on Rose's shoulder. 'Truly, I wouldn't hurt you for the world. But life is bloody at the moment and I'm afraid you got caught in the crossfire. Can you forgive me?'

'Yes… Yes, Mason. I'm sorry you're having such a bad time – and we're all still your friends and we'll support you, whatever you decide. Let's just put last night behind us because we have a show to do. Whatever else, that really has to go on now.'

'Thanks, Rose. I'm so glad we're still friends.' He leaned forward suddenly and kissed her cheek.

Across the road was a smart BMW parked at the kerb. A couple of seconds after Mason drove away, the BMW roared off, a white-faced John at the wheel.

John arrived back at the flat a few moments before Clive, who came in whistling and in high spirits.

'I presume you had a good night?' John called from the depths of an armchair.

'Yes, the best. But you obviously didn't.'

'No.'

'What happened?' Clive, concerned, came to sit beside his friend.

'I behaved like an idiot and hurt her feelings when she was already feeling mortified. But we got over that and I did believe her when she said there was nothing between her and Mason – except a bit of a buzz right back at the beginning.'

'Well, that's all right, isn't it? I mean, you surely trust her to tell the truth. Rose isn't the sort of girl to lead you on or tell lies.'

'When I went back to her place with her make-up bag which she'd left in my car, I saw Mason leaving the house - why? She only saw him at the hospital half an hour ago – he must have come straight round. And he kissed her goodbye.'

'It was probably just a social kiss.' Clive patted his shoulder. 'You shouldn't read too much into it, old man.'

'I don't know what to think.' John heaved himself out of the chair and went to look disconsolately out of the window. The grey, depressing clouds reflected his mood. 'I tell you, I'm ready to back off from this relationship. I watched what my parents went through and I always swore marriage wasn't for me. Then I met Rose and had a big re-think. But now…'

Clive tried to console him. 'There may have been any number of reasons Mason wanted a quiet word with her. He was leaving the house, not going in – which means he could hardly have been there for more than a minute or two.'

'I guess. But you told me weeks ago that you thought she was sweet on him.'

'This is the first time you've really felt like this, isn't it?'

'Yup.'

'And you thought it would be hearts and flowers all the way. Life ain't like that, mate, and if that's what you're expecting, you're in for a big disappointment. You have to decide whether to trust her or not – that's the bottom line.'

Clive gripped John's arm. 'You can't get in a cold sweat every time she smiles at another man or you'll go crazy. She's drop-dead-gorgeous and if you get together with her you'll be fighting them off for the rest of your life – not because Rose is flirting, but because she's the sort of girl most men would give their eye teeth for.'

'You think I don't know that?' He leaned his forehead on the cold window pane in an agony of indecision.

'Then keep cool – give her the lead and see what card she plays.'

'Thanks for the advice – but I'm not sure I can. I feel totally screwed-up and I always swore I'd never let anyone get close enough to do this to me. The first time I let my guard down, look what happens!'

'Give her a chance – it's probably quite innocent.'

'Yeah… Okay. How are things with you and Lauren?' he asked, changing the subject.

'We discovered we have a lot of things in common,' he smiled and winked. 'She's wonderful.'

'I'm happy for you, and envious,' John said sadly.

Stage Struck

It was lunchtime before Sam and Nick made it downstairs for much needed sustenance.

'There's pizzas in the freezer. Will that do?' he asked, slipping his arms around her from behind and nuzzling her ear.

'Oh, yes,' she giggled leaning back against him. 'But afterwards you'd better run me back to the hotel to collect my car.'

'If I must. Can't you persuade your parents to keep Ben for one more night?'

'He has school tomorrow – and anyway I miss him.' She turned to look at him, a serious expression in her eyes. 'This will be the difficulty for you, Nick. You have to share me and not be jealous or possessive. I told you Ben and I come as a package and I meant it; it doesn't mean my feelings for you are any less sincere – but Ben…'

'Sam, I do understand. And I like Ben and hope he approves of me, so please don't feel you have to justify how much you love him. I wouldn't think well of you if you didn't put him first. But just now, I'm so knocked out by how I feel – by the way we made love, which was quite extraordinary – that I selfishly wish that just for a little while, I could have you to myself. That's all.'

'As long as you understand. Now, feed me,' she pleaded, 'or I shall fade away.'

'At the double,' he grinned, opening the freezer. 'But you make the coffee, woman, before I die of caffeine deprivation.'

***

Late on Sunday afternoon, Lola was deemed fit to leave hospital and discharged. Her arm and shoulder were still sore and every joint seemed to ache; but even so she couldn't wait to get out of the place. She visited Leo before leaving and was relieved when he managed a crooked smile and asked how Gillian and Alex were faring.

'Gillian can go home tomorrow and Alex and I are leaving now. I'm going to stay with him, because his parents are still away and he chose not to tell them what had happened and spoil their holiday.'

'Does Mum know? She's gone shopping, thank God. I'm exhausted by her sitting next to me snivelling all the time.'

'No, but I don't care what she says. There is no way any of us can return to school before Christmas, so I'll go and be with Alex until his folks get back from Barbados.'

'God – that means I'm stuck with the pair of them on my own. Thanks a lot, big sister.'

'Sorry,' she grinned.

'Sis…'

'Yes?'

'When I was gradually waking up after the accident, I could swear Mum and Dad were having a row and he accused her of having an affair – with Nick.'

'So it *is* Nick!'

'You knew?'

'Yeah. Well, if you'd half an eye, you'd have seen it too.'

'Christ! Where does that leave us?'

'I don't know, kid; it's one of the many reasons I don't want to be around for a while. It scares me. How long will you be stuck in here, have they told you?'

'A few days. To be honest, my head aches most of the time and I'm quite glad to be on the happy pills they keep giving me.' His brow furrowed. 'Do you think they'll split?'

'Honestly, I don't know. But Nick brought a posh bird to the party,' mused Lola, 'so maybe it's over with Mum now and everything will calm down.'

'Can you believe it – Mum and Nick bonking? Yuck! I hate to think of old people doing it at all, don't you?'

'Revolting.'

'Are you and Alex…?'

'Yes. We spent two nights together last week when I was supposed to be with Caroline. You?'

'No. Gillian doesn't believe in it before marriage.' He pulled a face. 'Just my luck.'

Lola laughed until tears ran down her face – but suddenly those tears turned to real ones and Leo pulled her towards him. Unable to hug him because of the remaining drips and wires, she sat beside him sniffing.

'Don't worry, sis… We'll all come out the other side. Just think, we might have died last night. Nothing can be as bad as that.'

She sniffed again and rubbed her good hand across her nose. 'Poor Dad…'

'Oh, for God's sake go and find a tissue – you've got snot all over your face,' he said.

And with a giggle she leaned over and, in spite of his efforts to avoid it, she kissed him.

'I'll come and see you tomorrow.'

She left and met Alex, who had not been allowed into the ward, and together they made their way painfully out of the hospital and hailed a taxi.

At seven o'clock Rose drove to collect John from his flat and was met at the door by Clive. 'He won't be a minute – he's on the phone to his folks,' he said. 'Have you recovered from the traumas of Saturday night?'

Stage Struck

'Not really. But I gather you and Lauren…'

'Did she say anything?'

'She didn't have to,' smiled Rose. 'She has a grin on her face the width of the Forth Bridge and she seems to be hovering about a foot off the ground.'

'That's about how I feel too.'

'I'm so happy for you both.'

John appeared at the door and Rose smiled shyly at him. He looked tense and gave her a half-hearted smile in return. 'Shall we go? We're already late,' he said brusquely. 'I called Maureen and told her to expect us at seven.'

'Yes…'bye Clive.' She glanced at him and he was shaking his head gently at John, as if to warn him of something.

By the time they got into her car the air crackled between them, and instead of turning on the ignition she swung round to face John. 'Whatever is the matter? You look ready to burst.'

'You left your make-up bag in my car…' He held it up and she took it, thrusting it in the glove compartment.

'Oh, I wondered where it was…so, why is that a problem?' she asked, puzzled.

'I brought it back to your house in time to see Mason leaving.'

'I see. And you think that in the space of what…five or six minutes…he had come round, made mad, passionate love to me and left?'

John didn't reply, but glared mutinously at the windscreen.

'Mason came to apologise; to say that he hoped he hadn't done any permanent damage to our relationship.'

'I see,' he replied coolly, staring at the colourless street.

Furious, banging a hand on the steering wheel to emphasise her words, she continued, 'He has made sure Candy understands that there was *nothing* between him and me. Oh, and he also told her that he knows about her affair with Nick – so I expect his marriage is well and truly on the rocks. His life's in ruins and frankly he needs some friends to help and support him through this mess. Yes, he made a mistake when he kissed me, as I did when I allowed it - we were both feeling very vulnerable that night.' He turned to stare at her, his eyes indecipherable. 'I promise, that's all that ever happened and I'm not in love with him or besotted by him. I told you the truth, John, but it seems that wasn't enough.'

She blinked back tears and took a deep breath. 'So please get out of my car. I'll go and see Winston on my own and then have an early night.'

'Rose…'

'You and I must go back to being just friends because we have to get through this pantomime as we've made a commitment to it. But if you can't trust me now, you never will and I couldn't bear a half-relationship like that. Now please go.'

He seemed about to argue, but she glared stonily at him and his resistance faded. With a resigned sigh, to her relief he opened the door, climbed out and shut the door with a bang.

She drove down the road, glancing back through tear-filled eyes to see John standing, a dejected figure in the drizzle, staring after her.

Rose arrived at Winston's flat, her face puffy and red-eyed. Maureen let her in, took in her distressed state at a glance and firmly led Rose into the kitchen where Patsy was sitting at the table with a pile of costumes.

'Come and have some tea before you go in to see the old buzzard,' Maureen said. 'Patsy – I think she needs some sympathy to go with it. It's Mason, isn't it? We heard from someone else what happened after we left the party. What a shit.'

'No – I mean yes, he's part of the problem. But he was drunk and upset because of Candy.'

'Candy and Nick, you mean?'

'Does *everybody* know?'

'Everybody with eyes. She's a very stupid woman and if she loses her lovely husband over it, I'll have no sympathy.'

'I didn't have an affair with Mason, I promise you.'

'I never thought you did, my dear, you're not that sort of girl,' said Maureen staunchly.

'I have to admit,' continued Rose, 'there was a frisson of attraction when I first joined the group, but that's all, and now the only person I care about is John. But he obviously doesn't trust me and we've split up.'

'He's jealous, my dear,' piped up Patsy, handing over a mug. 'He's in love with you and can't see beyond that.'

She sipped the tea. It was hot and burned her lip but she didn't care. 'But if he doesn't believe me when I tell him the truth, I can't have a relationship with him.'

'No, you can't. But let things calm down for a day or two and then see what happens. He's a nice man – we like him very much, don't we, Maureen?'

Maureen nodded and said, 'So don't throw the baby out with the bath water.'

Rose drank her tea, repaired her make-up and went down the passage to the lounge where Winston was watching television.

'Rose! How nice to see you.' He switched off the TV and held out his hands.

Stage Struck

She wrapped her fingers round his and leaned over to kiss his cheek. 'You look well, Winston.'

'Which is more than I can say for you, young lady. What's the matter? Come and sit beside me.'

'Nothing... Oh, just boyfriend problems.'

'They told me about Mason. I'm sorry he said those things.'

'I didn't -'

'I never thought you did,' he interrupted. 'Take my advice – least said, soonest mended. Just let it go away because people soon forget things like that. Go to rehearsal on Tuesday as if nothing had happened.'

'Yes, I will. Do you think you might be well enough to come along? Everyone would love to see you.'

'After the way I behaved?'

'Winston, you should take your own advice!' she said sternly. 'You've been a member of that group for what, twenty years? I don't think they're going to hold one little tantrum against you.'

'Well, maybe I will. Yes, maybe I will.' He perked up and began to tell her stories of his past productions, and before long she was laughing and telling him he should write a book about his experiences.

'I suppose I might,' he mused. 'It would keep me busy, wouldn't it?'

'Have you heard any more from your children?' she asked finally.

'No. But I've made an important decision.'

'Really?'

He nodded. 'Yes, I'm going to change my will. I think Peggy would turn in her grave if she knew how I've been treated by them, so, as she was a fervent worker for MENCAP – in fact she got an OBE for it – I've decided to leave the bulk of whatever is left to them.'

'I can't say I blame you,' smiled Rose.

'Now off you go, dear girl, before I do something very ungentlemanly and fall asleep. Thank you for coming – it means a lot to me.'

She kissed him and returned to the kitchen where Patsy was putting the finishing touches to Lady Marian's wedding dress.

'Thanks for cheering me up. See you Tuesday – and Winston says he might even come along to watch.'

'Excellent. Things are looking up. Well done, Rose,' beamed Maureen. 'He just wants to see you in your fishnet tights – you do realise that? You'll have to be careful you don't give him another funny turn.'

Wishing them goodnight, she closed the door on their good-humoured laughter.

Rose felt much more cheerful as she drove home.

But that night, once again, she awoke with a scream, quite certain she could smell lilies.

***

Candy had left Leo to go to Boots to get a packet of aspirin for a splitting headache. She also needed some fresh air and time to consider the ramifications of Mason's declaration. After walking aimlessly up and down the road a couple of times, she noticed Aunty Mabel's Coffee Shop was almost deserted. She ordered a large latte and sat at a table in the far corner, contemplating it for a while, waiting for the aspirin to take effect.

She was very frightened. Suddenly the consequences of her affair with Nick were coming home to roost. And she didn't know how to deal with them. If Mason decided to end their marriage, the whole fabric of her lifestyle would crumble. The fine house, holidays abroad, expensive clothes - not to mention the disdain with which their friends would regard her. No-one would take her side against Saint Mason, she thought grimly. If Nick had done what she'd expected and asked her to move in with him, she'd have been all right. He had loads of money, an equivalent home, and liked the good life. But the swine had dumped her and now she was in grave danger of losing everything.

Well, she would deal with Nick sooner or later, she decided. In the short term, she simply must make her peace with Mason. She'd been shaken to the core when she heard him tell Rose he wanted to go to bed with her. It had simply never crossed her mind that he too might look elsewhere, and she was mortified. Mason and a younger woman... But in her heart she didn't believe it had been more than a fantasy. He couldn't – he was too level-headed, too upright in his beliefs to take advantage of someone like Rose. The poor girl had looked shattered at the very idea, probably revolted by the advances of a man so much older than her. Yes, that was it, Candy decided. He was trying to make her jealous, to show that he too could attract someone else. A typical mid-life crisis, she consoled herself.

But what if Rose had become really attached to Mason? What if she was just appearing in public with that American to cover her tracks? She recalled seeing Rose and Mason talking and laughing easily together a few times at rehearsal, and by his own admission she'd been to the pub with him and given him lifts home. Suddenly, Candy wasn't so sure any more. And then there was the cat hair... With a groan, she finished her coffee and walked back to St. Mary's.

Stage Struck

I'm going to hate it, she thought, but I have no choice but to do everything in my power to win Mason back – the alternatives are horrendous. Pinning a smile on her face, she went to see Leo, who was propped up on a couple of pillows eating a light lunch.

'Feeling better, darling?' she asked.

'Starving. I suppose that's a good sign.'

'Definitely.'

'Mum… Lola left last night…'

'What?'

'She's fine – don't worry. But she's gone to stay with Alex. His parents are still on holiday and he doesn't want them to know about the accident. So Lola and Alex are going to look after each other.'

'But…but… I want to look after her.'

'I think it's a bit too late for that, Mum.'

'Where does he live, this Alex?'

'In a mansion somewhere on West Common.'

Mason arrived at that moment and after a cool nod to Candy, he went to Leo and sat beside him. 'You have some colour back in your cheeks.'

'I'm okay, Dad. I still have a headache, but I can focus my eyes properly now. Don't worry, in a couple of days, I'll be home.'

'Thank God. Well, I'll just pop along to see Lola. I believe she can go home later today.'

Candy said, 'Apparently, she's already gone. She left to go and stay with Alex.'

'Did she indeed? Well, if that's where she feels most comfortable, that's fine.'

'You mean you approve?'

'She's safe and happy with him.'

'Meaning what?'

'You know exactly what I mean.'

Leo put his tray aside and groaned. 'Please don't start a quarrel here.'

'Sorry, old chap.'

'Just go home – both of you. I want to sleep and I can't with you two fussing around me.'

'If that's what you want,' his mother said, 'we'll come back this evening.'

'If you must,' he moaned, closing his eyes. 'But tomorrow would be better.'

143

Stage Struck

'He's improving,' said Candy brightly as they got into the car. 'What a relief. And if he doesn't want us to come back this evening, perhaps we could go out for a meal? We haven't done that for a long time.'

'People only do that when they want to spend time together, and frankly, I'd rather have a Chinese takeaway in front of the TV.'

'Oh...'

He pulled away from the car-park.

'Candy, I regret enormously the embarrassment I caused Rose the other night, and none of that would have happened if you hadn't been making life a total misery at home for the past six months.'

'So the fact that you fancy a girl young enough to be your daughter is my fault?' she said, trying not to scream at him.

'Yes. Yes it damn well is.'

'So you admit it then – you do fancy her - or is it more than that?'

'I should think any man with his hormones intact would fancy Rose, and when you add to that a sweet and caring nature, she is totally adorable. But I'd never have even thought about her that way if you'd been behaving like a loving wife.'

'Well I like that! How dare you speak to me...'

He ignored her, concentrating on the road, and went on, 'I presume your sordid little affair is over as he is toting a new woman around, and I can imagine the vitriol swilling inside you over that – so I think it would be better if we separated. I'll stay in Lola's room until I can organise myself and then move out.'

'No! Please, Mason, I couldn't bear it.'

'And I couldn't bear to stay. It's over, Candy. I could never feel the same about you again.'

'I don't believe that.' She began to sob. 'Please forgive me, darling. Lots of couples go through bad patches and survive. We could do the same, I know we could.'

'I don't think so.'

'What about the children? They'll be devastated.'

'They're not babies and they already have their own lives. They'll be sad, but they'll understand. And anyway, I don't intend to abandon them.'

'But...what about your precious pantomime?'

'What about it? I shall continue to work on that, as will Nick, I'm sure. I told you that too many people are committed, and I won't let them down.'

'And what about me?'

'Let me know by Tuesday if you plan to back out. I shall have to get someone else, which will be inconvenient – but no-one is indispensable.'

He drew up at their house and Candy got out and waited for Mason to do the same.

The window wound down. 'Have you got your key?' he asked her.

'Yes,' she said, leaning forward. 'Aren't you coming in?'

'No. I shan't be in until late.'

'Where are you going?'

'That is none of your business any more, is it?' And he left her crying helplessly on the pavement as the early winter darkness descended.

Stage Struck

Tuesday 16th December

It was a nervous and dispirited crowd that turned up for rehearsal. There was a low buzz of conversation and a complete silence fell as Mason came through the door. He strode straight to the front of the hall to address them.

'Right everybody. First I would like to thank you all for turning up here tonight, for your concern about Lola and Leo, and for the support Candy and I have received since Saturday night.'

There was a sympathetic murmur from the cast. 'Candy will be here shortly and, as I'm sure you're all wondering, she will still be taking part. Lola will be back at rehearsal on Thursday but Leo won't be fit and Barry Watson is bravely taking over his role.' He raised a hand to still a few low comments from the back. 'Gillian is fine and will be here next week. So, we're immensely fortunate that a tragedy did not rob us of four fine young people, and one way or another we're going to pull together and put on the best pantomime ever. Are we agreed?'

There was a roar of approval and a spontaneous burst of applause.

'What a relief,' said Patsy, rattling the green cups and saucers. 'Coffee and tea everyone. And I've made a huge box of mince pies – so help yourselves before we start.'

Mason was busy talking to Nick about props when Candy slipped in, having driven herself to the church hall. She watched the two men from a distance, as if wondering how to cope with being in the same room with them.

After a reviving coffee, Mason began the rehearsal from the beginning of Act One. John and Clive, both now in costume, ran their opening comedy routine and although the performance didn't sparkle, they got through it with a degree of aplomb. Verruca the witch and Candy as Tabitha did likewise, and when Rose had to make her first entrance, also in full costume, she remembered her lines and wasn't thrown by having a stand-in Lady Marian.

Then they did the slapstick routine where John as Mrs. Mixit got in a terrible mess making a birthday cake for Lady Marian. But the whole scene lacked pizzazz. Mason was trying to work out why the comedy was falling so flat on its face when the door to the hall creaked open and in walked Winston.

'Winston, you old fool!' yelled Maureen. 'You said you weren't coming – how did you get here?'

'I can still use a telephone and I called a taxi, dear one.' He grinned, and his smile broadened even further when rehearsal was temporarily abandoned as all his old friends surrounded him, obviously delighted to see him.

Stage Struck

'Right, Winston,' said Mason eventually, 'please sit there and see what you think of the slapstick scene. I've tried everything I can think of, but it doesn't work.'

'You wouldn't be patronising me would you, young man?' he asked mildly.

'No, I bloody wouldn't. I need some advice. Right, Jack and Mrs. Mixit, run the scene again – and this time, make it funny!'

The scene still didn't go well and the actors sat dejectedly on the edge of the stage, wiping the remains of a can of shaving foam off their faces.

'John, you have to play the scene for real,' said Winston thoughtfully. 'You're trying too hard to be funny and forcing it. Imagine you're really making a cake,' he said, exaggeratedly miming the stirring motion, 'but with the innocence of a child, putting in all the wrong ingredients and expecting it to come out well. You don't know the sugar has been changed to salt by Hansel and Gretel – but the audience does. You don't know the pepper is out of a firework – but the audience does… So let them enjoy the joke without shoving it in their faces. If you'll excuse the pun.'

He turned to Clive. 'And Clive, when you push the plate of shaving foam in his face, let the plate stick and slide off on its own,' he said, and slowly thrust out a hand in slow motion. 'You're rushing it – there's no time to enjoy John's reaction because you've moved onto the next thing.'

'Thanks, Winston.' Clive said, 'Can we try it again, Mason?'

'Yes… do.'

And the next time, it worked.

'Something so obvious – and I missed it,' grunted the director.

'You've had rather a lot to contend with the last few days. I was sorry to hear about your troubles.'

'Thank you – and thank you for coming along this evening. We need every ounce of help at this stage. Do you think you could take on coaching Barry who's replacing Leo? He could do with a bit of private tuition on stage craft and projecting his voice. It's going to be an uphill battle getting everything up to scratch in time.'

'Be delighted – yes, of course.'

'And, Winston – there's no question of patronising you. You know more about pantomime than any of us and we would truly value your contribution.'

Winston nodded and patted Mason on the arm. 'I say,' he chuckled, 'young Rose looks great in those fishnet tights, doesn't she?'

Stage Struck

Candy kept her distance from the others except when she was on stage, and to Nick's relief made no attempt to seek him out. Perhaps, at last, he prayed, she'd come to her senses. He had an enormous amount of work to do to get the set finished. There was still the Fire Officer to consult about using pyrotechnics on stage and he had to construct the special effects for the scene in Verruca's castle. Flying bats and coloured smoke from the witch's pot were required. He still had to finish three trees for the Magic Forest, which would be on wheels so that various characters could move the forest around the stage whilst hiding behind the structure. His private life had rather taken precedence over the show and now he was working against the clock to recover lost time.

Since there was little for him to contribute to the rehearsal, Nick went out to the property store which was freezing cold and damp, but where the cut-outs of fir trees were waiting to be painted. He switched on the single hanging light bulb which cast eerie shadows around the shed. Shivering, he hauled out tins of brown and green paint and a brush, and was soon busy slapping on a layer of paint. He left the door open to ventilate the small space as the smell was quite pungent and after a short while he thought he caught a glimpse of someone standing in the shadows just outside the door. Wearily straightening his back, he massaged it, went to the door to see who was there, and was hardly surprised to find Candy glaring at him.

'He's leaving me!' she spat. 'It's all your fault, you bastard.'

'Don't be ridiculous. I told you to let go of me weeks ago, Candy. If you'd done as I pleaded, none of this would have happened.'

'Well, if I'm losing him, there's nothing to stop you and me getting together, is there? You can get rid of your bit of fluff and…'

'Candy, are you completely insensitive to anyone else's feelings? Is it not obvious to you that I do not - repeat, do *not* - want you? I'm very happy with Sam and I beg you not to try to ruin that.'

'But we were so good together, Nick. How can you just cast that all aside? Not just the sex…'

'On the contrary, Candy, it was just the sex. For me it was just the sex. I'm sorry. With Sam there is so much more…'

'You said you didn't want a needy woman, didn't want commitment – or kids. And now you've got yourself all three. You're a cheating, lying, evil, self-centred user and I'll make sure everyone, including Sam, gets to hear what you're really like.'

She moved towards him, her eyes blazing and unexpectedly gave him a shove in the chest which caught him off balance and that was the last thing he remembered until Rose's face came

Stage Struck

into focus and he found himself surrounded by several members of the cast gazing anxiously down at him.

Hazily he looked around, half expecting to see Candy. 'What happened?'

'We were about to ask you the same question,' Rose said. 'Patsy came out with a cup of coffee to warm you up and found you sprawled on the floor.'

Nick massaged his head, surprised to find a huge lump at the back. 'I suppose I must've tripped and fallen,' he lied.

'Did you see anyone?'

'No.'

'Should we call an ambulance?'

'No, no, I'm fine.'

'No double vision or nausea?'

'No – just a sore head.'

'Well, someone should take you home.'

'Honestly – I'm quite all right. Please don't fuss.' He struggled to his feet and they helped him inside where he sat down on a plastic chair.

'Do you think someone attacked you?' asked Winston. 'You haven't been robbed?'

Nick patted his pocket. 'No – my wallet's still here.'

'Well,' said Patsy, 'you can't be too careful these days, there are some real weirdoes about. Perhaps they heard me coming before they could rob you. Maybe I scared them off.'

The image of little Patsy scaring off a huge burglar restored a collective sense of humour. In a surge of support, seven volunteers offered to come to the hall on the following Saturday morning to help Nick.

He was then hustled off home where he sat with an ice pack on his head, silently raging at Candy.

In need of some sympathy, he picked up the phone to call Sam but changed his mind, deciding that it might prompt a lot of questions he'd rather not answer. He'd already decided, regretfully, that as soon as the pantomime was over, he would cease to be a member of the group. It seemed the easiest way to ensure that Candy and Sam never came face-to-face again. What a mess! And now there was the complication of Sam's relationship to Rose, whom he was pretty sure had an inkling about his affair with Candy – something he couldn't possibly have anticipated. With a groan, he went to a cold bed wishing with all his heart that Sam was there to comfort him.

***

Stage Struck

Rose was pleased to see Winston enfolded again into the group. After they'd packed Nick off home, he thanked her for encouraging him to return. 'I feel back in control of my life now,' he revealed. 'Between ourselves,' he added, a finger tapping the side of his nose, 'I've stopped drinking and joined AA. They told me at the hospital it was essential but I didn't realise how much better I'd feel with a clear head.'

'You're very brave, Winston. I'm so pleased. Is Maureen still staying with you?'

'No. She went home a few days ago – only to phone me every half hour to make sure I haven't keeled over. It did feel strange at first, sleeping in the flat, knowing no-one was there at night. I'm glad I'm back on track - and a lot of it is down to you and John - as well as Maureen and Patsy.' Tears sparkled in his eyes. 'I know who my friends are now.'

Rose took his hand. 'At least something good has come out of something bad.' She smiled. 'It's often the way, isn't it?'

'Yes, it is. And you…and John?'

Rose shook her head sadly and glanced at John who was rehearsing a song and dance routine with Clive at the piano. His loud, tuneful voice belted out 'I'd Do Anything', the much-loved song from *Oliver!* which he sang to Jack the Jester with a few variations in the words to make them appropriate to the show. 'He's so talented isn't he?'

'He'll make a wonderful dame,' agreed Winston with a wry smile.

Just then they became aware of raised voices between Mason and Candy and Rose watched horrified as Candy burst into tears, slapped her husband soundly on his cheek and ran out of the hall.

An embarrassed silence fell, and they all watched as Mason climbed onto the stage, one side of his face aflame. 'All right – I think that was probably the last straw for me. Candy has walked out and there are no circumstances under which I would allow her back. It leaves us without a cat less than two weeks before the show – so unless someone has any ideas, I'm sorry, but I'm in favour of cancelling and giving money back to those who've bought tickets. Comments please.'

The rest of the company glanced at each other – at a loss – until a voice from the back asked, 'Does the cat have to be female?'

'Well no, Winston, I suppose not. Why?'

'Would you consider me?'

'What a bloody brilliant idea!'

'I'd have to play it differently, of course. A galumphing, ham-fisted fool of a Tom cat…but I could give it a go - if you're stuck.'

Stage Struck

'We're stuck.' Mason turned to the others. 'What do the rest of you think?'

There was a collective roar of approval and an encouraging buzz filled the hall as extra rehearsals were scheduled to give Winston a chance to practise his new role. They began immediately, and the spirit of the whole group soared as Winston capered round the stage, totally at home, relaxed and extremely funny. Clive and John had to stop their scene when they both collapsed laughing.

By the time rehearsal ended, they knew without a doubt that the show was saved and would be a huge success.

***

Candy drove home in a fury. She had arrived at rehearsal with her nerves frayed after three days of silence from Mason. He had merely given a grunt, implying 'yes' or 'no' to every attempt she made at conversation with him. Nick also ignored her and she'd finally followed him out to the shed in a last ditch attempt to make it up with him – and then he too insulted her. She regretted pushing him and hadn't realised he was so badly hurt when she left him lying on the floor. He must have cracked his head on a tin of paint. Well, he was obviously all right – so no need to feel too guilty, she thought, trying to comfort herself.

But the worst thing about the evening was the hostility from the rest of the group. And it seemed to be directed at her alone. Candy had expected a wave of sympathy after the children's accident, but Mason seemed to be on the receiving end of that and it was obvious that she wasn't welcome and everyone was blaming her for the disastrous state of her relationship with her husband.

'What has it got to do with anyone else?' she stormed, negotiating traffic lights which seemed to conspire against her. 'And then for the swine to tell me I had all the pace and charisma of a wet lettuce on stage! I'll never speak to him again. I hope the show collapses without me and they all go down with the flu'.'

Still cursing aloud, she pulled into the drive in a shower of gravel, scrambled out of the car and stormed into the house, slamming the door behind her. The house was also unwelcoming – no children, no Mason, and the central heating hadn't come on, so the place was freezing cold. But it wasn't the cold which was making Candy shiver. She switched on the hateful gas fire then poured a mammoth-sized glass of white wine to try to calm the waves of rage and fear.

Perhaps hitting Mason in front of everyone had been a step too far, even if he had asked for it. She knew he'd never forgive her for the humiliation. It was the very public and permanent end to her marriage. A solid lump of ice seemed to form in her stomach and she began to shake with fright.

Stage Struck

She finished her drink quickly and poured another with a quivering hand.

Supposing Mason threw her out of the house – how on earth could she survive financially? Where would she go; who would take her in? She knew she was having a panic attack and it was triggering her asthma. Calm down, Candy, just calm down, she told herself, but her breathing became more and more difficult and she began to sweat with the effort.

She grabbed the inhaler from her bag and breathed in deeply, feeling the drug hit her lungs, helping them to relax. But not enough… Still she was wheezing and gasping, so with great difficulty she struggled upstairs to her oxygen machine and sat for several minutes breathing in the pure gas. It made her feel a little heady but at least it eventually stabilised her asthma. She felt like an over-wound spring, and the anxiety passed over her in waves, making her nauseous and dizzy.

Making her way to the bathroom, she opened the medicine cabinet. Was there anything here which might calm her down and allow her to think clearly? Aspirin, anti-histamine, cream for athlete's foot… Nothing useful.

Disconsolately, she wandered into the bedroom where Mason's suit jacket was lying on the bed.

'Can't you ever hang anything up?' she muttered, picking it up and preparing to throw it in the corner. But then something rattled and she fished in the pocket and pulled out a bottle of tablets. Curious, she squinted at the label. Temazepam… Some sort of tranquilliser. So, Mason's been to the doctor for stress or depression. She bit her lip, knowing she was certainly the cause of his anxiety, but in her hand she held the answer to her immediate problem; something to quell the nausea, fear and inability to think straight.

Maybe an early night and a couple of pills would calm her down so she could talk to Mason in the morning without blowing up at him again. She still had her glass of wine in her hand and taking four tablets, she swilled them down in a couple of gulps. Perhaps two more would really knock her out. They were only very small tablets, she thought fuzzily, flushing them down with the remainder of the wine.

Throwing herself on the bed, she waited for them to take effect. Sleep – that was what she needed – a good night's sleep.

Mason locked the church hall, calling 'goodnight' to everyone as they left to make their way home. He couldn't face the idea of going back to the house, so he wandered down the High Street to McDonald's and ordered a two-thousand calorie meal – something he would never normally touch – which he sat munching, peering gloomily at the passing traffic.

Stage Struck

It was beginning to rain and a cold wind blew the last few leaves from the trees into a depressing pile by the bus stop outside. He hated eating alone, hated going home, hated his life and hated the fact that he now had to fulfil his commitment to the show before he could do something drastic to change his lifestyle.

Obviously, a divorce would be the first thing to organise, though he didn't know the procedure. He supposed he'd go and see a solicitor who'd ask all sorts of personal questions and want to know with whom Candy had been having an affair. It seemed sordid to reveal the true facts, but he supposed that these days there would not be an announcement in the local paper, nor the stigma his mother had suffered thirty years before when she'd divorced his father. Mason had never considered divorce before; his own childhood had been blighted by warring parents and after the split, an acrimonious relationship between them. Now he had to think about sharing the household effects, selling the house, downsizing his standard of living, supporting the children and possibly losing contact with them as they grew away from him. All of these thoughts were new territory and terrifying. But if he was honest with himself, life had been untenable for months, and he couldn't imagine ever reviving the feelings he'd always had for Candy.

She'd been a beauty at High School and he'd been overwhelmed when she consented to go out with him, delighted when she became his regular girlfriend and blissfully happy when, after university, she married him. Their relationship was tempestuous from the start, but they'd always resolved their quarrels, usually passionately, and he'd never even considered that she might cheat on him – or that he might betray her. In recent years, the passion had cooled, which Mason accepted as part of growing together and sharing the raising of children and running a home whilst being slave to a busy work schedule. Candy, however, had become more demanding and moody, to the point where the past nine months had been like walking through a minefield. Constantly, he checked every sentence, carefully phrased every request, and tried to protect the children from her more vile moments. He still hadn't considered she might be having an affair – but looking back he decided he must have been blind not to see it.

Angrily, he crushed the paper coffee cup in his hand before gathering up the detritus from his meal and tossing it into the bin. It was late. With any luck, Candy would be asleep and he could creep into Lola's room unheard. Another confrontation was more than he could bear.

He drove home slowly, calming himself, and was annoyed to see almost every light on in the house – a pet hate of his. Grimly, he clenched his teeth and went inside, turning them all off as he moved from room to room. There was no sign of Candy – please God, he prayed, she's sleeping.

Stage Struck

He tiptoed upstairs and glanced through the open door of the bedroom. Candy lay sprawled on top of the covers with the overhead light blazing down on her.

With a muttered curse, he reached for the light switch but before he flicked it off his eye was caught by a bottle of pills on the floor and an empty wine glass on the bedside table.

He picked up the bottle and with a gasp of horror realised they were his tranquillizers – and he had no idea how many were missing.

'Candy!' He shook her shoulder, but she flopped back on the bed. 'Wake up, for God's sake!' She was completely unconscious. 'Oh, no... What on earth do I do now?' He ran into the en suite, soaked a flannel in icy water then tried to prop her up while washing her face with the cloth – but there was no response. 'You stupid bitch – how much more can you hurt me? It would serve you right if I just went to bed and left you to die. I hate you, Candy – if you can hear me, understand it... *I hate you!*'

Angrily, he snatched the pill bottle and pounded down the stairs and picked up his diary, frantically searching for Rose's number. To his eternal relief, she answered on the second ring, sounding sleepy and confused. 'Rose... it's me, Mason. No, wait – it's Candy, I think she's taken an overdose of Temazepam and I don't know what to do. Should I call an ambulance?'

'Oh, good Lord...' Rose took a few seconds to gather her thoughts. 'How many do you think she's taken?'

'I don't know... Wait, there were thirty tablets and I've been taking one a day for a week... so there should be twenty-three left.' Quickly, he tipped the remaining pills on to the table top and counted them. 'I think there are about six missing.'

'What strength are they?'

'Ten milligrams.'

'Then don't panic – she'll sleep for twenty-four hours, I should think. Had she been drinking?'

'Yes – there's a half empty bottle of wine on the table.'

'I'll come round. I don't think we need an ambulance, but call your GP and tell him what you've told me.'

About five minutes later, he let her in. She was wearing a sweater and jeans and seemed short of breath. She must have run. Now she ran upstairs, straight to the bedroom. Candy's mouth was open, her breathing loud and laboured. Rose took her pulse and, satisfied, told Mason to help her get Candy into a sitting position.

'Doesn't she have an oxygen machine for her asthma?'

'Yes...'

'Bring it. We'll give her oxygen while we wait for the doctor.'

'Will she be okay?'

'I think so – it's not a massive dose she's taken, but combined with the booze it's knocked her for six. I'm more concerned that she can breathe properly until the effects wear off.'

The doctor arrived twenty minutes later and confirmed Rose's thoughts with a grim nod. 'She'll be sorry in the morning,' he said. 'She'll have the mother-and-father of all hangovers. Tell her to come and see me, Mr Fairfax. Maybe she needs some anti-depressants of her own.'

'I think mine have done enough damage. I shan't take any more, Doctor, so please will you take these away?' He thrust the bottle at the doctor.

'If you insist.'

'I do.'

The doctor nodded and pocketed the bottle. 'Then, goodnight.'

Rose and Mason watched the doctor drive away and then retired to the kitchen where Rose made Mason sit down while she brewed tea. 'Strong and sweet, that's what you need,' she said.

'Thank you for coming so quickly, I was in a total panic.'

'Understandable,' she smiled, handing him a mug of steaming tea.

'It's my fault she's done this.'

'Why do you think that?'

'I suppose I must have left a great gap in our marriage which Nick came along and filled.'

'It isn't for me to comment on that,' she told him as he sipped the tea. 'But we all have to take responsibility for our actions. If she's deliberately taken an overdose because you are threatening to leave her, then you have every right to be furious. It's emotional blackmail rather than a cry for help.' She eyed the clock. 'I must go now, I'm on an early shift.'

'Yes, of course... Thank you so much for rushing round...and Rose...'

'Yes?'

'Can we keep this between ourselves?'

'What do you take me for?' she asked, hurt.

'I'm so sorry...Of course you wouldn't... Silly of me, I mean...'

'Just get some rest, Mason. I'll see you at rehearsal tomorrow.'

Rose strolled home, noting with a smile that Clive's car was now parked outside Lauren's house. Min jumped onto her shoulder as she opened her front door and mewed loudly into her ear. 'Minny,' she groaned, ruffling the cat's ears, 'how much more complicated can things get?

I wish I'd never agreed to take part in this pantomime. I'd never have met John and I wouldn't be in this mess.'

But as she made a cup of hot chocolate to take back to bed she ached for John to be there with her. He'd barely acknowledged her at rehearsal. She had struggled to keep a bright smile on her face on stage, and waved to him and Clive as she drove past them on her way home, but he'd ignored her.

Rose tossed and turned in bed for an hour before getting back to sleep and woke late with barely half an hour to get to work. She was tetchy and snapped at her Staff Nurse, who, knowing this was out of character, persuaded Rose to take an early lunch break.

Gratefully, she went outside to get a breath of fresh air, taking cheese sandwiches to a bench in the hospital garden and sat, thoughtfully feeding crumbs to the greedy sparrows. At last, she wearily picked up the remains of her lunch and strolled slowly back to the hospital, just in time to see Mason walking towards the entrance. His shoulders were hunched and he had the exhausted expression of a man lacking a night's sleep.

'Mason!' she called and went quickly to him. 'How is Candy?'

'All right… Still sleeping, but she did wake once a couple of hours ago and I helped her to the bathroom. She says she has a headache.' He smiled with grim satisfaction. 'I'm here to collect Leo – he's being discharged.'

'I'm glad about that. At least he'll be around the house and keep you cheerful. Have you spoken to Lola?'

'Yes. She seems very content to be with Alex and I think it's better she stays with him for now. They're coming to visit Leo later.'

'Good… Well, I'll see you at rehearsal tonight.'

He nodded and disappeared into the building, leaving Rose to find her way back to the ward where three of her little patients had suddenly developed fevers with vomiting. Oh, no, she thought, just what we don't need – a bug on the ward when we're understaffed. What a day!

By the end of her shift another patient and two of the staff also succumbed. The ward was closed to visitors and Matron came to inspect. 'It's a virus… Pemberley Ward is also affected, Sister, so don't feel it has something to do with cleanliness on your ward. It's probably been brought into the kitchens by a member of staff. Can you stay on for a couple of hours while we arrange for extra bank staff to come in for the night duty?'

'Yes, Matron, of course.' It was almost eight o'clock before relief came and close to nine when Rose reached home. She was in no state to go to rehearsal, she realised. She was going to rise from her armchair and phone them, but she couldn't muster the energy and fell asleep there, only waking to hear someone knocking on her front door at ten-thirty.

Forcing herself out of the chair, she answered the door. He stood uncertainly on her doorstep and her heart leapt. 'John, what are you doing here?'

'You missed rehearsal without explanation – I was worried.'

'Come in,' she said, then raised a hand as if to ward him off, 'but please don't come near me.'

'I wouldn't dream of it,' he said stiffly.

'No. Oh, I didn't mean it like that. It's just that I haven't changed since I got home and we have an infection on the ward.'

'Oh, I see.' His shoulders relaxed as he took in the dark circles under her eyes. 'You look totally exhausted. Have you eaten?'

'I am… and no…well, half a cheese sandwich at midday.'

'Go and shower, while I get a fish supper from Charlie's Chippy on the corner.'

'But…'

'Just do it.'

'All right. Thanks.'

Twenty minutes later he was back and Rose, dressed now in a pair of pink pyjamas and a fluffy dressing gown, pulled two warm plates out of the oven.

They sat at the tiny table in her kitchen and she regarded John covertly as they ate. He said very little until they finished. Rose sighed contentedly and patted her stomach. 'That was wonderful. I shan't be able to get into my costume now – but what the hell.'

'I was worried about you.'

'I couldn't call before rehearsal… it's been a nightmare today. Thank Heaven I have two days off to recover.'

'Apparently, Leo went home this morning.'

'Yes, I know.'

'How?'

'As it happens, I saw Mason at the hospital when he went to collect him.'

'Oh. I'm sorry, I didn't mean…'

'John – I don't know quite how to say this but…' She paused, choosing her words and John got to his feet, anxiety in every angle of his body.

'Perhaps it's best not to say anything. I sure hope we can be friends and I'm sorry I made too many assumptions the other night. You never made me any promises but I behaved as if you had. Who you see is your own business and, well, I can only apologise. I'd better go now and let you get some sleep.'

She nodded. 'Thanks for supper. John, what I told you was the truth. I'm not involved with Mason – I don't want to be involved with him. Please can we give ourselves a second chance?'

'You sure you want to?' There was a flicker of hope in his eyes.

'I'm very sure. I've missed you so much.'

'Me too.' He took her hands. 'Can I kiss you goodnight?'

She nodded, and releasing her fingers from his, slipped her arms around his neck. He pulled her to him, holding her closely before seeking her mouth with his.

'I'll go, while I still can,' he said eventually and regretfully she released him and watched from the door as he climbed into his car and drove away. Even though she was exhausted, there was a small smile on her lips as she climbed the stairs.

Stage Struck

Wednesday 17th December

Candy took a full day to recover completely from her accidental overdose. She'd been woozily surprised to wake up and find Leo bending over her. But when she'd tried to pull him to her for a hug, he resisted and walked out of the bedroom.

Gingerly, she made her way down to the kitchen and lowered herself into a chair at the table, waiting for Leo to talk to her.

He came in from the lounge a moment later, avoiding eye contact with her, filled the kettle and put it on the hob in the central island. 'Tea?' he snapped.

'Please. How do you feel?'

'All right, I suppose.' He leaned against the black granite worktop and rubbed his temple. 'Bit of a headache.'

'Me too.'

The kettle clicked off, steam fronds hovering over the hob.

'Where's your dad?'

'Rehearsal. You've been asleep for nineteen hours, apparently. Well done, Mum.' He turned his back on her to pour hot water into two mugs.

'I didn't mean to harm myself. It was an accident because I was in a panic when your dad said our marriage was over.'

'Tried to blackmail him into staying, did you?'

'No.'

'Are you still seeing Nick?' he demanded angrily, plonking her mug on the table; dribbles of tea spilled over.

She stood up, pushing the chair back, aghast. 'Who told you that?'

'I was floating to the surface in hospital when you and Dad had a fight about him. I heard every word.'

'I'm sorry.'

Abruptly, the bravado dissolved and Leo turned an anguished face to his mother.

'We're frightened, Mum, me and Lola. Nothing is right any more – you're always fighting or not speaking to each other and we're afraid you're going to split. But what happens to us?'

'You're both grown up now…'

'I'm seventeen. I don't *feel* grown up.'

Stage Struck

And he suddenly seemed so young and vulnerable, this handsome, gentle son of hers. She took a pace towards him, wanting to hug him, but he held up a hand to ward her off. 'Leo – I'm so sorry. I know how hard it is for you – but I fell in love.'

'So did I, Mum, I fell in love with Gillian; but she doesn't think it's right to have sex before you get married and so I have to respect that. You could have controlled how you felt instead of behaving like a bitch on heat.'

She half-raised a hand to slap him but stopped herself in time. 'How dare you speak to me like that?'

'It's about time somebody did. You've ruined all our lives for a jerk like Nick Harrow, who's screwed half of Sipton. *I hate you!*' And he rushed out of the kitchen. She hastened after him but he was too fast, stumbling in his haste up the stairs to his bedroom. The door slammed shut.

From the bottom of the stairs she heard her son sobbing and her head and heart ached.

***

After locking the church hall Mason wearily made his way home. He had an early start for a meeting in Manchester the next morning, so somehow he had to get some sleep. The house was in darkness so he went in quietly and poured himself a small brandy nightcap before climbing the stairs to Lola's room. To his dismay, Candy opened the bedroom door and stepped onto the landing in front of him.

'Please, can we talk?'

'What is there to say?'

'The children have to be considered in all this.'

'Candy, that's the first time I've heard you say a considerate word for anyone else in many a long year. I have to get up at five so I have no intention of getting into a heart-to-heart tonight. Go to bed.'

'But the children...'

He gripped the banister rail, concern like a knife in his vitals. 'Is Leo all right?'

'Yes and no.'

'What does that mean, Candy?'

'He's distraught at the prospect of us splitting up. He's like a little boy, Mason, crying and pleading and I can't console him.'

He suspected that this was a vast exaggeration. 'So as usual I'm the one who is expected to sort out one of your messes.'

'It isn't good for him to be so upset when he's been critically ill.'

'What am I to tell him?'

'That's up to you, Mason. I want to try to repair our marriage, but I can't do it on my own.' She folded her arms, eyes earnest. 'I know it doesn't look like it, but I still love you very much, and although I lost my head for a while over Nick, I never wanted to leave you, I swear it. It was a mid-life crisis – me being stupid, wanting to know I was still attractive to another man. It got out of hand and I know I deserve everything I get; but the children don't and for their sakes I'm begging you to give our marriage one more chance. There's nothing between Nick and me any more – in fact, I wonder what I ever saw in him.'

Mason stood and stared at her, wanting to believe her, but reading her body language, which was cold and closed, it seemed that she was lying, using poor Leo as a way to make him stay. The image of her kissing Nick behind the church hall was still engraved on his memory.

He brushed past her and she flinched. 'I'll pop in and see Leo,' he said. 'Just get back to bed and out of my sight.'

But Leo was asleep, his face blotchy from crying and Mason ached to hold him as he had when he was a little boy, to make it all better and scare away the bogey man. But he knew it was too late.

***

The rest of the week passed in a flurry of extra rehearsals. The cast and crew were tired. Lola returned to the show and was gratefully embraced by her friends who tried to ignore the fading bruises on her face. Alex came with her to the Thursday and Friday rehearsals and professed himself impressed with her talent and also the high standard of the show.

'You're amazing, baby,' he told her in bed that night. 'I'm so proud of you.'

'Thanks…I'm so glad you were there.' Her arm was still sore but she gamely snuggled into his arms. 'Your parents get back on Sunday. I'll have to go home tomorrow.'

'I know,' he agreed miserably. 'I'm so used to you being here every morning when I wake up, it's going to be awful. What are we going to do?'

'My parents would never let you stay with me at home – and anyway, it wouldn't feel right.'

'I'll think of something. When you finish your exams, which drama school are you applying for?'

'I was thinking of RADA – but if you're going to Cambridge, I'd hardly ever see you. I might change my mind and apply to a university which offers a degree in the performing arts instead.'

'But you had set your heart on drama school. It would give you a better chance to make your name.'

Stage Struck

'You know, a few weeks ago I overheard Dad saying to Mum that I didn't have what it takes to be a great actress.' He tenderly stroked her flushed cheek with his hand. 'In my heart, I think he's probably right,' she said. 'If I took the other course, I could still act, but it would give me a better chance of a job as a drama teacher, among other things. So that's what I'm going to do. Then maybe we could share a house while we study – at least in the second year when they let you loose a bit more.'

'If you're sure that's what you want, it would be wonderful.' He kissed her. 'Since we only have one more morning to wake up like this, do you think we might discover a position which doesn't *hurt*?'

'I can think of one,' she smiled, 'like this…'

Stage Struck

Saturday 20th December

Mason woke early and stretched. Quietly he made his way to the bathroom and took a shower, after which he packed all his toiletries in a travel bag and returned to Lola's bedroom. He knew she'd be back that night, and since there was nowhere else for him to sleep – except the sofa, which he now viewed with disgust rather than affection, it was time to move out. He'd seen a nice two-bedroom flat a couple of doors from Winston's in The Brambles and made an offer. In the meantime, Winston had invited him to stay in his spare room.

So his agenda for the day was to move his clothes and breakable personal things to Winston's' place and to see an agent about putting the house on the market. He told Candy of his intentions and predictably she'd cried and wailed and begged his forgiveness.

He was sad that her ranting didn't touch his heart, but he now felt quite excited at the prospect of leading a single life again. He knew Lola understood. She'd been upset, but her love affair with Alex had softened the blow. Leo struggled with the idea of his parents splitting up and asked his father if he could live with him. Mason had told him that as he was seventeen he could choose, and would certainly be able to stay with either of his parents at any time. But Leo was angry, especially with his mother and called her a whore.

'Leo, don't let me ever hear you say such a thing again!' Mason shouted back at him. 'I don't doubt that some of the fault is mine – I've obviously failed her in some way – but, whatever the reasons, we can no longer live together. However, that doesn't give you the right to insult your mother like that.'

Fuming, Leo then left the house and cycled round to see Gillian, who quietly enjoyed the drama, but wisely kept her mouth shut.

Having packed his bags the night before, Mason now put them in the car. He stripped Lola's bed and remade it and left her room looking as normal as possible. Then, picking up his coat and briefcase, he left the house, gently shutting the door behind him.

He stood outside for a moment, waiting for a wall of regret to hit him – but it never came. He took a deep breath of damp, cool, fresh air and drove into the village for breakfast at the Inn on the Green.

Candy heard Mason moving around and knew what he was doing. She couldn't face him and buried her head in her pillow, disbelief washing over her in waves. Twenty years of marriage over – finished because of her stupidity. She staggered out of bed when she heard the click of the front door closing and watched from behind the net curtain as Mason drove away.

Wearily, she went down to the kitchen and made a mug of strong black coffee, but she couldn't face anything to eat. She sat looking round her home and knew that there were no options but to sell it. Mason had already found somewhere and she now needed to do the same. She knew she could have held out, demanded to keep the house as she still had two dependent children living with her – but there seemed very little point.

It was over. The week since the dreadful dinner dance fiasco had pushed everything forward at speed. The cracks in their marriage had become chasms and now there was no way back. She'd assumed that when she left Mason it would be at a time of her choosing when she moved in with Nick. Now the swine had left her and she had no-one.

Leo shuffled into the kitchen and made himself breakfast. He ignored her, and soon disappeared back to his room to turn on the radio; loud rock music filled the house.

Even her children were blaming her, she thought sadly, laying her head on her arms on the kitchen table.

She was still in that position when Lola found her an hour later.

'Mum! Are you all right?'

'Your father has left us.'

'No, Mum. He left *you*. I know - he just called on my mobile.'

'What are we going to do?' Candy whimpered.

'Personally, I'm going to pass my exams and then I've decided to apply to a university which does a BA in the performing arts. Alex is also changing his choices and looking for a law degree in the same university – or one close by.'

'Don't you care how I'm feeling? Can you only think about yourself?'

'Isn't that what you've been doing all these months you've been carrying on with Nick? Don't expect any sympathy from me, Mum. You blew it.' And she went to her room to begin studying with a renewed passion.

***

Sam replaced the phone with a soft whoop of excitement. Brian's mother Josie had asked if Ben could sleep over. 'They're playing a very complicated game,' Jo explained, 'and there were tears when I wanted to bring Ben home. It's the last day of term tomorrow – so if you can bear to be parted from him, he can stay and I'll take him to school with Brian in the morning.'

Stage Struck

'He can stay, thank you. As a matter of fact I'd love to be able to go out this evening…You're sure you don't mind?'

'Not at all. Ben's no bother, he's a good lad.'

'Thanks, Josie.' They hung up.

Wonderful, Sam thought, pounding up the stairs to shower and change – now I can surprise Nick and go over to watch the rehearsal tonight.

Twenty minutes later, she was on the road, heading towards Sipton, excited by the prospect of seeing Nick and, hopefully, spending the night with him. She'd barely been able to think of anything else since starting their affair. He was an erotic, sensual and intensely passionate lover who left her reeling. Her skin flushed at the memories she treasured and she murmured to herself, Oh, God, Nick, I want you…I want you!

The journey took half an hour, but at last she drove down the High Street and found a vacant parking space not far from the church. She tiptoed in through the side door and slipped unseen into the back of the church hall. The second act had just begun and she sat watching as Robin Hood, Hansel, Gretel and Mrs. Mixit made their way through the Magic Forest. Cut-outs of large trees were on the small stage and they were moved around by the punk baddies hiding behind them, trying to entrap the heroes and prevent them rescuing Lady Marian from the wicked witch.

It was a while before she saw Nick who was adjusting the sound equipment. An unearthly wailing came from the speakers and the children in the pantomime, dressed as little ghosts, ran on and off 'scaring' the characters on stage.

Mason stopped and re-started proceedings a couple of times until he was satisfied before Tom, the pantomime cat, scuttled onto the stage to lead his friends to safety.

Sam was puzzled. Clearly, the cat wasn't Candy but a rather large man. Briefly she wondered why the cast had been changed so late in the day, but just then Mason called a tea break and the cast gratefully gravitated to Patsy in her hatchway.

Shyly, Sam went up to Nick and tapped him on the shoulder. 'Hi…I hope you don't mind…'

'Mind?' He looked tired but delighted, and gave her a very unselfconscious hug. 'What a wonderful surprise. Where's Ben?'

'He's sleeping over with Brian.'

'Sleeping over? Then…' he raised his eyebrows and twinkled at her and she laughed and nodded. 'Oh, I wish we could leave here now, but I'll be about an hour.'

'That's fine. I want to see the show anyway. Rose!' she caught her cousin's sleeve as she walked by.

Stage Struck

'Sam! How lovely to see you.' Rose hugged Sam, gave Nick a tight smile and moved on. 'I'll catch you later, I have to speak to Lauren.'

'What happened to Candy?' Sam asked Nick, and he seemed startled.

'Candy?'

'She was going to be the cat.'

'Oh…I see.' He relaxed. 'Well, I think she and Mason had a major row and rumour has it they've separated. Winston has stepped in to take her place, even though he has only recently come out of hospital.'

'He was very funny.'

'Yes – I think we're all glad she's gone. Look out, here comes Mason.'

'Nick – can you check the sound tape again while the others are having coffee? Oh, hello, Sam.'

'Hello, how are the youngsters?'

'They're fine, thank you. Lola is over there somewhere, and Leo's just home from hospital.'

'What a relief. That was a terrible night.'

'Yes – we were both very grateful to you and Nick for getting us to the hospital.'

Sam thought Mason looked about ten years older than the last time she had seen him. She could imagine how awful she would feel if something happened to Ben – but then to have his marriage collapse and have to complete the production of the show at the same time, she could hardly imagine how terrible he must feel.

She felt deeply sorry for the poor man and decided to ask Nick whether they might invite Mason to join them for supper after the rehearsal. She watched as Nick went off to fix the recording of special effects, and wandered up to Rose, who was talking to John and Clive.

'I think it's going well, Rose,' she told her cousin. 'You were all excellent. Ben will love it when I bring him to see the show.'

'Thanks. I must admit we're all very tired, fitting in the extra rehearsals for Winston, but we're grimly determined that on Boxing Day the show will be as good as we can make it. Sam, what are you doing for Christmas?'

'I don't know for sure, but I hope to spend it with Nick and Ben.'

Rose led her gently away from the others. 'You're really smitten, aren't you?'

'Yes. He's wonderful – I never thought I could feel this way again after Josh died.'

'Just… I mean, don't get too…'

'What?'

'Nothing, Sam. I'm so glad for you.'

'Rose, is there something I should know?' Sam felt a quiver of anxiety pass through her and took her cousin's arm.

'No, no of course not; it's lovely to see you so happy again.'

'You would tell me, wouldn't you? For Ben's sake, I have to be sure this relationship is everything it seems to be.'

'I'm sure Nick is wildly in love with you. It's in his eyes and his body language.'

Sam had a feeling there was still a doubt hanging in the air, but rehearsal began again and she settled back to watch, trying to dispel her unease.

At the end, Nick mounted the stage to address the company.

'Don't forget, your presence would be much appreciated here tomorrow to finish the sets. We move into the theatre on Sunday, so all hands on deck please to help load the lorry here and then to move the set onto the Library Theatre stage. We'll be setting up for a technical rehearsal for Monday with full dress rehearsal on Tuesday. The first show's on Friday, Boxing Day afternoon with another in the evening. You'll be glad to know you get Thursday and Friday – that's Christmas Day – off to rest.' He received cheers, jeers and a few chuckles but soldiered on. 'There are two shows also scheduled for the twenty-seventh and then four shows the following weekend. It's going to be exhausting – but most of the tickets are now sold, so you can be sure of enthusiastic audiences. Right – everybody out of here and get some sleep.'

He jumped down from the stage and went straight to Sam. 'Come on, flower,' he murmured, 'let's go.'

'Whoa, Nick! We have all night and I wondered if we should ask Mason to come and have supper with us; he just looks so awful.'

Nick caught his breath and after a second shook his head. 'I'm sure he'll want to get back to Leo.'

'Nick, I'm starving and I don't suppose you've eaten either. Just an hour, please. We could pop into Pizza Hut or somewhere.'

'You wretch,' he grinned. 'All right – but just you and me.'

'No. These people are your friends and Mason looks almost in a state of collapse,' she said stubbornly.

Nick glanced at Mason, wondering how to divert Sam from what could be a catastrophic encounter. It was true he looked almost grey, but the last thing Nick could afford was for the three of them to chit-chat over supper.

'Okay. Stay there and I'll go and sound him out,' he told her. 'I suppose I should be grateful I've fallen in love with such a softie – but tonight I could wish you would save your sympathy for me. I'm tired and in need of a great deal of tender loving care.' He moved close to her, running a concealed hand up her thigh and she shivered.

'Stop it. Go and ask Mason – or I shan't be able to concentrate on you later for worrying about him.'

'That's blackmail,' he grumbled and reluctantly went over to Mason, glancing back at Sam to make sure she wasn't in earshot.

'Mason, will you be here for the theatre get-in?' he asked.

'Yes, of course I will.'

'You've been in overload this week – I'm sure we could manage without you.'

Mason shook his head. 'I'll be there.'

'Fine, if you're sure.' Nick turned away, but Mason called him back.

'By the way, I'm sure you'll be interested to know that Candy and I have separated – thanks to you. I'm staying with Winston for now, if you need to contact me.'

'Mason, I am truly sorry. I never meant…'

'She's all yours now, Nick. The field is clear.'

'I don't want her. It was all a flash in the pan, mate. Is there no way back?'

'No - absolutely not. So, you're going to ruin Sam's life now are you? Make a habit of this sort of thing, do you?' Anger flashed across Mason's face. 'Maybe she should be told exactly what you're really like.'

'I've tried for ages to drop Candy. She wouldn't let me go and she's still badgering me. Nearly every day I get phone calls and texts. I'm very sorry – really I am.'

'I wish I could believe you.' And he walked away, his fists clenched, and Nick had the distinct feeling that Mason had been aching to hit him.

Nick returned to Sam. 'He said thanks but no thanks – he's too tired. So let's go. I'll make you some supper at home.'

They left the hall, turning off the lights as they went, and Mason stood outside with the key in his hand waiting to lock up.

''Night, see you tomorrow,' said Nick, pulling Sam by the hand.

''Bye, Mason. Sorry you couldn't join us for supper,' she called over her shoulder and frowned at the confused expression on Mason's face.

They reached her car and Nick waited for her to get in. His Land Rover was parked further down the street. She peered up at him. 'You didn't ask him, did you, Nick?'

'No, I couldn't bear to share you. Forgive me?'

'I suppose so.'

'I'll make it up to you at home.' His hand cupped her face and he leaned through the open window and kissed her. 'I promise…and we'll see him another evening.'

'All right,' she whispered breathlessly. And she followed him home, aching for his love, but with just the faintest shadow hanging over her happiness.

Rose, John, Lauren and Clive decided to treat themselves to a late dinner at the Italian restaurant on the High Street. None of them had found time to eat and they were faint with hunger.

Lauren had been quiet all evening and Clive was concerned. 'What is it, Lauren?' he asked several times, but she had shaken her head and refused to talk.

'Tell you later.'

'Let's order some wine while we're choosing,' said John, perusing the menu. 'We can toast the success of the show.' He signalled a waiter and ordered a bottle of Chianti.

'I can't believe it's only a few days away. All these weeks of rehearsal and now it's almost show time,' said Rose. 'I'm terrified.'

'You'll love it,' smiled Clive. 'Once the curtain goes up and you have all those kids cheering you on, it's like the best champagne.'

'Can I ask you all something?' Lauren suddenly piped up. 'Would you come to my place for Christmas?'

'Yes, oh, yes that would be lovely – thank you,' said Rose, and John and Clive echoed her words. But Lauren was sitting with tears in her eyes, and she covered her face with her napkin. Clive put his arms around her while John and Rose glanced at each other in concern.

'What is it, Lauren – whatever is wrong?'

Lauren took a few seconds to calm herself, then told them. 'You're my best friends – the people I love most in the world. You all know that for the past few weeks I've been trying to trace my mother. Well, today I heard that she has been traced – but she's dead. I left it too late. Now I'll never have a family of my own.'

She wiped her eyes and tried to smile. 'So I want to spend Christmas with you guys because I know if you were all my family I couldn't love you more.'

'Oh, Lauren, I'm so sorry.' Rose took her friend's hand across the table. 'Did you find out anything else?'

Stage Struck

'No. They said they will try to discover if there are any other relatives but Mary – that was her name, never tried to trace me. There's nothing on the register of people trying to trace adopted children and she died of leukaemia a couple of years ago. There's no way of knowing who my father might have been, so I guess that's that. Poor little mongrel.' She sniffed and smiled through her tears. 'Right – that's that dealt with, so don't let's talk about it any more. We have Christmas to look forward to, and then the show. You know, I hate to say it, but I think Winston is going to be a great deal better than Candy.'

'I think he's amazing,' agreed John, accepting that Lauren wanted to change the subject. 'It's not too much for him after being so ill is it, Rose?'

'No. I think it will be the best thing for him. He mustn't lift things or run a marathon, but being in the show is the perfect antidote to his depression.'

'I expect Mason and Candy are feeling depressed too,' Clive said sadly. 'Christmas is a horrendous time of year if you're alone, and there are obviously huge problems between them. But this year we four will be together, so here's a toast to Lauren for suggesting it.'

'Thanks. Tomorrow I shall decorate my little tree and on Christmas Day cook an enormous turkey.'

'I'll bring the pudding and brandy butter,' volunteered Clive.

'Mince pies and Christmas cake from me,' piped up Rose

'Wine, chocolates, nuts and oranges…and anything else that tempts me in *Tesco*'s' said John. 'Oh, and a huge bone for Bugsy.'

'Do you think,' Rose asked thoughtfully, 'we might all go to my kids' ward on Christmas morning? We could go in costume and sing them some songs from the show.'

'Oh, yes!' cried Lauren, 'I could leave the turkey in the oven; there'd be plenty of time. But don't we need a Father Christmas?'

'I think,' smiled Rose, 'I know just the person.'

They ordered their meal and an hour later Lauren and Rose left in one car and Clive and John in the other.

'Wouldn't you like to spend the night with Clive?' Rose asked Lauren on the way home. 'I'm sure he's only waiting to be asked.'

'Not tonight. I just want to be on my own for a while. I guess it's a kind of mourning for the mother I'll never know. Stupid, really. I mean, I took all this time before even bothering to find her – telling myself she didn't matter to me. Now I know she's dead, I feel… lonely, bereft. Cheated. I don't understand.'

Stage Struck

'I do. I suppose I feel the same about my father – especially cheated. I trusted his integrity implicitly – and it was a pile of ashes in the end.'

***

Winston went home feeling tired, but content. The flat no longer oppressed him and he liked having Mason around. Although the urge to have a drink came over him sometimes, he felt reasonably in control, having only called his AA 'buddy' twice since joining.'

He knew that being included in the show had helped enormously but he did fear what he would feel like when it was over and he had nothing else to focus on. He also missed Maureen. His friend and sparring partner for so many years, she had bullied and cajoled him during the time she stayed with him. A week had stretched to almost three, although she had gone back to work after the first few days. He almost dared to hope that she might want to stay, but he just couldn't pluck up the courage to ask her. The evenings had been companionable, playing cards, watching television and arguing fiercely over politics – for they stood firmly on either side of the political spectrum – and to wake and hear Maureen singing along to Radio Two as she organised breakfast had made him feel safe and cared for.

He had been to see his solicitor and drawn up a new will which, he thought with satisfaction, would give his children a suitably nasty shock when he did finally get to meet his Maker. He realised that he no longer hoped that it would be soon.

Suddenly life had meaning again. The dark depression had gone. He knew he was a lucky man; he had survived his heart problem and been re-united with his friends in SADS. Now he had to find a way to lead a useful life again.

Just as he was about to go to bed, the phone rang and he turned and viewed it with suspicion. Who would call so late? Possibly one of his horrible children. Or maybe, he thought hopefully, it might be Maureen, checking he'd arrived home safely. After several rings, he nervously picked it up.

'Hello?'

'Winston, it's Rose. I'm sorry to call so late but I have a huge favour to ask of you.'

'Really? Well, my dear, for you, anything.'

'It's not exactly for me – it's for the children on my ward. I wondered whether you'd be willing to play Father Christmas on Christmas morning?'

'Father Christmas? Goodness me, I've never played that role before.' He chuckled, delighted.'

'It's just that you could do it with character. I thought maybe we could all go along and do a song or two from the show for them. Poor little things, they'll be in hospital on the most exciting day of the year... What do you think?'

'I think it's a splendid idea! How many presents shall I buy – how many boys and how many girls?'

'Oh, you don't have to buy the presents, the hospital has a fund for things like that and lots of toys are donated by the friends of the hospital. No, we just want your talent to entertain.'

'I would be delighted. Thank you for asking me, Rose.'

'That's wonderful. And I'm so glad you're in the show – everyone says it wouldn't be the same without you.'

'It's a good job I don't have lines to learn at such short notice,' he laughed. 'Even I can meow on cue.'

'I'll see you tomorrow – sleep well, 'bye, Winston.'

'Goodnight, Rose – and God Bless.' As he lowered the receiver, he realised those were the words he had used every night to his own children after reading them stories and tucking them in. What happy days those had been.

He got ready for bed, thinking about all those poor children in hospital, not just at Christmas but every day of the year. The germ of an idea was beginning to grow.

***

Nick groaned as he watched Sam dress. 'Don't leave me,' he pleaded. 'I shall die if you don't come back to bed.'

Sam giggled, 'Sorry, lover, your time's up. I have to go before my carriage turns back into a pumpkin. I also have to work in the morning and host a school Christmas party for my tiny tots.' She leaned over and kissed him passionately, a serious expression on her face. 'Nick, I'm in love with you, and feeling incredibly vulnerable. I'm scared of losing what we have.'

'Well, that makes two of us, flower. We need to talk seriously about where we go from here because I simply can't bear you disappearing in the middle of the night like this. I want to go to sleep with you and wake up with you for the rest of my life.'

'It's too soon for that.'

'Because of Ben?'

'Yes – and we've still only known each other a few weeks. This is the sort of love affair you're supposed to have when you're young; it's exciting and sexy and overwhelming. I'm scared stiff one of us will wake up one morning and find the spell has been broken. That none of this is what it seems.'

'You mean you're afraid that I'm not what I seem?'

'Are you?'

'Yes – yes, I promise you that what you see is what you get; a man who is helplessly in love with you and who wants to be with you forever.'

She smiled, reassured and after a final kiss she left quietly.

Nick had gone to the bedroom window to watch her drive away. A frisson of foreboding ran like ice through his veins as he returned to bed.

This evening had been an unexpected bonus. After the minor hiccup when Sam had wanted to invite Mason to join them for supper, he'd pulled out all the stops to give her a night to remember, telling her over and over how much he loved her. And it was true. To his everlasting amazement, the feelings he had for her grew stronger all the time. She had become an obsession and he had difficulty thinking about anything else. During the day his thoughts would return to her and he'd have to drag his mind back to business. At night, it was even worse. He would lie awake, suffering agonies of frustration, remembering her body next to his. Somehow, he had to dissolve her reservations, become best friends with Ben, and persuade Sam that they should at least live together and preferably marry.

After tossing and turning for half an hour he wandered downstairs and while the kettle boiled he looked around his immaculate house. He knew it would be difficult to cope with the trappings of a small boy; piles of toys, sticky fingers on the furniture, and simply having someone else to consider when all he wanted was to be alone with Sam. But the alternative was an empty feeling, a cold loneliness he had never experienced before, in spite of living alone for most of his adult life.

Now, back in bed, he sipped a mug of warm tea and he glanced at the alarm clock. Sam would just about be home, he calculated, and he called her number from the bedside phone.

She answered breathlessly, 'Hello?'

'It's me.'

'Hi,'

He could sense her smile.

'I just came through the door. Missing me already?'

'Yes – and I can't bear it. Can I take you and Ben out for the day tomorrow – I thought maybe London Zoo?'

'I thought you had to finish the set – all those people coming to help you, remember?'

'Damn! I forgot.'

'I suppose Ben and I could come and help too. I'm a dab hand with a paintbrush, and then you could come for dinner afterwards. If it goes well, perhaps you could stay over and leave early to arrange the theatre get-in?'

'If it goes well?'

'If Ben is comfortable with it. He's old enough to know I don't usually entertain men in my bedroom.'

'Glad to hear it. All right – I'll see you at the church hall any time after nine-thirty on Saturday morning. I love you.'

'I hope so. 'Night, Nick.'

He switched out the light and buried his face in the sheets where she had been laying, breathing in the lingering scent of her. Being in love was torture.

Sam put the phone down with a smile and made a mug of cocoa. If only that little niggling feeling would go away – that unquantifiable something. There was a reservation in Rose, she could just sense it and she didn't think it could be jealousy. Rose was obviously dating the handsome American and anyway Nick was far too old for her little cousin. But since Rose was such a sunny person who rarely took exception to anyone, Sam couldn't understand why she plainly didn't like Nick.

She'd also been mildly upset at Nick's deception when he had tried to fool her into believing he had asked Mason to eat with them that evening. He wanted her to himself, that much was plain. He should have simply refused to ask Mason at all, rather than tell her a lie.

No-one's perfect, she told herself. I'm a typical Virgo; an idealist and expect perfection in others. Be realistic, Sam, or you will end up a lonely old woman. But Josh had never lied to her. Why, oh, why did he have to die? She sighed, switching off the lights as she went upstairs.

Quite a crowd turned up to paint the remaining parts of the set. Nick's own boring task was to fix new wheels on all the trees for the Magic Forest because they swivelled too much, like those on a wayward supermarket trolley, raising the nightmare scenario of one of them careering off the stage into the audience. Then there was the backdrop for the village scene to be finished. Lauren was assigned to that.

Several flats for the Warthogs Castle needed a second coat of black paint. Rose was busily engaged with that when Sam popped her head round the corner and whispered urgently, 'Please, come to the front of the church – I really need a word with you.'

Rose downed her brush and, making a vague excuse to Mason about needing the loo, she joined Sam in the church foyer.

'Hi! Where's Ben?'

'Gone to spend his pocket money in the sweet shop. He'll be back in a few minutes.'

'What's the matter?'

Sam drew a deep breath, then said, 'I want to know if I'm imagining the fact that you have something against Nick.'

Rose's stomach lurched. This was a conversation she had been dreading. 'Nick? Well, nothing really. Apparently, he has a bad reputation with women in general. I don't want to see you get hurt, that's all.'

'What do you mean – a bad reputation?'

Rose was flustered. 'I just mean – Oh, you know, he's known as a flirt and ladies' man. Apparently. He used to have a string of glamorous arm-candy girlfriends.'

'Talking of Candy, she dropped some pretty heavy hints when we met at the dinner dance.'

'Candy is a bitch. She and Mason have split up.'

'I know, Nick told me.'

'Where did you meet him?' Rose asked. 'I wouldn't have expected your social paths to cross.'

'Strictly between ourselves, through a dating agency.'

'A dating agency! Why would Nick need a dating agency? I'd have thought he could take his pick of a dozen girls any day of the week. Come to think of it, Sam, why did *you* go to a dating agency?'

'Usual reason, I guess; it's hard for single mums to meet anyone. I thought I'd try it for a few months and Nick was the third date – and the only one I would have ever considered. And, like you, I've wondered why he used Meet Your Match.'

'Odd.'

'I love him, Rose. I've been so happy the past few weeks and I never expected to feel like this again. But I have to know I can trust him. Even if there was something he didn't want me to know at first, I now need to know that he can tell me, whatever the consequences. He has to be honest with me. I can't stand deception and there's something he isn't telling me, I can just feel it. Already Ben is very attached to him and I dread him getting hurt if Nick and I split up. He isn't married, is he, or separated?'

'No, I've never heard rumours about that. On the contrary, he's reputed to have a pathological fear of matrimony. Give it a little while, Sam. Maybe if there is something he

Stage Struck

hasn't told you, it's because he's scared of losing you. Give him a chance to get round to it. But you have to accept that a bloke like him doesn't get to his forties with a lily-white past.'

'No – I do know that, but he really seems to want to settle down now. He's talking about us moving in together and so on. I do believe he cares for me. But it wouldn't be enough if he's keeping something important from me.'

'Have you asked him?'

'Indirectly – but he just smothers me in love and kisses and takes my mind off it,' she giggled. 'And honestly, Rose, he knows how to do that in spades.'

I can imagine, thought Rose wryly, he's had a lot of practise. 'Well, I should give it a week or two and create a few opportunities for him to tell you. If he doesn't, then you have to pin him down and ask. Don't get too drawn into long-term plans until you're satisfied.'

'I'm so scared - that something's going to burst my bubble.'

Rose gave her a hug and felt like Judas. Her instinct was to tell Sam about Nick's affair with Candy, but she couldn't bring herself to do it. The poor girl was so happy and Rose felt enraged with Nick. 'Take it a day at a time,' she said firmly and decided that the only thing she could do to help would be to talk to Nick. She must convince him that he had no choice but to come clean to Sam if he wanted to keep her. She just hoped that she wasn't saving Sam from heartbreak now, only to set her up for it later.

'Hello, Rose.' The small boy came bounding up to her and grabbed her hand.'

'Hello, Ben. Come on – we'll go and find the others.' She drew him and Sam round the back of the church where the rest of the group were still beavering away.

'Look who I found,' she called. 'Another helping hand.'

'Two helping hands,' chimed in Leo as he walked up behind them, and everyone rushed to surround him and welcome him back.

'Hello, Sam – is this your boy?'

'Yes. Ben, this Leo.'

'Ah, Leo,' Nick greeted him when the hubbub died away. 'Since you're still clean, could you go down the road to the DIY shop for a tin of black emulsion please? We're getting low.'

'If you like,' Leo said ungraciously, with a glance at Mason, who shrugged and nodded his consent.

'Thanks. Here's some money from the kitty.'

Leo snatched the notes from Nick and pocketed them. He turned to Ben. 'Do you want to walk down the road with me - if your mother doesn't mind?'

Ben eyed his mother hopefully.

'No – I don't, if you don't,' said Sam, amused. Ben was so confident these days and growing up fast. A year ago he would have clung to her legs in the face of half a dozen people he didn't know.

Leo placed a hand on Ben's shoulder and led the boy down the street.

When they reappeared half an hour later Ben had tomato sauce all round his mouth and professed to like his new friend, who had treated him to a burger and chips at McDonald's.

'He was hungry,' grinned Leo with a shrug.

'He's always hungry,' said Sam with a tender smile at her son. 'Thank you, Leo. That was kind. I'm so glad to see you fully recovered.'

'Thanks. I still get a few headaches, but we were all very lucky. Thank God you saw us that night in the blizzard. You went back to fetch my parents, didn't you?'

'Well, yes. Nick spotted the car overturned in the hedgerow.'

Ben sat listening open-mouthed, having been told nothing of this. 'Nick and Mum saved your life? Did they really?'

'In a way.'

'So you do like Nick, then. I thought you said you hated the bastid when we walked down the road?'

'I'm sorry, Ben, I was just talking to myself.' Leo looked embarrassed. 'I forgot you were there.'

The set was finished and the weary workers made their way to the pub or to their homes. Sam and Ben said their farewells and Nick hugged them both, saying he would see them later for supper.

Rose watched Sam drive away before calling Nick over to her. 'Can I have a word?'

'Of course – can I buy you a drink?'

'No thanks. It won't take long. Just come into the props store where we can be private.'

Nervously, he followed her and perched on the edge of an old table as she shut the door and stood facing him.

'What can I do for you?' he asked, knowing before she spoke what she was going to say.

'You're seeing my cousin. I gather it's a serious relationship. At least for her it is.'

'And I promise you, Rose, it is for me too. I'm besotted.'

'She doesn't know you've been having an affair with your friend's wife, or that you're responsible for their marriage break-up.'

He blanched. 'Are you going to tell her? It's been over for weeks, since before I met Sam. Although Candy has been very upset about it. I promise you, I love Sam and I wouldn't hurt her for the world.'

'Maybe so.' She looked askance at him. 'Sam has had a terrible time since Josh died. We all loved her husband dearly and I can tell you he's a hard act to follow. She seems to think you might be the one to do it. However, she knows something is being hidden from her and, if you're not honest with her, she'll drop you like the proverbial hot potato. And she's within an ace of finding out.'

He lowered his eyes, embarrassed and frightened. 'What can I say…?'

'I think you're a first-class shit, Nick,' she interrupted icily, 'but she loves you and I don't want to see her hurt. So either you come clean with her this weekend - or I will.'

And without giving him a chance to reply, she walked out and slammed the door.

Nick sat there stunned and knew she was right. After a moment's thought, he tidied away the remaining debris from the set, locked the shed and went home, calling in at a florist on the way to order a huge bouquet of flowers to be sent to Sam.

He would tell her tonight after dinner – get it all out in the open and hope that she would understand. He felt sick with anxiety that she might not.

***

On their way home, Sam and Ben got stuck in traffic that was heading for a football match and the little boy was soon bored. They played 'I spy' and counted red cars and had spelling tests. But still the traffic crawled and Sam was running out of ideas to entertain him. She had been wondering all the way how to broach how Ben perceived Leo's comment about hating Nick, but eventually he brought it up himself. 'Why does Leo hate Nick?'

'I don't know, darling. Did he say anything else? '

'Well sort of, but it didn't make any sense.'

'Why? Tell me what he said.'

'Well – see, he wasn't really talking to me. He was sort of muttering and saying rude words under his breath, like he didn't see why he should go and get the paint. But…well, what does "screwing" mean? I know it means screwing in screws and things, but Leo said, "I hate you Nick, you bastid." What's a bastid?'

'I think he meant bastard, darling. It's a very rude word you're grown-up enough to hear, but not grown-up enough to use. Understand?'

'Yes, Mummy.'

'But what has that got to do with screwing?' she asked, puzzled as she finally turned into their driveway.

'Leo said something like, "I hate you, you bastid – bastard - you've been screwing my mother".'

***

Candy was well into her second glass of white wine, watching the late afternoon film on Channel Five. She had spent the morning house hunting and found a small Victorian terrace which had been tastefully re-furbished. She was sickened by how much it cost, and it wasn't even in a particularly nice street. Mason had told her he had made an offer on a flat in The Brambles, and since today there had been a viewing of the house, she knew her days there were numbered. She could hardly believe the changes she was going to have to adjust to. Neighbours she could hear through the wall – and worse they would be able to hear her. No driveway for the car, no en suite bathroom and a kitchen you couldn't swing a cat in.

She knew in her heart it was her own fault, but she still felt a burning hatred for Nick – and an ongoing yearning for the swine. Why wouldn't it go away, this feeling? Why, in spite of his cruelty to her, did she still dream about him? Why did she ache to feel his glorious hands on her body and relive the amazing heights he had taken her to in bed?

'He's a bloody demon,' she sighed, remembering the incredibly erotic things he had said and done. Things she had never experienced before and which still stirred her. And now he was saying and doing them to someone else. Candy was almost physically sick at the thought.

Just as she was pouring a third glass of wine the phone rang, causing her to start violently and slop wine down her clothes.

'Bugger,' she muttered, grabbing the receiver. 'Hello?'

'Candy?'

'Yes, who is this?'

'I expect you'll remember me. It's Sam.'

'Good God.' Speak of the devil, she thought. 'Well, what can I do for you?'

'I know it's an absolute cheek to call you – but I wondered if you'd mind confirming whether or not you're having an affair with Nick.'

Sam's voice wobbled, and for a brief second Candy felt a pang of sympathy for her. 'Who told you that?'

'That doesn't really matter.'

'Well, yes, I'm afraid I am. It's why Mason and I split up. Sorry.'

Only silence from the other end.

'You see,' she continued, improvising, 'Nick decided to find himself a pretend girlfriend to tote around in public to avoid any suspicion about him and me because one or two people in our circle were beginning to smell a rat.'

'I see. Is that why he went to a dating agency?' Sam asked in a small voice.

'Dating? Yes.' Candy was thinking fast. A dating agency – so that's how he did it. Now it was beginning to fall into place. 'It was an obvious way to find someone who didn't already know him and who wouldn't realise they were being used.'

There was a muffled sob from the other end of the phone and she decided it was time to go in for the kill.

'I'm sorry, Sam. I'm afraid you must prepare yourself for the worst. Now that Mason and I have split up, there's no need for the subterfuge. We're just giving my children time to get used to the idea, and then Nick and I will move in together. I expect he had you completely fooled because I know he's a very convincing liar and, to be honest, the man's a bastard.' She gave a sigh and studied her fingernails. 'I really don't know why I love him so much.'

'I can't believe it,' Sam whispered.

'He's a philanderer, there's no denying that. But you see, I know what I'm taking on. I'll have him at any price, Sam. He may play away sometimes, because that's what he's like; but at the end of the day he'll always come back to me, and that's all I care about.' She grinned and shifted in her seat, loving her moment. 'Tell me, when he was making love to you – and I know he did because he described it to me in delicious detail – did he call you "flower"?'

The receiver at the other end went down with a bang.

Candy smiled grimly. Revenge was supposed to be sweet – but, to her surprise, it had a bitter after-taste.

Sam packed bags for her and Ben, hid the Christmas presents in a pillow case in the boot of her car and asked Mrs Evans to look after Pebbles the hamster. She worked on autopilot, trying to keep her distress to herself, although she was simply longing to scream and cry and shout. She really had no idea where she was going until a few minutes before leaving when she suddenly realised that her parent's house in St. Albans would be empty. They were staying with a friend in Nantes – and Sam had a key.

Knowing she'd be welcome to use the house she had grown up in, she set off, leaving strewn around the garden the huge bouquet which had arrived with a message reading, 'To the only one I've ever loved'.

Stage Struck

Nick arrived at Sam's house at seven o'clock as arranged. He opened the front gate, expecting Ben to be at the door waiting for him. But the house was in darkness, Sam's car had gone and there were red roses strewn all over the front step. A white bow was caught on a bush, twirling in the breeze, and the little card with his message had been torn to pieces and scattered on the path.

It seemed that Rose had not kept her word and given him a chance to talk to Sam. He felt ill and sat on the step, trying to catch his breath. He wondered whether to wait. Perhaps she'd come back. Somehow, he didn't hold out much hope.

He saw a curtain twitch next door and he stood up signalling to Mrs Evans to open her window, which she did with a knowing smile on her face.

'Have you any idea when Sam will be back?' he asked, trying to sound nonchalant.

'Not till after Christmas,' she said, adding self-importantly, 'I've got the kiddy's hamster to look after.'

'I don't suppose you know where I can contact her? It's very important.'

'No. She never said. Upset, she was.'

'Thanks.' He went back to his car and sat for a long time wondering how on earth he would cope with life without her.

As the bells of St. Albans Abbey struck nine, Sam tucked up Ben in the spare room at his grandparents' house. She stared at the flickering television unseeingly and cast aside an unread magazine of her mother's.

At midnight she went to bed in her old room and tried to sleep, but all she could do was weep into her pillow and storm about what a fool she had been. She writhed in anguish at the idea of Nick in bed with Candy – and presumably arousing the horrible creature by telling her about the way he'd made love – no, had sex - with Sam. What a revolting thing to do.

Stage Struck

Sunday 21st December

At nine o'clock an early mist still hung over the quiet High Street. Mason opened up the church hall and the side gate, waiting for the local man-with-a-van to arrive. Fred always moved their sets in and out of theatre for a reasonable price, plus a pub lunch and a couple of free tickets to the show. Predictably, his large van rumbled into sight just as Rose and Lauren arrived, closely followed by John, Clive and a couple of others from the cast. There was no sign of Nick, so they began to load the van with stacks of flats which, being made largely of canvas, were light though awkward to manoeuvre, together with props and the group's own small stock of spotlights.

By ten o'clock the van was ready to go, but since they didn't have access to the theatre for another hour, Fred parked and went with Mason and most of the crew to a small café for breakfast. Rose decided to wash her hands after the loading and when she came out of the Ladies John was waiting for her in the church foyer.

'Come and look at the church,' he said, taking her hand. 'It's all decorated for Christmas and it's very beautiful.'

'I'd rather not,' she said, glancing at the internal, glass double doors which members of the church were opening up for the morning service. 'I've never been able to go into a church since that day.'

'If I come with you, and we just go through the door a little way... See how you feel? I promise, if it's too much for you, we'll come straight back out.'

For a moment she struggled with the desire to turn and run. Her heart rate soared and she went very pale, so much so that John put his arms around her and held her gently.

'I'm sorry, honey; I should never have mentioned it. Let's go for breakfast with the others.'

She shook her head. 'No. You're right. I should face it out, because every time I come here for rehearsals and I have to walk across the foyer past the entrance to the church, I feel sick. It's a blight on my life and I know that I won't really recover from all the trauma until I face it. It's ridiculous.'

'No, it isn't. It was a terrible experience.' He took her to sit on a bench seat in the foyer almost opposite the church entrance so she could see the flowers around the door. 'But I want you to be whole again and able to forgive your father so you can be at ease with him. Let the past go – let him rest in peace.'

'Don't you think he can?'

'Who knows? Maybe he's just longing for you to say you forgive him, and that you still love him. Hate is so destructive.'

Rose began to cry and John held her as she sobbed against his chest. The elderly Minister approached and asked gently if he could help.

'Maybe later, thank you,' John said.

At last Rose's sobs subsided and she dived back into the Ladies to blow her nose and rinse her face. When she came out, John was talking to Mr. Stevens, the Minister, who came over to her and took her hands.

'My dear – your friend told me briefly what happened to you and I do so hope I can help.'

'If you mean can you pray for me – well, yes. I haven't been able to pray for myself since my father died. Nor for anyone else.'

'That, certainly. But you know you don't have to go into a church to be with God and for sure He understands what you're going through. Have a chat with Him – just try it and see what happens. Maybe He'll show you the way.'

With a nod and a brief smile, she took John's hand and together they went outside to walk slowly down the High Street. 'I'm sorry I upset you,'

'It was only because you cared,' she said, squeezing his hand tightly.

'I do care – so much.'

'I know.' She struggled to compose herself, longing to tell him that she loved him too, but she knew she would just burst into tears again, and feared that he might think the words had simply sprung from her emotional state. So she contented herself with reaching up gently to kiss his cheek as they walked along. 'Me, too,' she whispered, and he smiled contentedly.

The cast and crew arrived at the Library Theatre as the caretaker was opening the doors and by lunchtime everything was inside, stacked around the stage. They took a quick break for a pub snack, after which Fred drove off in his van, and they re-grouped to try to work out what went where.

'Where the hell is Nick?' fumed Mason. 'Today of all days – and not even a phone call. He isn't answering at home, so I've no idea what he's playing at.'

Rose was also concerned, wondering whether her threat to Nick had anything to do with his absence. She took Lauren, Clive and John aside and told them what had happened, so John decided to drive round to Nick's house to see if he was all right.

'Did you tell Sam about Nick and Candy?' Lauren asked her.

'No, of course not. I promised him the weekend to tell her the truth.'

Stage Struck

'Perhaps we should call Sam,' Lauren suggested. 'Maybe they're together after a passionate resolution of the whole problem.'

'That's a good idea.' Rose fished out her phone and called first Sam's home number, to which there was no reply, and then her mobile, which was switched off. 'They've both gone to ground,' she said. 'What on earth is going on?'

John arrived at Nick's just in time to see him emerging from the house and walking towards his Land Rover.

'Hey, Nick, are you all right? We were real worried about you.'

'Migraine. I had a lot of pills last night and they knocked me out. Sorry – I'm on my way.'

'Do you want a lift? It's pointless taking two cars and someone can drop you home later.'

'Thanks – that might be for the best.'

Nick knew, and John guessed from the whisky fumes, he was probably still well over the limit after the half bottle of scotch he had single-handedly consumed the night before. He avoided conversation on the short trip – grunting in reply to a couple of trivial comments John made, and both of them were very glad to arrive at the theatre.

'Sorry – everyone,' he said, shooting a vitriolic glance at Rose. 'Migraine pills knocked me for six. You've done a grand job so far; let's get the flats in place. Clive, can you and John get the village backcloth straightened out? We'll fly that first.'

He began to wind down a bar from the fly tower overhead and when it was at waist height they all helped to attach the backcloth by means of the dozen or so ties along its length. 'Right – raise it up, would you, Mason?'

And before their eyes, the Keepumlarfin village street scene, designed and mostly painted by Lauren, unfolded before them.

'It's fantastic, Lauren,' said a proud Clive.

Once that had been wound up out of the way into the fly tower above them, they began to arrange the flats and prop them up with stage weights, and before long most of the basics were in place.

Mason paced anxiously. 'We're cutting it fine, Nick. Are you going to be ready for technical rehearsal?'

'Yes. Roger and Paul – they'll be running the lights and sound desk - are due here in a few minutes. We'll stay and get them rigged as far as we can. You can all go. Thanks.'

'Right.' Mason walked away and dismissed the others. 'Thanks everybody – you've done a great job. Technical rehearsal tomorrow evening. No costumes or music, we'll just be working

Stage Struck

out scene changes, lighting and sound cues. Full dress rehearsal Tuesday, when Barbara will be here with her little musical quartet. Go home now and get some rest – see you tomorrow.'

While they began to disperse Rose went back into the theatre to see Nick.

'Nick, do you know where Sam is? I can't reach her.'

'She's gone. I don't now where she is and I'm nearly out of my mind with worry. What did you say to her?' he demanded furiously.

'Me? I haven't seen her or spoken to her since she left yesterday with Ben. I thought you were seeing her last night for supper.'

'Oh.' He sat down on the edge of the stage. 'I'm sorry. Well, someone must have said something because the flowers I sent her were thrown all over the garden when I got there last night, and a neighbour said she'd packed the car and gone away for Christmas.'

'Who else might have said something?' asked Rose.

'Candy, I suppose. But she doesn't have a phone number for Sam.'

'Then I have no idea. She hasn't been in contact with me. Perhaps she's gone to her parents. But no, they're away in France over Christmas.'

'If she does call you, Rose, please try to tell her I was on my way to explain things, to tell her about Candy. I know I should've done it in the first place. I thought she might not let me get past first base if she knew I'd been involved with a married woman. Then it got more and more difficult to tell her as time went on. I got more and more afraid of losing her. And now it's too late.'

'You're right; you should have been honest with her. She's not a naive little fool and she would have understood if only you'd told her at the beginning.'

'I don't know what to do.'

'Well, she has to come back to her house eventually so I should just give her time to cool down and then see what she has to say.'

'Yes, thanks, Rose.' As she made to leave, he gently grabbed her arm. 'And if she calls you…?'

'I'll do my best.'

John was waiting for Rose outside.

'Sam's done a bunk,' she told him. 'Obviously she got wind of what he's really like. But I do feel a bit sorry for him now. I think he really loves her – but he's an idiot.'

'Yeah, honey, love makes idiots of most men.' He grinned and she playfully punched his arm. 'Hungry?' he asked.

'Starving.'

'Let's drive out of town – there's a nice restaurant by the lock.'

'Sounds a bit posh. Can we change first?'

'Sure, I'll drop you off and come back when I'm also sweet and fragrant.'

They drove down the High Street where the doors to the church were flung open as early worshippers arrived for evening service.

She touched John's arm. 'Can you stop a minute?'

He pulled into a space opposite the church and Rose sat watching for a while, steeling herself. Then she opened the door and got out of the car, leaning on it for support.

John came round to join her and held her hand. 'There's no rush, Rose.'

'There is. Suddenly there is. Will you come with me?'

Together, they crossed the road and walked slowly through the heavy oak outer doors to stand in the foyer. The organ was playing as people chatted to their friends and made their way to their favourite pews, and then the kindly Minister was at her elbow.

'Ah, Rose,' said Reverend Stevens.

Despite her misgivings, she was impressed that he not only recognised her but also remembered her name. Her mouth was too dry to speak but she smiled in response.

'Reverend,' John nodded.

'Would you like to sit at the back for a while? You can leave any time you want to. I'll make sure the glass door is left open for you.'

Mutely, she nodded and, gripping John's hand as if her life depended on it, she walked the few yards to the nearest pew and gratefully slid into it. Her hands were shaking, but she took a deep breath and fought down the panic.

The Minister moved away from them and walked down the aisle to the vestry doors as the last few members of the congregation found their places and the organ struck a chord. The people rose to their feet and the choir processed from the back of the church singing 'Lord of all Hopefulness, Lord of all Light,' and Rose found the words coming back to her without the need to glance at the hymn book John was holding in front of her. She sang along in a small voice and gradually she felt calmer and more in control.

Reverend Stevens climbed to his pulpit and prayers were said, for the world, for each other, for the church's embattled mission in Zimbabwe – and 'for our new friend Rose, that she may find peace again in the love of God.'

And in that moment, she did.

***

Sam thought she'd never experienced such pain since Josh's death, and she could barely move from her bed until ten-thirty that morning, when poor Ben came in to ask for something to eat.

'What's the matter, Mummy? Are you ill?'

'No, darling, but you're old enough to understand that I'm very upset with Nick, and I don't want to see him or talk to him.'

'Isn't he our friend any more?'

'No. No, he isn't. I'm sorry if you're disappointed.'

'A bit. I'm hungry. Can we have breakfast and go and feed the ducks?'

Kids are so pragmatic, she thought. At least Ben wasn't in shreds over the wretched man.

She took a shower, plastered some make-up over her blotchy face.

They went to the coffee shop at Morrisons for a snack and to buy some bread for the ducks in the park.

It was a cool, sunny day and as she and Ben wandered around the beautiful lake in Verulam Park, she thought back to happy childhood days here. Picnics with her friends and with Rose and her parents. As a teenager, she'd played tennis in the public courts and walked with her first boyfriend through the wooded pathway around the Roman wall. How simple life had been then.

She wondered whether she should call Rose, but for the moment she just wanted to lick her wounds in private and find a way to put Nick-bloody-Harrow behind her.

She sat on a bench and was watching Ben running away from a swan which wanted more than its share of his bread, when a voice behind her asked, 'Samantha – is it really you?'

Turning, she squinted into the sun to see who was speaking.

'Cathy? I don't believe it.' She rose and hugged her old school friend. 'What are you doing here? I thought you'd moved to Australia.'

'I did, blue.' Cathy chuckled, putting on a broad accent. 'But I missed old Blighty and I'm back for three weeks to stay with Adam, my brother. You remember him!''

'I do,' laughed Sam. 'I was so in love with him when I was fifteen. Where's… um… what was your husband's name?'

'Greg. I'm afraid I lost him in Walkabout Creek. The bloke was just so unhygienic. But I like Oz, so as I have my own business I'm allowed to stay and it's okay for the time being. But I'll probably drift back here in a year or two – the British blokes at least don't call you Sheila and treat you like shit.'

'That's a matter of opinion,' said Sam bitterly.

'Blimey, that was loaded.'

Stage Struck

'Yes, it was. Believe me, getting back into the dating game as a single mum is a nightmare. I wish I'd never bothered.'

'Do tell,' Cathy coaxed her. 'Look, we've got lots to catch up on – why don't you come back to Adam's place for a bite of lunch. He's cooking, and I saw enough spuds going in the oven to feed the five thousand. That your boy?'

'Yes, that's Ben.'

'Hi, Ben. You hungry – and do you like roast lamb?'

An enthusiastic nod affirmed that, and the three of them walked the short distance through the park, past the glorious cathedral, to Adam's terraced Victorian house in nearby College Street.

Sam hadn't seen Adam since she was fifteen and he eighteen, and she remembered with a wry smile the colossal crush she'd had on him then. At nearly forty, he had hardly changed except for slightly thinning hair and still had the crooked smile she'd loved so much.

'Samantha!' He kissed her on each cheek.

'I found her and Ben in the park,' Cathy told him. 'Thought you wouldn't mind if they join us for lunch?'

'Delighted. Gin and tonic?'

'What a good idea – thanks.'

'Sam's nursing a bruised ego and an aching heart.'

'Oh, God. Sorry to hear that, Sam. I'll put in more G than T in that case, then you can tell us all about it. Sit by the fire in the living room.'

She settled in a pine rocking chair next to the beautiful, original fireplace.

'You have a lovely home,' she said admiringly, taking in the elegantly draped curtains and leather sofas.

'We like it. I restored the floors and fireplace myself.'

The door opened to admit a man who looked like a matinee idol; tall, blue-eyed and muscular.

'Oh, there you are!' Adam greeted the newcomer.

'Sam, this is Mike, Adam's partner,' Cathy said.

Mike hugged Cathy and smiled at Sam.

'You know they say all the gorgeous men are gay? Well, it's true.' Cathy curled up on the sofa. 'Now – dish the dirt.'

Sam took a gulp of her drink and tried to gather her thoughts, glad that Ben had been diverted into the study next door, having been given a computer game to play with.

After downing rather too much of her drink she told Cathy and the others about her disastrous relationship with Nick.

Adam sat opposite her, swilling ice around his glass and then asked her a question she had not yet put to herself.

'Did you believe him, when he said he loved you?'

'Yes.'

'Did you know this Candy before?'

'I met her once at a party.'

'And what was your first impression of her?'

'That she was well-cast as a pantomime cat. I didn't like her.'

'Or trust her?'

'Well, no.'

'So why have you taken her word before that of the man you're supposed to love? You never gave him a chance to answer his case.'

'Adam's a lawyer,' apologised Mike.

'Well, he's always promised me there was no-one else lurking in the background,' Sam answered slowly. 'It was my biggest fear – meeting him through a dating agency - that he might be married or something. I only found out about Candy by chance, because of what Leo blurted out, forgetting that Ben was there and old enough to understand.'

'Doesn't that strike you as a bit odd? That Leo would say something like that in front of a small boy – unless he had planned for it to be repeated.'

'You mean…?' Sam suddenly realised that Leo might have overheard her conversation with Rose in the church foyer.

'Maybe Leo, having seen you and Nick happily together, decided to try to spike your relationship. Nick clearly has been at least part of the cause of his parents' marriage break-up, so possibly Leo wanted to get his own back. If he saw you were chatting merrily to other members of the drama group, including Candy's husband, you obviously didn't know about the affair.'

'So, you're saying Nick *did* have an affair with Candy?'

'Probably. But it may not have been recent. If it was over before he started going out with you, it isn't a problem, is it?'

'Well – no, I suppose not.'

'And you said the woman is a cow – sorry a cat.'

'Oh, yes indeed. Almost the most painful thing was when she asked if he called me "flower". She could only have known that if he'd told her; or if that's what he called her too.'

'If he'd called you both "darling", would you have been upset to find out?' he asked craftily.

'Well…no. It's a common term of endearment, isn't it?'

'Case closed,' grinned Adam triumphantly. 'One man's *flower* is another man's *darling*. He probably calls all the ladies of his acquaintance "flower".'

'Lord, I'd hate to be up against you in a court of law.' Sam smiled, feeling slightly better.

'Well, if you follow me to the kitchen you can pass judgement on the roast lamb.'

They watched as he lifted the roast, sizzling and smelling of garlic and rosemary, from the oven. 'Mike – can you carve? Sam and Cathy, set the table please? *Muchas gracias.*'

'We've just come back from Gran Canaria,' apologised Mike. 'It takes him a week or two to get over it.'

Sam and Ben drove back to her parents' house. She spent another sleepless night, wondering whether Adam had been right in his assumptions. Was Nick really as black as he'd been painted? Could he really have made love to her so passionately and then gone to another woman? Was it in his nature?

Yes!

No.

Maybe.

Dawn was a long time coming.

Stage Struck

Final Dress Rehearsal

After three exhausting practise runs on the stage, lots of false starts and inevitably, all manner of glitches no-one had anticipated, the cast wearily assembled for their very last rehearsal. They would have Christmas Eve and Christmas Day off and then two shows on Boxing Day, the first at two-thirty, the second at seven o'clock.

Rose was especially tired after fitting in extra shifts at the hospital to make sure she could have the time off for the show. She was in the dressing room putting on her make-up when her mobile phone rang and Nick put his head round the door looking annoyed. 'No phones back stage – that applies to everyone. They can be heard in the auditorium.'

'Sorry – I'll switch it off,' she apologised, removing it from her bag. But before she turned it off, she glanced at the screen to see the display: *Sam calling*. She rushed outside the building, away from the mêlée in the girls' dressing room and answered. 'Sam! Where are you? We've all been so worried!'

'Sorry, Rose. I had to disappear for a while – to get my head together. I'm in St. Albans, staying in my parents' house.'

'What happened? Tell me quickly because dress rehearsal is about to start.'

'Leo may have overheard my conversation with you and he dropped a hint – a huge one to Ben - that Nick was, as he put it, "screwing his mother".'

'Oh, no! How awful.'

'I knew something wasn't right, and that seemed to be a possible answer. I absolutely had to find out, so I found Candy's phone number in the book and called her. She told me she's still having an affair with Nick and that he told her all about the things he did with me… in bed.'

Rose gasped. 'What a bitch!'

'Right! She said I was a cover for the fact that he was her lover. Now they plan to move in together since her marriage has broken-up.'

'Oh, Sam, no wonder you were so upset.'

'Do you know if that's the truth?'

'That's nothing like it, Sam. I knew Nick was seeing Candy before he met you because Mason told me. I didn't tell you because you were so happy and, to be fair to him, he seemed really smitten. Now Nick is in bits and he says he ended it with her before he met you, but she won't let go. To be honest, he isn't my favourite person, but I think he's telling the truth.'

'Truly?'

Stage Struck

'Sam, I wouldn't lie to you. In strict confidence, I know that Candy took an overdose a couple of weeks ago so she's very unstable and quite capable of making up a story like that.'

'So you think I should believe Nick?'

'That's for you to decide.'

'I suppose so. Rose, has Nick ever called you "flower"?'

'Yes. He calls everyone "flower". Why? Surely you don't think …?'

'No, of course not. Thanks, Rose, I'll let you go. Good luck with the show.'

'Thanks. Shall I tell Nick you rang?'

'If you like, but don't tell him where I am. I need time to think. Have a good Christmas. I've been invited to spend it with an old school friend, her brother and his partner. I'll feel more able to relax and enjoy it now.'

'Good. Let me know when you get back.' She switched off her phone and tried to re-engage her mind to connect with the show.

When she returned, she found the girls' dressing room was heaving with children in ballet costumes, Lady Marian was begging someone to zip up her dress and Verruca the witch was grumbling because she couldn't get to the mirror to attach her wart.

Lauren eyed Rose's mobile. 'Has Sam been in touch?'

'You must be psychic - yes, she's all right. Candy told her a horrible string of lies.'

'That sounds in character. Poor Sam. Well, think yourself into Robin Hood now, girl, and slap those thighs. We've got a show to do.'

To everyone's relief, the rehearsal went well.

Afterwards Mason gathered them together in front of the stage and seemed quite emotional. 'You've done sterling work, every one of you. I'm so proud of you.' They all beamed up at him. 'What can I say? Thank you all. It's been a long day.' His voice croaked a little. 'Have a happy Christmas.' As they applauded, he strode into the shadows backstage.

Gradually, everyone dispersed. They changed, removed make-up and left the theatre wishing each other a merry Christmas.

Rose caught a glimpse of Nick on his knees tightening up the screws on a market stall ready for the village scene opening the first performance. He looked drawn and pale and she felt a pang of sympathy for him.

'Nick…'

'Rose. You did well tonight, flower.'

'Thanks. Look, I had a call from Sam.'

He stood up quickly. 'You did?' Anxiety was in every line of his body. 'Where is she?'

'I can't tell you that, but she's all right. Candy told her a pack of lies. She said you were still having an affair with her and you planned to move in together.'

Nick scowled. 'What a baggage! I suppose it's in character. What did you tell Sam?'

'That I didn't think it was true – but I can't tell her what to believe. Give her time.'

He gave her a thin-lipped smile. 'Thanks, Rose.'

With a nod, Rose left the theatre and went to join John, who was leaning on his car parked across the road from the theatre. She was very aware of an added intensity in his gaze as he watched her approach and her heart began to beat a little faster. They'd become even closer since Sunday. After the service they'd gone to dinner and then back to his flat where they'd talked for hours, sitting cuddled together on his sofa. At last, Rose had been able to talk about her parents, to remember the love she felt for them, and to begin the process of forgiveness. She'd returned to her flat with regret, but she had to catch a few hours sleep before an early shift.

Now, she approached John who still had the remains of his make-up round his eyes and looked rather exotic. She laughed and, reaching in her pocket for a tissue, she gently wiped the blue shadow away.

He took her hand, turned it and pressed his lips to her palm. Amazingly, something inside her totally dissolved into a hot fire. She gasped and looked at him, seeing an answering longing in his eyes. For what seemed like an eternity they stared at each other.

'Is it the right time, Rose?' he asked her softly, and she knew exactly what he meant.

'Yes. Yes – yes,' she murmured and regardless of who might be watching, he drew her into his arms and kissed her with a tender passion which left her weak at the knees.

Breathlessly, they both scurried back to their cars and headed for Rose's house. Once inside, nerves almost overcame her. She turned to him at the foot of the stairs. 'I'm so afraid you'll be disappointed, John. I'm not exactly an expert.'

'You couldn't disappoint me if you tried, honey. Relax…I love you.'

'And I love you.'

'Then nothing else matters, does it?'

He led her upstairs to the warmth of her bed where Rose discovered for herself what all the fuss was about. She felt free at last, as though a ghost had gone from her shoulder. Her spirit soared joyfully and all her anguish lifted. Giving herself totally to John was the most wonderful thing she had ever done, and afterwards she snuggled in his arms knowing she was safe. It felt like coming home.

'Rose,' he murmured, some time in the early hours after a slow, ecstatic reprise, 'I can't bear the thought of letting you out of my sight ever again. Will you please, please, marry me?'

'Oh, yes,' she whispered. 'As soon as possible.'

Stage Struck

Christmas Eve

Sam was grateful that Ben had found a playmate called Jake a couple of doors away which meant she could spend her time deciding what to do with her future. She knew that whatever else had fallen off the shelf, she loved Nick – and that life without him was going to be bleak. She also realised she'd given him a tough manifesto. No dark secrets, no sordid love affairs, squeaky-clean past - how unrealistic was that? Adam was right. Whatever had happened before he met Sam was none of her business. If he'd had an affair with Candy and it had truly ended when he met her, did it matter? Her gut twisted at the idea of him 'screwing' Candy, as Leo had put it, but the alternative of not seeing him again hurt even more.

Ben came back from Jake's house and she pulled him onto her lap. 'Ben, tell me honestly – did you really like Nick?'

'Yeah – he's cool. But you don't like him any more do you?'

'It's hard to explain, Ben. Although I'm upset because of something someone said about him, I actually miss him very much.'

'So call him.'

'Would you be unhappy if he and I spent a lot of time together; if he maybe lived with us?' Ben thought for a moment. 'Would he be like a new daddy?'

'Would you like a new daddy?'

'I don't know. I don't remember my daddy because he went to Heaven when I was a baby, didn't he?'

'Yes, darling, he did.'

'If Nick was like my daddy, that would be okay. You would still love me the same?'

'Of course I would. Oh, Ben, I love you more than life itself and that will never change.'

'And Nick likes football. Do you think he would take me sometimes?'

'I'm sure he would,' she smiled.

'When are we going to see him?'

Stage Struck

Christmas Day

John and Rose woke, blissfully, having not spent more than an hour apart or in the company of anyone else for two days. His Christmas present to her was a diamond and sapphire ring which they bought the day before. So far, they'd kept their engagement a secret. But today they had to emerge to meet up with Lauren and Clive before going to the children's ward. They took a leisurely bath together.

When they were ready, they wandered hand-in-hand along to Lauren's house, where Clive too had obviously stayed overnight.

Lauren opened the door, took one look at them standing on her doorstep and instantly knew that these two glowing people had spent the night together. She raised her eyebrows and smiled knowingly, causing Rose and John to burst out laughing and throw themselves on her and Clive with delighted hugs.

'What – may I ask - has happened?' demanded Clive, with a broad grin.

'This!' beamed Rose, holding out her hand to show off her sparkling ring. 'You're the first to know.'

Lauren sat on the sofa, tears brimming in her eyes. 'It's the best Christmas present I could have. Oh, Rose, I'm so happy for you.'

'Thank you. I'll tell you all about it later – but we have to go and entertain the children now. Shall we change here, since you've got all the costumes? The others are meeting us on the ward.'

Half an hour later, the neighbours were somewhat surprised to see Robin Hood, Mrs. Mixit, Jack the Jester and Gretel bundle into Clive's car and head off down the road.

They entered the hospital to stares and giggles and met up with Winston, dressed as a very fat Father Christmas with a huge bag of presents, Barry and Gillian as punk baddies and Maureen as a toned-down witch. 'Don't want to scare anyone into wetting the bed,' she croaked.

As arranged, Father Christmas stayed outside and the others went in to delighted shrieks and squeals from the children, many of whom were with their parents. The cast went round to each child and then, to taped music provided by Barbara, they sang songs and did a handful of sketches from the show.

At last, John announced, 'Well, children, we have to go back to Keepumlarfin, but there's someone outside to see you. I think he's just giving some sugar lumps to the reindeer.'

Stage Struck

Then Winston entered to a roar from those children who were well enough to roar, and broad smiles from the rest.

'That was great,' said an exultant Clive. 'What a start to Christmas! Right - it's definitely time to get back to Lauren's to check on the turkey and to crack a bottle of champagne – or two.'

Arm-in-arm they headed for the car, leaving Winston to entertain the children, which he did for over an hour. He then walked back to the car park where Maureen and Patsy were waiting to take him home to lunch - which was being cooked by Mason.

'I loved that,' Winston beamed, 'and as I have the freedom these days, I'm going to ask Rose if I can spend some time on the ward, reading to the kids and helping out.'

***

Candy woke with another hangover and shambled downstairs mid-morning. The house was empty as Lola had gone to Alex's for Christmas and Leo to Gillian's. Neither of her children, it seemed, wanted to see her on Christmas Day, and she felt incredibly depressed – and guilty. The things she had told Sam had come back to haunt her and kept her awake for several nights. Pangs of conscience were a new experience for Candy and she was discovering how it felt to be isolated and alone.

She made coffee and forced down a slice of toast. For the past week her appetite had reversed and she'd hardly been able to eat anything, restoring her weight to normal, but leaving her looking pale and ill. Candy could hardly believe how her life had disintegrated in the past two months; Nick dropping her had been a terrible blow, and she knew she'd dealt with it badly. Haunting him, threatening and demanding had been undignified, to say the least. Then to lose her husband – whom she missed more than she'd have believed possible. Now the house was under offer and she'd have to move to a rabbit hutch. Her children despised her and she knew she wouldn't be able to show her face at SADS ever again. How the hell had all that happened? She wondered how she could ever make amends?

For a couple of hours she wandered round the house. You've hit the bottom, Candy, she told herself – now there's only one way to go and it's going to take every ounce of courage you possess.

Finally, deciding there was only one place to start, she dressed with care and used a minimum of make-up to cover the puffiness round her eyes and give her lips a touch of colour. She took a deep breath, climbed into her car and headed for Nick's house.

He answered the door in his dressing gown, unshaven and bleary-eyed. 'What the hell do you want?'

'Can I come in? Please, Nick, it's not what you think.'

Uneasily he stepped back and allowed her to walk through to the lounge. The usually immaculate house was a mess; dirty crockery, a lot of empty beer cans and general debris littered the room. 'Well?' he demanded.

'I've come to apologise. I told Sam a pack of lies and I want to tell her the truth; try to put things right.'

'Am I hearing things?' he asked.

'Where is she? I'll go and see her.'

'I don't know where she is. She left the same day she spoke to you. Tell me, why the change of heart? Christmas spirit?'

'Not particularly. Maybe I just came to my senses. I feel a shit.'

'You should.'

'I know. I've lost everything and it's all my own fault.' She sat on the sofa, her head in her hands. 'I really loved you, Nick.'

'Candy, be honest with yourself; you enjoyed the fun, the sex, the secrecy and so did I. Flower, we had a great time, but I don't believe you were ever in love with me, nor I with you. It wasn't in the same league as the way I feel about Sam – and I don't mean to hurt you by saying that.'

She shook her head. 'Ironic, isn't it. Now we're both free to have an affair.'

'Don't even think about it.'

'No... I'm not. I'd better go.' She rose and walked to the front door and he followed her.

'Go and talk to Mason,' he advised.

'He hates me – there's no prospect of reconciliation.'

'I'm sorry.'

He opened the door and Candy turned to leave.

On Christmas morning, after opening Ben's presents and making an apologetic call to Cathy, who understood instantly and begged to be kept informed, Sam packed everything back in the car and headed for Sipton. She'd decided to arrive unannounced, calling first at Lauren's, where she knew Rose and the others had gathered.

Stage Struck

'Can I leave Ben for a while?' she asked as Rose and Lauren welcomed them into the hall draped with festive decorations.

'Of course you can,' Rose said. 'There's plenty of food so you can both join us for lunch. On the other hand, if you don't re-appear we'll assume - otherwise…'

Sam flushed and, smiling weakly, she left them, thinking in passing that Rose had a particular glow about her.

She drove with her heart in her mouth, wondering how on earth to approach Nick. Should she go in and ask him outright about Candy – or simply throw herself in his arms and tell him none of it mattered as long as he loved her? She parked a few yards down the road to make the surprise complete. She walked to the gate and stopped there to take a few deep breaths. Then she began to walk up the path, her heart hammering so loudly she was sure he would hear it. She almost had her hand out to ring the bell when the door was flung open.

Nick, still in his dressing gown, stood slightly behind Candy who seemed about to leave.

The three of them stared at each other for a moment, and then Sam turned and ran down the path, through the gate, along the pavement to her car. She fumbled in her handbag for the keys, found them and triggered the remote unlock. Swinging the door open, she jumped in and then activated central locking. A little breathless after her run, she tried inserting the key. Why couldn't she get the blasted thing into the ignition? Her hand was trembling. At last it slid in - just as Nick reached the car and yelled at her not to go.

She swore at him, started the car and pulled away with a screech of tyres.

Candy was standing at his gate, waving at her – the bitch.

Well, that was that. Now she had seen the situation with her own eyes and it was every bit as bad as she had feared.

Nick turned to Candy. 'Quick, we've got to follow her. I've no idea where she might go.'

'Dressed like that in your dressing gown? The house is open…'

'I don't bloody care! Just get in the car and drive. Please!'

With a slightly hysterical giggle, she did as he said and they reached the end of the road in time to see Sam turning towards the park.

'Don't get too close. I don't want to frighten her into some sort of car chase,' he begged, so Candy slowed down and kept Sam's car in sight until she stopped in the large car park next to the river.

They waited until Sam, shoulders hunched, took a few paces away from her car. Then Nick told Candy to drive up and intercept her.

Sam looked startled, then furious as Nick climbed out of the car and strode towards her.

Stage Struck

He held his arms up as if in surrender, his eyes wide and beseeching. 'Sam, I know how that looked but I promise you – on oath, if you like - Candy came to see me for quite a different reason to what you're understandably imagining.'

Candy stood by his shoulder. 'I came round just now to ask Nick where I could track you down. I told you a lot of lies the other day and I've felt bad about it ever since.'

'Am I hearing things?' Sam asked sarcastically.

'Nick has been trying to get rid of me since before he met you, but I wouldn't let go. Now I've buggered up everybody's lives and today I decided enough was enough. I must try to put things right, at least for you and Nick – it's far too late for Mason and me.'

Then she turned and walked shakily to her car. She gave a tearful last look at Nick, climbed in and drove away.

Sam eyed Nick, who was shivering in his dressing gown. 'You look ridiculous,' she said at last.

'I feel ridiculous. Not just because I'm standing in the middle of a public place in my pyjamas on Christmas Day – but because I've been such a fool.'

'You won't hear me arguing with that.' She folded her arms and stepped away from him, leaning on her car.

'I was terrified that if you found out about Candy you'd consider it a capital offence. I promised you there was nothing sordid in my background and I lied to you on day one.'

'Go on,' she said.

'The truth is I joined Meet Your Match to find a girlfriend I could bring to the dinner dance. I was hoping that if Candy saw me with someone else she'd believe I really didn't want her any more. I'd expected to take weeks to find someone I could tolerate – and then I met you on the first date. I think I fell in love with your voice before I even saw you and when we met I was blown away. I can't tell you what I've been going through since you left.'

She regarded him more softly, taking in the bowed shoulders, pleading expression and she noted, biting back a giggle, a pair of very shabby carpet slippers.

She kept him in agony for a few more moments before walking slowly, finally, into his arms.

'Happy Christmas, Nick,' she murmured.

'Happy Christmas, flower.'

As he held her she felt his tears on her cheek.

Back at Lauren's, Ben enjoyed being spoilt. They played games all afternoon and as the light faded they collapsed by the fire, with Ben leaning sleepily against Rose, Bugsy's head contentedly on his knee.

'I hope Mummy is all right,' he mumbled.

'I'm quite sure she is more than all right,' grinned John. 'Don't worry about her. Let's tell each other scary stories!'

Ben perked up and proved to have a fertile imagination, inventing monsters and ghosts which were far more frightening than anything the others could dream up. They were laughing so much they didn't hear the phone ring until the last minute. Lauren rushed to pick it up, but it was too late. Puzzled, she dialled one four seven one, but the number was withheld. 'Funny,' she mused. 'Who could that be?'

'Probably Sam,' said Clive. 'Asking us to keep Ben for a while.'

'She doesn't have this number – and its ex-directory.'

'Stop worrying about it. Probably a wrong number.'

'I expect so.' A strange feeling caused her to quiver and cuddle up to Clive.

'Someone walk over your grave, poppet?'

'I hope not.'

Then Rose's mobile rang and she answered with a smile. 'Hi, Sam.' An expectant silence fell among the others as they waited to hear the news. Infuriatingly, Rose replied simply with, 'Uh huh…hmmm... Oh, dear…no! I don't believe it. Yes, of course,' and then rang off.

'Well?'

'What?' she asked, smiling.

'Rose!'

'Candy confessed. They're back together and Ben is staying with John and me tonight.'

A cheer went up and they decided that Christmas Day had finished on a high. With two shows to do the next day, Rose, John and Ben left and walked down the road together, the small boy in the middle, holding each of their hands.

'We look like a family,' observed John.

'Yes, we do,' she smiled up at him. 'Give me a year or two.'

'As long as you want, honey. Anyway, I'm not ready to share you yet.'

Stage Struck

Boxing Day
The First Show

At one o'clock sharp the caretaker turned up to open the theatre and a very nervous crowd of actors drifted into their dressing rooms. There were cards for each other and from friends and supporters wishing them luck, and flowers for the girls from the men in the cast; a long-time tradition in the group.

Rose felt as though a herd of elephants was charging through her stomach and she kept rushing to the loo. But half an hour before curtain-up, they were all in costume, joking among themselves and beginning to calm down. They could hear a buzz of anticipation from the auditorium as the first of the audience arrived – and the buzz quickly grew to a deafening level as two hundred brownies and guides, their usual first house, filled the seats.

'They're less critical than our later crowds and it gives us a chance to get the show up to speed,' Mason told them. 'Now, you've all worked incredibly hard and been through some tough times. I can't tell you how proud I am of all of you. And now I want you to go out there and have fun. Enjoy the kids. Play to them and reap the rewards of all your efforts. Break a leg!'

They surrounded him, thanking him for his own hard work and Rose handed him two envelopes: the first one contained a card signed by all the cast, which made him smile; and the other which had been delivered to the dressing room earlier, removed his smile as he recognised the handwriting. Before he could open it, however, he was called away to make a last-minute adjustment to the Maypole on stage, so he put it in his pocket and rushed off.

Winston, dressed as Tom the Cat, with long whiskers glued to his face, popped his head into the girls' dressing room and grinned at them. 'You all look lovely – and Rose, if I were forty years younger…'

She sashayed smilingly over to show off her costume and kissed him. 'We haven't told the rest of the cast yet,' she whispered, 'but John and I are getting married.'

'My dear, I'm so happy for you – and honoured to be let into the secret. It's been quite a journey for us all this past couple of months, hasn't it?'

'Yes. A roller coaster – but I wouldn't have missed it for the world.'

'Five minutes!' called the Assistant Stage Manager. 'Beginners on stage, please.'

'Break a leg,' grinned Winston, disappearing into the wings.

The overture began with a medley of songs from the show, and then Jack the Jester walked down through the audience to 'oohs' and 'aahs' from the children.

Stage Struck

'Hello, children,' they heard him say. 'My name's Jack... Well, say hello, Jack.'

'*Hello, Jack!*' they screamed, and after his introduction the curtain went up on the spring celebration in Keepumlarfin. The children in the show, together with the chorus, gave a rousing rendition of 'Zippity Do Da', before John, looking truly magnificent in his patchwork dress and pink wig made his first entrance. He showed not a trace of nerves and the children loved him. He came offstage grinning triumphantly and watched as Verruca the witch made her entrance with a flash and bang which evoked squeals of delight and then loud 'boos' and hisses from the children.

Then it was Rose's turn. Taking a deep breath, she strutted confidently on stage to loud wolf whistles from a few of the dads in the crowd.

'Well, what have we here?' she asked, slapping her thigh. 'Beauty and the Beast, by the look of it. Why, it's the lovely Lady Marian – but what is she doing with this horrible hairy heap?'

'Quick! Give her a kiss,' yelled a small ginger-haired boy in the front row, 'otherwise she'll have to marry that horrible man.'

Cast, crew and audience howled with laughter, and Rose somehow managed to get back to her script and pull the scene together. She came offstage with Lady Marian to rapturous applause and heaps of praise for surviving her little heckler.

The bug had bitten; she knew she would be addicted – stage-struck - for the rest of her life.

All too soon they were taking their final curtain call. Robin Hood and Lady Marian in her wedding dress entered last to roars of approval and they reprised the final song from the show. The small boy at the front jumped up and down and she gave him a special wave. He really was very cute and she could see him grabbing his parents' hands and bouncing to the music.

As the curtain came down on an elated cast, they hugged each other and embraced stickily. The heat backstage was suffocating, but no-one minded. They'd done it – the show was a huge success!

It was hardly worth changing out of their costumes as the next show was only an hour and a half away, so after the audience had left, they scattered around the auditorium where it was cooler.

But then Joe, one of the front-of-house staff, came looking for Lauren. 'There's someone outside for you,' he told her.

'I can't go outside in costume, Joe. Who is it?'

'He wouldn't say. But there's no-one else around to see you. He seems quite anxious you should come.'

Lauren glanced at Clive and Rose. 'I'd better go and see.'

Stage Struck

In the deserted foyer a man, perhaps a year or two younger than her, stood waiting with a pretty brunette whom Lauren took to be his wife – and the exuberant little boy from the front row.

'Hello,' she smiled. 'Did you enjoy the show?'

'Yes we did – especially Jasper,' said the boy's father. 'Could you and I go and sit down over there a minute. I know it seems odd, but there's something I need to say to you.'

'Well, yes, all right.' Puzzled, she followed him to a quiet corner and sat opposite him.

'Lauren... this is going to be a bit of a shock to you. I did try to call you yesterday, but there was no reply, so in the end I decided we'd come and see you today. I simply couldn't wait any longer to meet you.'

'I don't understand...'

'You've been trying to find your mother, haven't you?'

A quiver ran down her spine. 'Yes. How do you know?'

'It's a long story. But you and I are rather in the same boat.'

'You mean you're trying to find your mother too? Well, I hope you have better luck than me. I found out my mother died two years ago.'

'Yes, I know.'

'How? And how did you find out about me? I thought the agency was supposed to keep things confidential.'

'Lauren...my mother died two years ago too - of leukaemia.'

'But...'

To her surprise, he came to sit beside her and took her hand. 'I'm not making a very good job of this,' he said. 'I'm your brother. My name is Tony and over there is my wife, Linda and our son - your nephew, Jasper.'

Lauren gazed at him in disbelief, a flush spreading to her face which she covered with her trembling hands.

Tony knelt in front of her and gently gripped her shoulders. 'I'm sorry. This must be a colossal shock for you – as it was for me. I didn't know anything about you until a few days ago. It was quite by chance that a letter from the agency was forwarded to me from our mother's old address asking her to contact them. I phoned to say she had died and they apologised and said the letter had been sent by mistake. They'd already discovered from St. Catherine's House that she was dead. Then the lady asked who I was and there was a stunned silence. Eventually, she told me I had a sister, and believe me, I was as shocked as you are now.'

'Why didn't they contact me?'

'That was my fault. I too was stunned and didn't know if I wanted to get in contact. I needed time to think about it. In the end, I went to see them and asked for all the information they had about you – which incidentally included the fact that you were in this pantomime. You sounded so like Jasper in personality, I just knew I'd like you. And so I called you yesterday. When you didn't answer quickly, I chickened out and decided to come here today. We were lucky to get the last tickets.'

Lauren looked from Tony to Linda and little Jasper, who was hopping from foot to foot with impatience. 'Can we go and see her now?' he pleaded with his mother.

Shakily, Lauren rose to her feet and faced her brother. 'Do we have a father – or even the same father?'

'I don't know who your father was. You're about two years older than me and I know my mother married my father when she was pregnant with me. He left her a year after I was born – so I have no idea where he is now. Are you all right? Can I get you a drink?'

'Oh, yes, I'm all right, Tony. I'm astonished, shocked. And absolutely delighted. I have a family.' With tears and smiles she went to meet her sister-in-law and little Jasper, who was suddenly overcome with fright and put his thumb in his mouth. Linda, also tearful, embraced her, and then they included Tony and Jasper and stood together unable to believe that they had found each other.

They were still like that when Clive came looking for Lauren.

Somehow, they all got through the second show which went as well as the first and the audience rose to its feet in a storm of applause at the end.

Exhausted, the actors changed, hung up their costumes and retired to the pub – all except for Lauren and Clive who slipped away with some people no-one had seen before.

Mason left the theatre – last as usual - and fished in his pocket for his car keys. He wasn't in the mood for the pub, he decided. Everyone was so happy and he felt depressed. He couldn't rise to the self-congratulatory mood of the others and decided to call it a day and go back to Winston's flat. Then his hand closed over the smaller envelope which Rose had given him earlier. He stood under the streetlamp and opened it.

Dearest Mason, it read.

I wanted to tell you that I know what an idiot I've been. I don't expect you to forgive me but I wanted to say how sorry I am. I ruined our lives for nothing and I can't ever make that up to you. I am ashamed of myself and I have decided to go away, probably to Scotland to stay with my Aunt until I can find a little house there.

If you can bear to see me one last time, so that I can say sorry in person, I'll be waiting across the road from the theatre in the little café. If you don't come, I'll understand.

Love, Candy.

He glanced across the street to see a small figure in a white raincoat, standing outside the café under the opposite streetlight.

For a long moment they stared at each other, and then he turned and walked away.